BENCHED

SARA ELIZABETH SANTANA

Sara Elizabeth Santana

Sara Elizabeth Santana

www.saraelizabethsantana.com

Printed in the United States of America

Publisher's Cataloging-in-Publication data

Santana, Sara Elizabeth

Digital Version of BENCHED

ISBN:978-1-7349833-4-0

Fiction > Romance > New Adult

Print Version of BENCHED

ISBN: 978-1-7349833-5-7

Fiction > Romance > Contemporary

First Edition

BENCHED

Book One

Sara Elizabeth Santana

DEDICATION

To Dad.
Thank you for my never-ending love of baseball, without which I could not have written this book. I'm sorry for the steamy scenes.

EPIGRAPH

"Love is the most important thing in the world, but baseball is pretty good, too."
    Yogi Berra

PROLOGUE

People often say that in small towns, everyone knows everything about everyone, but that isn't always true. However, if you live in a town that is obsessed with its college baseball team and you just happen to be the coach's daughter, then yes, people will know *everything* about you.

Santa Isabella is a town tucked along the central coast of California. For years, the town was known mostly for pulling oil out of the ground and not much else. But like most things, that didn't last. The town needed to find something else to bring money in and that's when the boardwalk was built, and the state college followed soon after. Santa Isabella became a tourist destination, and how could it not? It was just close enough to San Francisco for a day trip and was known for beautiful weather all year long. The small college town of Izzy was perfect—the best of both worlds. With ease, tourists could lounge on the sandy beaches and hike through the thick redwoods on their way out of town. Despite its small size, the town was full of tourists, from the very beginning of spring to the end of summer. They often outnumbered the locals but even then, the people in Santa Isabella found way to gossip about the tourists too.

Nowadays, it's known for that very same college and for its baseball team, the Quakes. The Quakes won their very first college world series in the eighties and ever since, they've been the only thing that mattered in this town. Everyone lives and breathes baseball all year long. They camp out in the stadium during the season and count down the minutes until it's spring again. The whole city is decked from the sky to the ground in green and black. The baseball players are rock stars.

Santa Isabella is where I grew up.

Santa Isabella is where I go to college.

Baseball was once the most important thing in my life.

Now, I'd do anything to avoid it.

CHAPTER ONE

I'm late. There is sweat dripping down my back—very attractive—and I'm almost afraid to glance down at my watch because it will tell me the level of trouble that I'm in. I'm not just five minutes late. I'm so incredibly late and I'm pretty sure that I've missed the entire practice. I don't have a good excuse and I'm confident that my dad is probably going to kill me. Or make me participate alongside the boys during Hell Week. I can't decide which one would be worse. On one hand, Hell Week would get me back on the field, doing what I love. On the other, the field was the very last place I wanted to be. It was a melancholy feeling and I briefly begin to wonder if there is leniency in Santa Isabella for the coach's daughter being late on her first day of work before the season starts. Probably not, but I'm not going to think about that right now. I just need to get into that locker room.

I've spent so much time on this campus, yet I still have managed to get lost going from my English class in the McPherson building to the bookstore, and from the bookstore to the locker room. It's honestly very easy to get distracted while on campus. I basically grew up right here, spent more days here on campus with my dad, on the field, than at my own home, yet I still am mesmerized at how gorgeous it is. California State University, Santa Isabella fits the bill rather perfectly for a college on a sunny coast — palm trees everywhere, people hurrying across campus in a pair of shorts and tank tops, and not one person is walking around without sunglasses framing their faces. Salt from the sea breeze is present with every new breath, and sometimes I think it looks like something out of a Hollywood movie, but on a much smaller scale.

Izzy might be popular with the baseball players but it's still a relatively small campus, and I'm glad for that fact alone. I don't need to be any more lost than I already am. I race past the main quad and shake my head when I spot an older classman lounging in a hammock strung between two trees. *Of course.* It's January, the beginning of a new semester, but the sun is giving off a heat more suited to summer. My dark blonde hair is sticking to the back of my neck and all I really want right now is some good air conditioning and a cold bottle of water.

The thought of the air conditioning that is already pumping in the locker room spurs me to quicken my pace. I'm getting closer but I'm nearly ready to admit defeat — I'm too late at this point to salvage myself. Sure enough, the guys are already leaving the locker room by the time I get there, and that's when I absolutely know for a fact that I'm going to get it. Dad runs a tight ship as coach and as his new assistant, I'm expected to be the perfect first mate.

I reach for the door handle, resigned, but it swings open before I can. I jump back and feel my face flush.

Jesse's smile always hits me like an unexpected camera flash in my face. He's a senior, the starting pitcher for the Quakes, my twin sister's boyfriend, and someone that I actively try to avoid. This can be difficult to do, considering all three of us attend CS Santa Isabella. However, since I'm working for the baseball team, I don't have much choice in the matter. Seeing Jesse is unavoidable at this point. "Hi Evie."

"Hi." The word traveling from my brain to my lips and out into the air in front of me feels like the most difficult thing I've done all day.

"You're late," he remarks. His hair is still wet from his post-practice shower and I can see the faint outline of his chest through his dampened shirt. Jesse has always been so distracting, and that's no different now. His dark brown hair is sticking to his forehead and the back of his neck and is nearly black when wet. His shoulders are wide, hips narrow, and he has strong, muscled legs but its *more* than that. It's his warm brown skin and the way his mouth turns up at the end when he's teasing or the way his long fingers hold the baseball right before he releases a pitch.

It makes me feel out of control.

As a person who has spent the last three years doing everything they can to be in control, I don't like it.

I bite my lip and force myself to look away. These are not good thoughts to have right now. This is exactly why I avoid face to face contact with him as much as possible. "I know. Is anyone else left in there?"

He shakes his head. "No. But, hey, when has that ever stopped you from going in there?" He winks at me.

I ignore the wink, walking past him to enter the locker room, uttering a soft '*thanks*' as I pass. My heart is pounding wildly in my chest at the brief encounter. It's been three years and I still manage to become nothing more than a walking sack of skin and organs with no brain around him. It feels like I haven't changed a bit. I rush through the row of lockers, my mind wandering. I'm not prepared for whatever lecture my dad is going to give me, I have textbooks to buy and I don't particularly want to wait in the long lines and the brief conversation with Jesse has totally knocked me off balance. I'm not on my game and I'm hardly paying attention to anything around me so when I take a sharp right, I hit something warm and solid. I stumble backwards, somehow managing to keep myself upright. "Shit, I'm sorry…"

I look up and immediately blush, turning my eyes to the floor. Whatever I was about to say has died at the tip of my tongue and I realize that my mouth is wide open, and I shut it quickly, the flush on my cheeks deepening.

"Well, that's okay, princess," comes the answer. There is a twang to the unfamiliar voice. I want to look back up at him, but the fact that he was stark naked really talked me out of it. As in, *hello-that-part-of-the-male-anatomy-that-I-tried-not-to-look-at-but-kind-of-seems-impressive-and-my-god-I-didn't-want-to-see-that* naked. "You're one of the coach's daughters, right? Evangeline, I'm assuming?"

I nod, my eyes glued to the ground and the suddenly fascinating pattern in the polished wood floors beneath my shoes. "Yeah. That's me. Just Evie though."

"You're a little late. Coach was looking for you. I didn't know anyone would willingly get on Coach's bad side like that." There is amusement in his voice. "You can look now, by the way. Unless the floor is just that interesting to you. It *is* a pretty pattern." He's practically laughing at this point.

I chance a glance upward and am relieved to see that he's decent now if you can call someone like him merely decent. He's gorgeous and he's still damn naked. I don't want to look at him…down below so I find myself studying his face. He's unfamiliar to me so he must be new to the team. His dark hair is thick and styled in that perfectly messy way that looks like he hasn't tried at all, but you just know that he's definitely trying. His eyes are a deep brown, set against tanned skin—his skin is too pale without any clothes on for that brown to be natural—and a scattering of dark freckles across his cheeks. I'm tall but this guy practically towers over me, his chest just at eye level. He's in shape, fit and muscled but also lean. He's probably fast on the field. I'm considering what position he might play as my eyes skim over his tan chest, his abs and the dark hairs leading down to…I cough loudly and raise my eyes back to his.

He falters for a moment. "Whoa. Your eyes…"

"Yes," I say almost monotonously, before he can continue. It's the same reaction every time. "They're weird, I know." It's an old thing, I can almost predict what people say about it at this point. Lucy and I are identical in all but one way. I was born with a rare mutation, heterochromia.

For some crazy, rare reason, I was born with one brown eye and one eye that was a mix of brown and blue. Lucy, on the other hand, was born with two normal brown eyes. Besides this minor difference, we are nearly identical. We are Mexican on our mother's side and Spanish on our father's side and I've always thought that we look like both sides pretty equally—dark, dirty blonde hair, light brown skin that darkens in the summer and brown eyes, *mostly*. We are both tall like our father, but our large breasts and wide hips are definitely from our mother.

The heterochromia is usually the first thing that most people notice about me and don't get me wrong—it's kind of cool. I don't know any different either, but I do have moments when I've been incredibly irritated to be *different*. I feel that, sometimes, people just stare.

Exactly the way this guy is staring at me right now.

"It's really cool," he says, finally, a casual lilt to his voice. "Heterochromia."

I raise my eyebrows. "I'm impressed. They must have good schools in…" I paused, waiting for him to fill in the blank for me. I still didn't recognize him, which could only mean that he was one of two things: He was either a freshman or a transfer student. After practically living and breathing baseball my whole life, members of the team weren't exactly strangers.

"Kentucky," he supplies, the wide grin returning to his face. He practically blinds me with that perfect smile. "And Texas, I guess, too."

I frown for a moment and then it dawns on me. "Wait, are you…"

"Young!"

The two of us jump at the loud, booming voice and turn around. Dad is standing there, watching us. The guy is wearing a towel but that's it and it's slung very low on his hips. He has the decency to look a little embarrassed and hitches the towel a bit higher. "Coach, I was just…"

"Why don't you get dressed, Young?" Dad says firmly. He has a way with words, never straight demanding but always obeyed. His word is law in this locker room and on that field. "Next time, I better see you covered up around my daughter."

I turn around to hide a small smirk behind my hand as the he stammers out, "yes, sir."

"Evie, in my office. *Now*."

I resist the urge to roll my eyes and start to follow him. I look back once, and my eyes meet with the young player again. He winks at me and blows me a kiss. I look away, quickly, huffing into Dad's office, slamming the door behind me.

Dad sits down in his chair, propping his feet up on his desk. He knows I hate when he does that to his desk, the coffee table at home, the dashboard in the car and so on but he still does it and I refuse to let it get to me. He's smiling and I know he's just enjoyed the little show of power he's put on in the locker room. I've spent so much time in this locker room that the sight of half-naked baseball players doesn't tend to send me into fits or anything.

Except when they look like that guy did. *Damn it.*

"Who was that?" I ask, covering a yawn with my hand nonchalantly. I would be lying if I said I wasn't curious about him. "Freshman?"

He shakes his head before answering me, when he does his answer is quick and almost snappy. I can feel the mild irritation radiating off him. "Austin Young. Shortstop."

This information flips a light switch in my brain; suddenly the naked stranger didn't feel so much like a stranger. When Dad and I had gone over who we thought would be the strongest players of the season, he had brought up that we were getting a new transfer this go-round. "Right. He's the University of Texas transfer. He's a junior, right?"

It's so weird to get a transfer student, especially here. The team is hard enough to get on without trying to come in as a junior. It only made me more curious.

He nods in response. "Yeah. He was a good pick. He got more bench time than anything over there so he could get some real good play time here, *if* he raises his batting average." There's a long pause before he continues. "That's not important right now. Why are you so late?"

Damn it all to hell, I thought to myself. "Got lost," I say, breezily. "It's my first week."

He narrows his eyes at me. I know that his athletes find him intimidating, maybe even a little bit scary, at times, but that's laughable to me. He's just my dad. Outside of the locker room, he looks like your average All-American dad—dark blonde hair, blue eyes, dad shorts, you know the drill.

It's my short, fiery Mexican mother with a temper that people really should be terrified of, if I'm being honest. "You know where the stadium is; you grew up on this campus. Besides, it's your second semester. How on earth did you manage to get lost?"

"It was the first practice," I say, deflecting. "I'm sure you didn't miss me."

"Not the point," he answers, using his coach's voice. "I hired you for a reason. Well, for many reasons. So, I need you here. It doesn't look good for the team obeying me and being on time for practice if one of my own coaching staff members can't be on time, especially since she's my daughter. We had batting practice today and now I only have my own notes."

Not to mention an entire coaching staff...

This time I really do roll my eyes. "I'll be there tomorrow, okay?"

He sighs. "Fine." He rifles through some papers on his desk and I wince again at the absolute disaster that is his office. How can someone who is so obsessive about his team be so unorganized in the office that he's given to run the team? It literally makes no sense, but I've learned that arguing with him about it is a losing battle, so I say nothing. He finds what he's looking for and hands it to me. "Our first away game is coming up. I need you to start booking the rooms—make sure everything is all set, rooms are assigned and all that."

I nod, tucking the papers into my folder. "Okay." I start to stand up, but he stops me.

"Hey, did you get into that journalism class?"

I freeze and my heart drops from its normal place in my chest all the way into my stomach. "Um, no, I didn't. It was full. Maybe it's just a super popular class, which makes it

hard to get into. Especially since I *am* a freshman after all."
I shrug casually, hoping he'll drop the subject.

He doesn't. Instead he frowns. "You need to get into
those classes as a freshman, Evie. You're a sports journalism
major; you don't want to fall behind. Do you want me to
pull some strings?"

I'm actually undeclared at the moment, but he doesn't
know that. All it would take is a quick search on his
computer to find that out, but my dad has been so sure of
my career in sports writing and broadcasting for so long
that he would never doubt that it would say anything else.
"Dad, no. I'd prefer to just be a normal freshman here,
okay? I'll get all my general ed classes out of the way and
then we can worry about the journalism classes, okay?"

Please drop it. Please drop it. I fidget back and forth for a
moment until he nods. "All right, I guess you're right. Just
make sure to be on time, tomorrow, okay?"

I nod, firmly. "Of course. No problem." I make my
escape from his office. The locker room is empty now and I
feel a little disappointed. I shake this off. Nothing good ever
comes from a baseball player. Especially when they look
like Austin Young…

CHAPTER TWO

Some people really need to learn how to wear shirts.

Not that I'm staring at any of their bare chests anyway.

Today, I managed to make it on time to practice. Actually, I do one better. I'm early. I find a seat on the bench in the dugout and pull out my roster, ready to take notes on these boys. The last place in the world I want to be is here, but I'm getting paid and even though I get free tuition because my dad works at the college doesn't mean that I don't need money for life expenses. Books. Food. Venti green iced teas from Starbucks. The real necessities of life.

Dad usually spends the first few days of practice exclusively on batting. Mostly because he wants to see what his players are capable before sending them off to the assistant coaches to work on their specific positions on the team. Today I'm watching them bat and I'm bored as hell. These are the Quakes, after all. We have a reputation to maintain and therefore, we tend to get the best of the best when it comes to players around the country. Sure, everyone is a little rusty from the off-season, but they look good.

In more ways than one.

My eyes are drawn to Austin and not just because yesterday I saw him full-fledged naked. He's a new addition to the team, but he's not a freshman so he just seems…*bigger* next to the new freshmen he stands amongst. He's had some college playing experience, though admittedly not a lot. He came from UT in Austin, also a school known for good baseball, and played with some incredible players, though he was a benchwarmer more than anything else.

I'm curious about him and it is driving me insane. My interest in baseball has dwindled over the years but I know more about baseball than, well, the average person knows and my inherent love for the game keeps me watching him as he swings the bat.

I've determined one thing about him.

He kind of sucks.

It's a bit harsh and I feel bad even thinking it. I can't even consider saying it out loud because it sounds mean even in my head. He doesn't *suck*. He doesn't truly anyway. When he manages to connect with the ball, he has power. He's well built—broad shouldered and strong arms. He holds his elbow too low and it is causing his swing to be incredibly awkward. He's missing pitches that are right down the middle—ones that he should be hitting with ease. The problem is familiar to me and totally fixable, but he doesn't even seem to realize he's doing it.

It's driving me insane. How can he possibly be comfortable swinging that way?

I pull out my phone and begin to Google him. Not much comes up, but there's a little bit. I learn he was an All-American in high school, breaking pretty much every single record his school had. He pitched in high school, as well as playing shortstop, which makes me wonder why he chose one over the other. I'm curious to see if he can still pitch.

He's incredibly fast, according to some articles from his local newspaper.

"Wow, Evie, Googling the new guy? In public? Shameless."

I jump, startled, and look up and into the eyes of the last person that I want to see. He looks so good in his practice uniform and I can literally feel the heat radiating off his body, inviting me in, like it remembers oh so well what I really want it to forget. "It's my job to know everything about you guys, isn't it?"

"I guess so. Let's get real, sweetheart," Jesse shrugs, leaning closer to me across the dugout, the movement pulling his jersey tighter across his chest. "I haven't seen you google a new Quakes player in years." He looks away from me, his eyes landing on Austin as he misses yet another pitch. "He's a good-looking guy. If you're into that all-American white boy thing." He glances back at me to gauge my reaction.

Blood rushes to my cheeks, but I refuse to play into this game of his. I've known him long enough to know better. "Sure," I say shortly. "I'm not really here for that."

He doesn't answer and for a moment, I believe he'll let it go and walk away. After a moment however, he speaks, so low that I almost don't hear him. "No. Not anymore, anyway."

I stand up abruptly. "I have to go find my dad." I rush out of the dugout and onto the field. I weave in between players, all of whom toss out '*Hey Evie's*' as I walk by. Dad is on the opposite side of where I was previously sitting, working with another one of the Quakes pitchers. He looks up as I approach and smiles. "What have you got for me, button?"

"Hey Coach, I need to talk to you about…oh, hi, Evie."

I turn around and even though I'm pretty sure my face

color has finally returned to normal, it flares a fire engine red again. "Hello, Austin."

That wide smile is quickly in place. "Aw, you took the time to learn my name, baby. That's so sweet." A hand comes up to cover his heart over his bare chest because seriously this guy has no idea what clothes are, apparently.

"And you took all of three seconds to forget mine," I say, drily, passing my notes over to Dad. "It's *Evie*, not *baby*. I'm not anybody's baby and I'm definitely not yours."

"You could be," he replies, easily. "If you wanted to be."

I'm almost impressed at his ability to flirt shamelessly in front of my father, who speaks up before I can throw anything back. "Young, stop flirting with my daughter. What do you want?"

Austin's tone turns serious as he faces Dad and starts asking him a question. Now that my job is done, I turn to make my exit. Austin winks at me as I leave and my fists clench as something swoops dangerously in my stomach. I've known the guy less than twenty-four hours and he's already managing to both annoy and charm me at the same time.

"What's on the agenda today?" my roommate and best friend, Sydney, asks me.

Lying on my bed upside down with my legs propped up against the headboard, I stretch my arms over my head and look at her from across the room. "Two classes and then I have work."

It's warm again today and I doubt that I'll ever wear anything other than summer clothes ever again. I'm comfortable, don't get me wrong, but I miss hoodies and scarves and wearing a normal bra instead of a sports bra because sweating through my regular bras is getting irritating and at least a sports bra is made for sweating. *Sigh*. At this point, I just want to be comfortable and a tank top, sports bra, and cutoff shorts seems to be the best way to do it.

Sydney, on the other hand, looks adorable, even with her changing her outfit three times already. Everything looks great on her, no matter what it is. I almost wanted to be jealous of her.

"I don't know why you let your dad convince you to work for the team. I know you don't want to be there," she remarks, examining her reflection in the mirror on the back of our dorm room door. Like me, she's tall but that's also where the similarities end. Her slim body fits easily within the frame of the mirror and her dark red hair spills down her back, a stark contrast against her pale skin. Her green eyes are narrowed as she studies her outfit from every angle. Her black jeans hug her narrow hips and give the impression that she has a curve to her butt, but the shirt does nothing but accentuate her small chest. Just as I'm thinking this, she makes a face and yanks the shirt she's wearing over her head and tosses it to the ground. She grabs another one from the miniscule closet we share.

"I need the money and really, it's not that bad. Also, Syd, we barely have enough room to move around without you tossing your shit all over the place." I gave a pointed look at her discarded shirt.

She looks over her shoulder at me, rolling her eyes with a small smile. Her side of the room is a disaster. Clothes are everywhere, textbooks are stacked on her desk and chair so she can't use them for their intended purpose. There's even more crap on her bed and I question, not for the first time, how she can be comfortable sleeping on it. It's only our second semester at this school and I still am struggling to accept that our split personality dorm room is here to stay.

My side of the room, on the other hand, is incredibly neat. My bed is made, corners pulled tight. My textbooks for this semester are stacked neatly on my desk, next to my laptop, which is closed. The only thing askew is my Harry Potter poster, which I hung crookedly the first weekend in this place and haven't bothered to fix since then.

We're almost polar opposites. I know that sounds cliché, but it's true. Sydney is loud, messy, and certifiably insane, always down for whatever the next adventure is. She has her reasons for that. I'm a lot quieter, neater, more likely to stay at home and watch Netflix than go out and party. But we make it work, mostly because our mutual best friend, Drew, is a nice mix of the two of us and the three of us are basically unstoppable together.

Sydney finally decides on a shirt and then turns to me. "There are other jobs on campus, Evie. You don't *have* to do this one."

I pause, considering what she's said. "I know I don't. How else do I explain to my dad that I would rather work in the campus library or the coffee shop instead of the base-ball field. He's used to his daughter who used to…who loves baseball. The locker room is where I should be so I'm there."

"Not the way you should be," she points out. I gave her a look; she knows why I had practically given up anything to do with baseball after Jesse. "Yeah, I said it. Are you sure *that's* not the reason you're there?"

"I have no idea what you're talking about." I ignore the sinking feeling in my stomach.

"Well, is it about Jesse then? Is that why you're there?"

"Of course not," I say sharply, sitting up. She winces at my tone. "Jesus, Syd."

"It's been three *years*, Evie," she replies, softly. "You gave up your dream. And you can still barely stand to be around him. Forgive me for pointing out the obvious reasons that you're denying to yourself."

"It's not because of Jesse. And it's not because...because of the other thing, either," I repeat. It's not. *It's not, it's not, it's not.*

"He's not going to leave her," she says, and the words nearly break my heart. I've repeated those same words over and over to myself throughout the past three years. They have become more and more the truth as the years have passed, as they've stayed together. Lucy and Jesse are solid, stable and that's not changing anytime soon. It's not surprising, considering what they've been through together, the heartbreak they endured together three years ago, the kind of heartbreak that only the two of them *could* endure together. I can't help it though; I would be lying if I said that they're not the words I want to hear. He made me promises too.

I stand up quickly, my hair flying all over the place in the sudden movement. I run a hand along the back of my head to smooth it and grab my book bag off my desk chair. "I have to go."

"Oh, come on, Evie, don't be like that," Sydney protests.

"I have to go," I repeat, this time more insistently. "I have class in twenty minutes on the other side of campus." Before she can reply, I'm out the door and halfway down the hallway. I punch the button for the elevator, hard, and wince a little. The door slides open immediately—a rare occurrence—and I step in. There's no one inside and I take this opportunity to sigh rather loudly. I regret the way I spoke to Sydney. It's not her fault, not in the slightest, and I have to stop taking these things out on people that don't deserve my anger.

The walk to my class is short. A blast of cold air hits me as I open the door to the auditorium. My classes this semester are simple: English Lit, Calculus, Psychology and Art History. A weird combination but I'm hoping something will jump out and scream, *CAREER*! I knew for so much of my life what I wanted to do and knew how totally unlikely it was. Now I'm on a search again and I've had no luck so far.

It's the first day of my Art History class, which is a popular class, as most of the seats are already taken and I'm a good ten minutes early. I'm actually kind of excited about this class, more so than the other classes I've signed up for this semester. So far, college has just seemed to be a repetition of high school—math, reading, writing, *blah blah blah*. But I've heard great things about this class and the professor and apparently, I was lucky to have even enrolled in the class. I always liked history in junior high and high school, so I have high hopes for this class. I'm more than ready to really feel like I'm in college already. Maybe it's the familiar surroundings but it feels like nothing has changed. I want things to change. I need things to change.

I head up the risers, to a seat in the back. There's a group of desks that are empty and I slide into one of them, taking out a blank notebook and pen.

I wonder for a moment if Sydney is right and I'm truly just being a masochist by choosing to work with my dad. I could work some other job on campus to earn money. There are plenty of them. There's two Starbucks on campus, as well as a regular cafe and a *ton* of food places. The bookstore and library are always hiring student workers, yet I chose to stick with the baseball team. True, it would be hard to explain to my dad why I wanted nothing to do with the team I've spent my entire life loving, but he would live. *Ugh*. It can't be because of Jesse or because I used to want… what I still wanted. There's no way. That was the old Evie and that was three years ago. I'd moved on.

I had. There was no other option but to move on.

I'm so lost in my thoughts that I almost don't notice when someone literally plops into the seat next to me, loudly, causing me to jump a little. I turn involuntarily in their direction and my mouth drops open. *You have* got *to be kidding me.*

"Well, hey there, princess."

Austin's smile is wide as he stretches his legs out. He barely fits into the desk and it's no wonder. He's not particularly large, not surprising for a shortstop but he's all legs and he's bulky enough to make the desk he's sitting in look like it was made for a five-year-old.

"What are you doing here?" I ask, stupidly, unable to think of anything else to say. I'm starting to wonder if the guy even knows my name. All he has managed to do so far is call me baby and princess. I wanted nothing more than to roll my eyes at the trivial nicknames.

"Well, crazily enough, I'm actually *enrolled* in this class," he replies, his smile stretching even wider across his face. He has this devilish sort of smile, like he knows a big secret. It does funny things to me every time I see it and I don't like it. "I am a student here too, you know."

"Are you following me?" I regret the words almost before they even leave my mouth, but it's like word vomit and I tend to have that, like, pretty much all the time.

Austin's eyebrows raise and there's something extremely sexy about it and I have the sudden, irresistible urge to run my fingertips over them. It's a stupid thought and I shove it away as quickly as I can. "Now, how on earth would I know you'd be in this class? Though I'm pretty glad you are." His accent is thick as hell and I get the image of him on the back of a horse with a cowboy hat on shirtless. *Damn it.* This will be fodder for my dreams for a while.

I turn away from him. "You have this sort of weird thing of showing up wherever I am."

"Today is just a coincidence, princess," he laughs. "I can't help it if you walk into locker rooms while innocent baseball players are taking showers. You work for your daddy and I play for him. Not exactly weird that we'd bump into each other. This campus isn't exactly huge anyway."

"You're irritating," I spit out, under my breath, as the professor walks in.

"I'll take that as a compliment," he replies.

"It was most definitely not intended as one." I roll my eyes and flip my notebook open to a clean page before taking a copy of the syllabus from the large pile as it's passed down the rows. I turn to hand the slowly depleting pile over to Austin and find him mere inches away from my face. I gasp, a heat flooding through me at his proximity.

"Do I intimidate you, princess?" he asks, a wide grin on his face. His face is mere inches away from mine, his lips are right in front of me and my god…it had been so long since I had been kissed—that has to be the reason I'm feeling all of this…warmth spread through my chest as the sudden desire to close the distance between us overwhelms me. It's not that I haven't been with anyone since Jesse…but also, I don't think anyone has made me want to kiss them this strongly, this soon into having met them, and I'm unnerved by it.

I'm unnerved by *him*.

"Of course not," I say, sharply, pulling away from him, "and stop calling me *princess*."

He chuckles under his breath. "*Liar*." He takes the stack of papers from me, his fingers brushing against the sensitive skin on the inside of my wrist. The contact is brief but it's enough to send a jolt up my arm. I yank my arm back and he smiles knowingly before taking his own copy of the syllabus and passing it along to the girl on his opposite side.

Austin doesn't speak to me for the rest of the class. The professor drones on and on and on, reading every single word on the syllabus, even though we all have a copy in front of us and should, logically, be able to read and understand it on our own. I can feel Austin's eyes on me several times. His gaze makes me uncomfortable, like every inch of my skin is on fire, and I'm squirming in my seat. I glance his way, and the corners of his mouth turn up a bit. I flush and turn away from him.

Suddenly my sloppy, comfortable outfit from this morning doesn't seem so sloppy anymore. Austin's eyes are all over me, drifting over my shoulders, across the swell of my breasts, to the curve of my hips to my bare legs and he makes me feel indecent. I am torn between loving the attention and wishing that he would look at anything else in the room besides me. I cross and uncross my legs several times, feeling the heat throughout my body as he stares at me. *Is he even trying to pay attention to whatever the hell our professor is saying?*

I nearly jump out of my seat when the professor finally dismisses us for the day and my notebook goes flying off my desk, skidding to a halt a good five feet in front of me. Several people look in my direction and I blush furiously. Some of my dark blonde hair spills in my face as I reach for it, but a large hand reaches it before I do. "Here you go, princess."

"Stop calling me that," I say, firmly, reaching for the notebook. He holds it tightly in his hand, as we engage in a sort of tug of war. "Let go."

He laughs and let's go. I'm unprepared and I stumble backward a little, hitting my hip against the desk behind me. The pain shoots through my back as my mood shifts from annoyed to pissed in no time at all. Frustrated, I turn away from him and promptly march down the steps, ready to be as far away from him as possible.

"See you at practice!" he calls out after me. I scowl, making my exit as quickly as possible.

I try to ignore Austin during practice, but this is so much easier said than done because I can't seem to tear my eyes away from him. He's decided, yet again, that a shirt is completely optional today and his skin has a beautiful golden-brown tan and even I'll admit—his chest and stomach are a gift from the gods. No one should be able to look that way, not even a baseball player—*especially* not a baseball player. My mind flashes again to him astride a horse, with the damn cowboy hat. Austin catches me looking at him and smiles and my face burns while I scowl and look away.

My eyes fall back on Jesse, who is pitching not too far from where I'm sitting. He throws a pitch that's wild and Jackson, our starting catcher, glares at him. Jesse laughs easily, tossing out words to Jackson that I don't quite catch. He must say something funny because Jackson laughs a beat behind him. I watch them for a bit longer, a smile spreading across my face. Jesse has always had a way of making me smile, even when I didn't want to or didn't feel like it. From the moment I met him, he felt like something special. I pause in the middle of my work, laying my pencil down on the clipboard, as a memory from three years ago makes it way forward. I inhale sharply as I try to repress it, but no matter how hard I try, my heart pounds in my chest as his voice fills my head.

"Is that right?" Jesse asks, his eyebrow raised. He looks me up and down and it sends a shiver up my spine. His eyes meet mine and they flick both and forth between the two colors. He seems surprised

but he doesn't say anything. "I don't know many girls who really know and love baseball."

I feel a slight annoyance at the statement. "I know that you had eighty RBIs this season, the most in Quakes' history and that you ended the year with a .332 batting average, just a few points shy of the record as a freshman, if you hadn't gone zero for four in game four," I blurt out.

Dad bursts out laughing, and Jesse is a beat behind him. "I guess I shouldn't be surprised in this town," Jesse says, looking impressed. "Thanks for pointing out my fantastic performance in game four. I seriously appreciate that."

With another shaky breath, I wipe the palms of my now sweaty hands on the front of my shorts. Shaking my head, I turn back to the paper in hand, determined to divide up the players evenly when they hit the road for their first away stay. There's only one other woman on the staff, Jane, the team's athletic trainer, so I'll be bunking with her, if I even decide to go, that is. I can't make up my mind if I should go with the team for the weekend or stay here on campus.

How did I get myself so mixed up in this team? All I've wanted to do is avoid baseball and now I'm considering putting myself in a position where there's *more* baseball. I consider that it has to do with Jesse or Austin…possibly even both of them, but I really don't want to let those thoughts go any further.

Dad walks up beside me, peering over my shoulder. "Tomorrow is the first game," he says, after a moment. I nod. "I'd like to have you in the dugout with the team." It's phrased as a request, but his tone makes it more like a demand. I resist the urge to sigh but nod again. *Well, I guess that decides on whether I'm staying or going.* Baseball, it is. "Is everything all right?"

I look up at him, surprised. My dad is an amazing guy. He is, but the fact that he hasn't noticed how much I've changed over the past few years shows how much dedication goes into watching every small detail of his team on the field and less on the team he has at home. "Yeah, I'm fine."

"You just seem…tired or something."

I deflate a little. It's more than just being tired but it's not worth attempting to explain, especially now. "Yeah, I'm a little tired. The beginning of the semester and all of that."

He nods, clearing his throat, looking decidedly less uncomfortable than he did a moment ago. My dad has always liked when things are wrapped up in a tight box that he can understand. It's always kind of baffled me, considering the kind of family he has, but I'm used to it by now. "Makes sense. You'll get in the groove of things before long." There's a long pause and I'm hoping he's going to say more than that, but he just continues. "What do you think of Bennett's swing?"

I sigh and flip through the pages on my clipboard. "There are definitely some issues there."

"Alright." He says, taking a seat next to me. "Hit me with it."

"HEY! THERE'S MY GIRL!"

I whirl around, my ponytail smacking in my face, and I immediately blush. The Quakes have just won the College World series for the first time in years and everyone in town is buzzing about it, especially about our new freshman pitcher, Jesse Valdez.

Jesse Valdez.

He's the most beautiful person I've ever seen in my life. He's tall, handsome as hell, with dark brown hair that's nearly black, deep-set brown eyes, and caramel colored skin. Not to mention how talented he is on the pitcher's mound. I haven't seen a fastball thrown like that in the Quakes Stadium in years. He's three years older than me but it's not that much of a difference. I'm determined to finally meet him.

It seems like destiny is on my side. As I push my way through the celebrating crowd toward Dad, I see him. He's surrounded by a ton of people, congratulating him on the win, but my eyes are only on one person: Jesse.

"Hi Dad!" I squeal, running into his arms. He lifts me in a big bear hug, and I laugh. "Congrats on the win!"

"Thanks, button!" He has an incurable smile on his face, looking around with pride. The last time the Quakes won the World Series was when he was in college and I know he's happier than ever to bring that trophy back as a coach. "Evie, have you met Jesse yet?"

I feel my heart slam hard against my ribs and the butterflies that had already been flying aimlessly in my stomach all day start beating their wings with a fervor I didn't know could exist before. Jesse was right there, right next to my dad, with a smile on his face. "No, I haven't had the chance to," I say, faintly, staring up at him. It's so hard to string words together when he's around. I stick my hand out to him. "I'm Evie. Evie Cordova."

"Ah, Coach's daughter," he answers. His smile grows wider and I take this time to admire him. He's at least six-foot-two, maybe even taller, with broad shoulders, a flat stomach, and extremely well-built arms. His hair is a deep black, falling into dark brown eyes, complimenting his perfectly tanned skin. He's perfect in every way, the exact sort of perfect that you have in your mind when you're sixteen years old. "I remember you from the games. I didn't know you were the coach's daughter."

"One of them," I manage to say. "I'm a twin."

"Double trouble?" Jesse asks, but he doesn't seem that interested in this fact, and it immediately makes it a thousand times more attractive. Lucy and I have heard dirty jokes and suggestions all my life. It's also just nice to be treated as a separate person from my sister, which is a rare occurrence.

"Oh, yeah, I got two girls ready to send me to an early grave,"

Dad jokes. "Especially that Lucy. Evie makes my life easy. She likes baseball, like her old man."

"Is that right?" Jesse asks, his eyebrow raised. He looks me up and down and it sends a shiver up my spine. His eyes meet mine and they flick both and forth between the two colors. He seems surprised but he doesn't say anything. "I don't know many girls who really know and love baseball."

I feel a slight annoyance at the statement. "I know that you had eighty RBIs this season, the most in Quakes' history and that you ended the year with a .332 batting average, just a few points shy of the record as a freshman, if you hadn't gone zero for four in game four," I blurt out.

Dad bursts out laughing, and Jesse is a beat behind him. "I guess I shouldn't be surprised in this town," Jesse says, looking impressed. "Thanks for pointing out my fantastic performance in game four. I seriously appreciate that."

"Any time," I pipe, a small smile on my face. "And I don't just know baseball. I play baseball."

Jesse shoots an incredulous look over at my dad, who beams proudly. "She plays for her high school team. They just won their CIF championship game, thanks to her. She hit a double to score the winning run."

I turned to Jesse, my face flushed in both pride and embarrassment. I square my shoulders back and try to exude confidence. I know how to act around boys; I spend most of my time with the guys on the team but it's just so different when you actually like them.

"Well, okay, I'm impressed. Are you going to join the Quakes someday?"

Jesse and Dad laugh like it's the funniest thing in the world and I frown. Why else have I been playing so long and working so hard if not to play for the Quakes one day? I open my mouth to say something back, but someone calls out to the both of them and they're distracted.

Dad turns away to talk to someone else and now I have Jesse's *full attention. He takes this opportunity to lean close to me. "Are you going to the bonfire tonight?"*

I suck in my breath, my skin tingling at his proximity. "I think so."

His hand is on my arm as he whispers in my ear. "I hope you do." He pulls away, walking backward. "Nice to meet you, Evie."

CHAPTER THREE

My back is stuck to the vinyl chair I'm sitting in. The day is hot and we're already into the fourth inning, and the boys are doing spectacularly. It's just a preseason game, so it doesn't count toward our record or anything but the guys are still giving it a good show. The papers, ESPN —*everyone* is going to be talking about the team this season. A clipboard lays across my lap, with the batting order on it, and I'm taking notes. I'm doing a terrible job at pretending I don't care about this game.

After all these years of avoiding the damned sport, I've learned that it's easier to pretend you don't care when you're not around it. But when being here, on the field, watching the game and smelling all the familiar smells—the newly popped popcorn, the freshly mown grass—and hearing the satisfying crack as the ball makes contact with the bat—it's just hard to ignore how baseball makes me feel. I spend so much time filled with dread at the thought of coming back to the locker room, the practice field, the stadium but once I'm here, I forget why I dreaded it in the first place. I used to love baseball so much; being here used to be like a kid in a candy store inside of Disneyland. It doesn't feel like that anymore. It hasn't for a while, but I'm remembering that feeling—the true feeling of home.

"Are you okay?" Drew is leaning against the fence of the dugout. His eyes are concentrating on the field in front of him, but his words ring with sincerity and genuine concern. Drew has never been what some people call conventionally attractive but he's attractive in his own way. He's cute, so incredibly funny, with dirty blonde hair, green eyes, and a ton of freckles. But once he got on that pitcher's mound, he became something else. Any girl would fall in love with him when he was on that pitcher's mound.

Plus, I could attest to the fact that he was a really good kisser. Or at least he had been when we were fifteen. I had experience with that.

"I'm fine," I say, breezily, aware that both Austin and Jesse are mere feet away from me. "Why wouldn't I be?"

He tears his eyes away from the field for a moment and gives me a knowing look. He, like Sydney, is one of the few people who know the truth of what had happened three years ago. He hates Jesse, almost as much as I wish I could, but he holds it in as best as he can. After all, he's a freshman on the team, not even a starter yet, and he worships the Quakes as much as everyone else in this town. Drew's been pitching for as long as I can remember and he works his ass off all the time, trying to get better, determined to be a starter eventually on this team. He has to respect his captain, even if he secretly hates him.

"I know you don't want to be here," he says, under his breath and I raise my eyebrow at him. "Well, I know you didn't want to be here like *this*." His eyes are back on the field, watching intently as Jesse stands on the mound and throws a pitch. It's a bit outside but the umpire calls it a strike, much to the approval of the fans in the stands. It's the last out of the inning and the boys coming running in. I busy myself with the batting order in front of me, calling out names as they come strutting into the dugout. They've effectively ended my conversation with Drew, and I am grateful. I adore my best friends and I know that they are looking out for me, but I'm tired of being asked if I'm okay. I *am* okay.

I have to be okay.

Austin, on the other hand, does not seem okay at all. He's having a terrible game. It's the bottom of the fifth and we are winning the game, but only by three runs. Jesse is pitching and he's only allowed one run. Austin hasn't contributed on offense at all. His first at-bat was fine, a walk, not great but not the end of the world. His second and third chances at the plate were just awful though. He's swinging at wild pitches—pitches that aren't even in the strike zone. His elbow is too low when he's up there and it's making his swing all kinds of awkward. He's up for the fourth time and, for some reason, I'm hoping he'll change his luck. I tell myself it's because I want to spare myself from having to watch his awkward swing and nothing more.

I learned from Jane recently that Austin had been recovering from a shoulder injury from his first season at UT. They have some of the best trainers in the college system at that school...there really shouldn't be any reason why it would still be bothering him. That is, unless he didn't let it heal right, unless he wasn't honest about his injury, unless he's afraid of hurting it again, *unless, unless, unless*. Whatever it is, I need to figure it out so it can be fixed.

By the batting coach. Not me. *Definitely not me.*

"Nervous much, Evie?" a voice comes from above me as Austin steps up to the plate. I look up, my eyes meeting Jesse's. He's thrown his jacket over himself, keeping his arm warm until he's back on the mound. He's leaning against the fence behind me, next to Drew.

"What are you talking about?" I ask, ignoring the look of concern on Drew's face.

"Your boy out there," Jesse answers, nodding his head in Austin's direction.

My tone has a little more bite in it when I repeat myself, pausing after each word. "What. Are. You. Talking. About?" The ball goes flying straight down the middle of the strike zone and Austin doesn't swing.

Strike one.

"Well, you *were* Googling him the other day…"

"You're ridiculous," I say, tapping my pen against the plastic of the clipboard in my lap. "He's just another one of the players." *Just like you,* I want to say but, of course, I don't. It always seems so useless to say anything…*more* with Jesse. It's like starting an argument you'll never win. I've had way too much experience with this. I'd rather not repeat it.

"Good," Jesse says, his voice soft. It's meant for only me, but I can tell that Drew hears him by the way his lips are pressed tightly together into a thin line. "Not just anyone can date my Evie."

I ignore him but my body betrays me, and butterflies erupt in my stomach.

Austin steps out of the box for a moment, adjusting his batting gloves before stepping back in. I can see him taking a deep breath, his shoulders lifting slightly, before getting back into his stance again, elbow way too low once again. We seriously need to figure out what is going on with that old shoulder injury because he could be a real decent batter if he just stopped swinging so weird. The Fullerton pitcher throws the ball to first, where a runner is waiting, before turning his attention back to Austin. The second pitch is a little outside; Austin fails to swing and luckily the umpire calls it a ball.

"Come on, Austin!" Jesse calls out from behind me. There are a couple of cleat chasers—baseball groupies, though I do feel kind of bad calling them that—sitting behind the dugout. Earlier, they'd been making appreciative comments about Austin and, now, encouraged by Jesse, they call out to Austin. One of them even yells *'take it off,'* which makes me roll my eyes.

Another pitch is thrown and Austin swings wildly for a pitch that's definitely low. He twists uncomfortably for a moment and I wince. That's going to hurt later.

"Come on, Austin!" Jesse repeats and a few more people in the crowd call out as well. Jesse is the hometown hero and if he's cheering for the newbie, you can bet the others will follow.

I focus on Austin, as he watches a ball that's too high fly past him. I breathe a sigh of relief and wait for the next pitch. Austin's bat connects with it and I feel my fingers gripping the edge of the clipboard tightly as the ball goes flying up and up and up and comes down, straight into the glove of the second baseman. Austin rips off his batting gloves and stalks back to the dugout, passing me on his way in. Our eyes meet for a moment and I try to smile encouragingly at him.

"Well, that was embarrassing," Jesse remarks under his breath and I barely catch his words. I shoot him a glare from the corner of my eye, but he doesn't see it. He's tossing his jacket to the side and grabbing his glove, ready to return to the field. His comment lingers however and leaves me annoyed. I remember a certain pitcher with an incredibly low batting average just a few years ago.

Austin is behind me as well and he looks angry as he makes his way onto the field. I'm close enough to see there's a crease in his forehead and his mouth is set in a straight, grim line. It's jarring after all the smiles and charm he's been giving me all week and I have a feeling it's directly connected to his performance—or lack thereof—tonight. Jesse strikes out the first batter, easily, within four pitches. Austin yells and pumps his fist into his glove a few times. He's ready, waiting, angry and yet poised. I can't stop watching him. I'm supposed to be watching the whole team, but Austin is mesmerizing and I'm drawn to him. He knows everyone is watching and he looks determined.

Jesse throws a ball, looking truly pissed. He takes his time with the next pitch and sends it sailing down the middle, but the batter makes easy contact with it. It goes out like a shot toward center field.

I'm already groaning in disappointment when I see Austin go into a dive. He reaches for the ball and grabs it, rolling into a somersault. The crowd behind us goes wild and he sits up, yelling triumphantly. I feel a jolt go through me and I can't help the small smile that stretches across my face. He's too attractive for words and that catch…that catch was stunning. I completely miss the last out, distracted as I am, as the guys return to the dugout. A hand brushes over my thigh as they pass, and I know who it is. I suck in a breath quickly and stand up, retreating into the dugout.

Maybe this job really *is* a bad idea.

The locker room is a disaster after the game is over and I'm cleaning up the best I can when I hear someone slam a locker door shut. It echoes in the empty room, startling me and I pause for a moment, waiting for footsteps or some other kind of noise to let me know who else is in here. There's no other noise though so I walk around and find Austin sitting in a chair, by himself. He doesn't notice me at first, so I clear my throat.

He looks up and a smile stretches across his face, though it does seem a little forced. "Hey princess."

"What are you doing here?" I ask. "Everyone else is gone. I think they were going down to Mitch's to celebrate the win." Mitch's is the local pub, located close to the beach. The owner serves pizza, burgers and cheap beers and it's where most of the students go to hang out after a game.

"Don't really feel much like celebrating," Austin admits, shrugging. He's shirtless again and I can't help admitting, to myself anyway, what a beautiful sight he is. My lady parts are way too happy to look at him, and my brain has to scold them, reminding them that he's a baseball player, no matter how pretty he looks without a shirt on. He shifts in the chair and his muscles ripple slightly. I have a sudden, over-whelming desire to run my tongue over his stomach and I blush, turning away. It's amazing how easily this guy can work me up.

"Well, what's wrong?" I ask. He doesn't answer and I feel a sudden flash of irritation, both at myself for caring and him for not answering, for keeping me here. I can't lock up until everyone is out and I'm tired and I don't want to be here. "Okay, well…" I turn to leave.

"Wait, don't go."

"What?" I say, sharper than I mean to. "What do you want, Austin?"

He hesitates and there's a hint of something in his eyes, something I can't quite identify. His hands run through his dark brown hair and it looks like he's done that quite a few times tonight. "I just…need someone to talk to. Someone *not* on the team."

I blink a couple times, surprised. I've known the boy all of three days, if that, and our interactions have been limited to blatant flirting on his part and staunch denial on my part.

"Um. Okay." I manage to answer. "I guess I'm here. I'm not technically part of the team. Talk."

My eyes are glued to his abs and I can't look away. I'm too distracted for a serious conversation. I'm not even boy crazy; I've always been one of the boys. I don't act like this. What the hell is wrong with me? He doesn't say anything for a second and my irritation flares up again. God, who the hell is this guy?

"Tonight sucked," he finally says, his words barely audible in the nearly silent room. They come out quickly, as if he can barely stand to say them.

This is not what I'm expecting, and I pull back, my eyes springing to make eye contact with him. "Wait, what?"

"Evie, tonight…was not good. It's not what it needed to be. I was not what I needed to be." He pauses. "I sucked."

I shake my head, hearing the anger and pure disappointment in his voice and I feel the sudden urge to make him feel better. "You didn't suck, Austin…"

"Yeah, I did, actually," he says, cutting me off. "Zero hits? Not exactly a winning start to the season." His anger thickens his accent and I'm having a harder time understanding him.

"It's the beginning of the season," I point out. "That wasn't even a real game. No one expects you to be a superstar. No one expects you to be perfect."

"I do. I expect me to be perfect." His voice is firm and sharp, and it catches me off guard. He sighs. "Not to mention what the *entire* town is expecting, right? The Quakes are supposed to be perfect."

"You're being incredibly too hard on yourself," I say. My hand seems to have a mind of its own as it reaches forward to pat him on the knee. "It's only one game."

Austin pushes my hand away before I'm able to touch him and I'm disappointed and relieved. Touching seems like a very bad idea. He stands up, a quick sudden movement, and the chair clatters to the ground with a loud crash and I jump. "No! It's not just one game!" He starts pacing back and forth. "One game and I'm back on the bench and scouts won't even look my way. Goodbye MLB! Goodbye every-thing I've worked hard for—*everything* that my mom sacri-ficed for! Goodbye to the one and only thing that I've ever been good at! I don't want to be on the bench—I *can't* be on the bench. I'm a nobody in this town, they don't have to keep me in the game or even trust me to get my job done."

It's the most personal thing he's said to me in the short time we've known each other. In all honesty, it's the most personal thing anyone has said to me in a while. "You're not a nobody," I say with conviction. "You killed it in high school, made All-American and you did even better in Texas. You probably would have done better if you had the playing time, which you *will* get here. And tonight? That catch was phenomenal."

He stops pacing and looks at me, his eyebrow raised. How on earth is an eyebrow raise sexy? "What are you talking about?"

I roll my eyes, resisting the urge to check my watch. God, I'm exhausted. I had barely, officially, met this guy and already he had me acting like a complete fool and I just wanted to go to bed. "Austin," I say, slowly, "you made the All-American team in high school and broke the record for stolen bases and home runs in one season, as a junior, no less. You got into UT, one of the *best* baseball programs in the country and now you're here, in Izzy, as a transfer, which, by the way, isn't common either. You're not a nobody."

"Did you look me up?" Austin asks, a smile spreading across his face.

I roll my eyes. He hasn't even been listening to a word

I've been saying. "Don't get excited, ball boy," I say, drily. "My dad's your coach, remember? I have easy access to information, and the information I saw—it's impressive, Austin."

"I can't believe you looked me up. I heard you knew everything about everyone here at this school," he remarks, picking up the chair and tucking it against the wall.

"Who told you that?" I ask, eyeing him carefully.

"Nobody important," Austin replies, the smile on his face stretching until it's almost too blinding to look at. "You really thought that catch was great?"

"Austin, everyone in Izzy tonight thought that was great. It'll be front page news tomorrow," I admit, sighing. I glance at my watch, standing up and pulling my keys from my pocket. "You seem happier. Does that mean we can go home?"

"Well, it does make me happier to hear a pretty girl telling me that I made a good catch tonight," Austin answers, grabbing a t-shirt from his locker and yanking it over his head. I try not to be disappointed in him putting on a shirt for once.

"Austin…" His name is a sigh on my lips.

"What?" he asks, holding his hands in defense.

"Please stop hitting on me," I say, as we walk out of the locker room.

I'm fitting my keys into the lock and turning it closed when he replies, "I'm not hitting on you."

I scoff, tossing my keys into my backpack after pulling on the door handle to make sure it locked.

Austin grabs my arm and turns me around so that I'm facing him and we're mere inches apart. "Seriously, I'm not hitting on you. Not right now anyway." A grin spreads across his face. "You'll know when I'm hitting on you."

I try to pull away and he pulls me close and I notice how

thin his white t-shirt is. His hand is wrapped tightly around my waist, his thumb under the hem of my shirt, rubbing the bare skin on the small of my back and I have to remind myself to breathe.

"Evie, I'm just saying, the guys on the team talk. They say you know baseball and not just because you're a girl but just because you—you're well…you're *you*. You really love baseball; it's why you're helping with the team. Getting a compliment from you? It feels like a big deal around here."

"Oh," I manage to say, stupidly, trying so hard not to notice how close we are and that everything in my body is screaming at me to close what little space is left between us. My hands are reaching for him before I can catch myself. I clear my throat, flushing, and pull away. "Well, it was an incredible catch. You *should* feel proud of that. That was something that people will remember, not whether you hit the ball tonight."

"Right. So now I'm happier than I was before," he answers.

"Fabulous," I answer, flatly, rolling my eyes once more. "Does that mean I can go home now?"

Austin laughs. "Yeah, princess, you can go home now." He pauses. "Where are you at?"

I hesitate before answering. "Fletcher Hall."

His smile returns, just the corner of his mouth. "Perfect. I'm in Houser. I'll walk you."

"Oh, no, you don't have to…" I start to protest, but his hand slips into mine easily and he starts pulling me in the direction of the dorms. I lose my train of thought and the small contact we have through our hands is driving me insane. Who is this guy that thinks he can just touch me so easily? And why am I not pulling away?

The walk to our dorms isn't too far from the stadium but we remain in silence the whole way. His hand stays linked with mine and I can't figure out a way to extract it without seeming rude. I don't want him to hold my hand…do I? I can feel my heart pounding in the center of my palm and I'm sure he can feel it too. I'm hyperaware of how sweaty my hand is, and I'm embarrassed by it. His thumb makes a brief sweep across the top of my hand occasionally, and it sends a jolt through me every time. The guy unnerves me.

He walks me all the way up to the door of Fletcher Hall and I expect him to leave as I slide my ID through the scanner at the front door. Instead, he reaches for the door, holding it open for me. I walk through it wordlessly and make my way through the front halls to the elevator, with him at my tail. I'm not sure what he's doing but every nerve ending is boiling, and the elevator seems crowded as we make our way up to the fourth floor.

Sydney and I managed to score a room tucked away from most of the action. The first couple of weeks of school had "majorly sucked" in Sydney's words because no one walked down our way, no matter how many times we left our door open, but it also had the advantage of having what little privacy was available in a dorm hall.

Technically I could have stayed at home instead of moving into the dorm, but my room at home didn't feel the same when my sister decided to move out after high school graduation. She was always the braver one, jumping off cliffs into the ocean when we were preteens, cutting her hair a million different ways, never knowing if it was going to look right. She's the exciting, thrill-seeker out of the two of us. It only made sense that the moment we turned eighteen, she moved out into an apartment off campus with her boyfriend. My parents didn't care either. They had already dealt with much worse than their barely legal daughter moving in with her boyfriend of two years.

Instead of staying at home, in the room that Lucy and I

used to share, I took up Sydney's offer to be her roommate. Syd always had good reasons to not want to be at home, not that she spoke about them much, and pretty much escaped to the dorm hall the moment that she could. This new room was a good, clean slate for the both of us.

I pause in front of our door, staring at the white board Sydney hung up before she did anything else with our room. There's a message for her, a scrawled-out phone number with a crooked heart and I resist the urge to laugh. Damn social butterfly. My keys are dangling loosely in my hand as I turn to say goodbye to him.

"Can I see you tomorrow?" His hands are shoved deep in the pockets of his jeans and he suddenly looks shy.

I blink in surprise. "Why would you see me tomorrow?"

"Well, we do have a class together tomorrow," he points out, "and practice."

Art History. Right. Damn. "I guess you have your answer then."

"What about after practice? We could hang out."

"Austin," I warn.

A corner of his mouth lifts slightly. "Remember how I said I wasn't hitting on you? Well, I lied."

I sigh, loudly. "I don't really *do* baseball players."

His small smile transforms into a full, megawatt smile. "Well, that's an interesting rule, Evie," he says, taking a step forward. I move away from him but there's nowhere to go and my back hits the wall behind me. "Who *do* you do…"

"That's not what I meant," I reply. His hand comes up to my waist and he pushes me tighter against the wall. The pressure burns me, the heat of it is overwhelming through my thin shirt and I look up at him.

"Do you think you can make an exception?"

I shake my head, my heart beating a heavy metal rhythm in my chest. "I never make exceptions."

"I think you will, princess," he says, his voice low. He moves closer to me, and his body is flushed against mine. I gasp, my hands reaching up on their own accord to grab his arms. His muscles flex under my fingers and my fingernails dig into his skin.

My lips part and my eyes are fixated on his lips, the lower lip fuller than the upper. I want to take it between my teeth and the urge causes butterflies to erupt in my stomach. "I don't know where you get your confidence, cowboy," I say, trying to ignore how he feels against me, soft in all the right places, hard in all the oh so wrong ones.

"I'm not going to lie, I like it when you call me cowboy," he says, a low growl in the back of his throat. I didn't think guys actually growled like in romance novels but apparently, they do and it's sending shivers up my spine.

"Well, I don't like…" He cuts me off before I have a chance to finish my sentence and his lips are on mine and I can taste the salt from the coastal air on his lips. A small moan escapes from the back of my throat as he deepens the kiss, his lips sliding against mine, probing my mouth to slide his tongue in. His kisses are fast and feverish, but his lips are impossibly soft against mine. His tongue drags against the roof of my mouth and I moan again, my hands sliding up his arms to his shoulders and pulling him down tighter against me.

We kiss for what feels like ages and I have no need to stop. God, how long has it been since I've been kissed— really and thoroughly kissed? The kiss is hard and bruising and I can feel it all the way to my toes. There's a dim reminder in the back of my brain telling me that this isn't really something that I should be doing and that someone could walk out and see us at any moment but my focus is solely on his lips and how I don't think I've ever been kissed like this before. I'd be content to sit here, pressed up against the wall, his body pressed hard against mine, and kiss him for hours. That's how seriously great the kissing is.

Austin seems to have other things in mind, as his hands begin to explore different areas of my body.

His leg slides in between my legs and it rubs up against me in all the right ways. I gasp at the sudden sensation; he's definitely aroused, and I can feel it against me. I roll my hips and a shudder goes through him.

"Fuck, princess," Austin manages to say, his tongue darting out across the pulse on my neck. His head dips lower and lower, his lips drifting across my collarbone and into the dip of my tank top. His fingers tug at the collar and he's yanking it down before I can protest. I briefly am grateful that I'm wearing a nicer bra and not one of my old beige ones. His hands reach up and grab me, his thumbs rubbing softly over my nipples. The sensation causes me to gasp.

He leans down, taking a nipple into his mouth through my bra and my hands are wrapped tightly in his soft, thick dark hair. Little whimpers are escaping my lips and my hips are flexing over and over against his leg. I'm riding his leg, in the middle of my dorm hallway where anyone can see and I know I should be way more concerned about getting caught, but his teeth close against the skin of my breast peeking out over my bra and I lose track of where I am.

"Wrap your legs around my waist," he says, sharply. I obey without question and his lips fall back on mine. One of his hands is on my waist, his fingers spread across my hips and his other hand is gripping me by the back of my neck, pulling me in as our kisses grow faster and deeper. His tongue swipes against mine and his name leaves my lips in another gasp. Everything feels good, it feels amazing and god it's been so long and all I can think of, all I can focus on is the sensation of his lips against mine and the way his hips are moving against me.

New sensations are rippling through my body and I'm desperate, my hips grinding up against him. I haven't felt like this in a long time and not without taking at least some of my clothes off. It's like a hot war zone down there and I can't help the moans and gasps that are escaping my lips in between kisses.

"Fuck, you feel good, Evie," Austin breathes out, his lips hovering over mine. "You feel good right here." I nod again and again as my fingers tangle in the hair that curls at the nape of his neck. His hands are spread across my ass and he's pulling me against him, and I can feel the pleasure building up and…

"I'm…" I gasp. "*Shit*. I'm going to…"

"*Fuck*." He mumbles against my ear, pulling me tighter, harder against him and my fingernails dig into the firm skin of his back. "Ride me, baby. Come for me."

I feel a flush in my face as he says the words; I've never had such harsh demands directed my way but I find it sexy as hell and I gasp loudly when I do come, and the feeling spreads deliciously all over my body. I'm clutching him tightly and my hair has fallen in my face. We stay like that, propped against the wall, breathing heavily.

"That was…unexpected," I say, pulling away just far enough to look at him, my legs still wrapped tightly around him. I blush, the red spreading like wildfire across my cheeks and he catches it, grinning as his fingers brush against the heat of my skin. He leans down to kiss me and I'm helpless to it right now. He's a damn good kisser and I'm basically a wet noodle in his arms.

"I hope it's a good kind of unexpected…" Austin says, softly, his lips still on mine.

"Uh..." I'm distracted, too distracted for coherent conversation. "What about you?"

"Seeing the face you just made when you came, princess, that was enough for me," Austin said. His fingers sweep my hair over my shoulder as he bends over, his lips back on my neck. "That will be featured in my dreams for weeks to come..."

"Well, hello there..."

I yank myself away from Austin and he stumbles, dropping me in the process. I manage to stay upright, pressing myself tightly against the wall. My hands fumble with my tank top, pulling it back up. Sydney is standing in the doorway of our dorm room, her arms folded across her chest and her eyebrow raised. There's a small smile on her lips, just enough to be seen by me, but I'm sure I'm the only one who notices. Austin is running a hand through his hair, looking both sheepish and like a model.

"Hey Sydney—I was, uh..." I can barely get the words out and I really need to just get into the room and shut the door. Possibly—no, *definitely*—change into a new pair of underwear. "I was about to come in."

Sydney nods, her smile growing a little more noticeable. She turns her gaze to Austin and her eyebrows nearly disappear into her hair. "And you are?"

"Austin Young," he says, at the same moment I blurt out, "Nothing. No one."

She looks back and forth between us, a knowing look on her face. "Right. Nice to meet you, Austin." Her eyes meet mine. "You have an early class in the morning."

"Right," I agree, quickly, wiping my palms on my shorts. My eyes are glued to the floor, the wall, the ceiling, anything but Austin's eyes. I can't look at him right now. I can't believe what we just did. I don't do things like that. *Ever*. I haven't even done anything since...I'm not the kind of girl who randomly hooks up with an admittedly hot base-ball player in the hallways of her dorm. I can't think straight as I start walking toward Sydney.

"God, say good night already, Evie," Sydney says, and I can hear the barely concealed laughter in her voice.

I stumble and turn in Austin's direction. "Right. Night, Austin."

Austin's hand is in mine suddenly and he's pulling me toward him. His lips brush my forehead and I jerk back in surprise. "Good night, Evie."

Sydney drags me into our room and shuts the door behind us. "Evangeline Maria Cordova. Explain." Her hand is still wrapped tightly around my arm and tugging on it does nothing to free it from her grip. Apparently former high school cheerleaders are too strong for their own good.

"There's nothing to explain." I tug on my arm again and it budges maybe half an inch.

There is a wide, triumphant smile on her face. "You're so full of shit, Evie. You were just hooking up with a super-hot guy in our hallway. Not just any guy, but a baseball player at that."

"How did you even know…" I shake my head. I don't know why I'm even bothering to ask. Everyone knows the baseball players here, even the new ones. I shouldn't be surprised. "It was a momentary lapse of judgement."

"Was it at least a *good* lapse of judgement?" she asks, finally letting go of my arm and sitting on her bed. She leans against the wall, shoving some clothes toward the end of the bed. I resist the urge to grab them and fold them.

I sigh and collapse on my own bed. "That is completely beside the point, Syd."

Sydney's eyebrows raise and they nearly disappear again into her wild mane of red hair. "So, it *was* good?"

I can still feel the heat of Austin's body on mine and he's

not even here anymore. My legs ache but in such a good way. "Again, besides the point. Ugh!" I grab my pillow, burying my face in it and groaning loudly. "I'm so stupid."

"What? Why?" she sounds confused.

"Why?" I cry out, though my voice is muffled by the pillow. "I just made out with some random guy in the hallway of our freakin' dorm? What is wrong with me? I don't do that, Sydney, *especially* not with a baseball player. Let alone a player on my dad's team!"

"Oh, who cares if Austin is a baseball player, Evie? He's *hot*!"

Despite the panic steaming through my veins, I laugh. "That's all that matters, right?"

She shrugs but there's a mischievous gleam in her eyes and I laugh again. Sydney is the party animal of our small friend circle; she always has been. She flourished in high school. She cheered for the football, basketball and, of course, baseball teams. She was the Homecoming Queen and was barely beat out for Prom Queen. She's loud and boisterous and it seems like Sydney is constantly on the hunt for her next conquest.

Making out with a guy she barely knows outside her dorm room? That's PG and completely normal for Sydney. Drew, on the other hand, is hilarious and goofy but always serious about his grades and baseball and is the most loyal friend in the entire world. He, like everyone in this damn town, grew up obsessed with baseball and the Quakes and now that he's on the team, living out his dream. *My dream*, I couldn't help but think to myself. My best friends literally could not be any different from each other and I'm the middle child, a mix of them both.

It really is no wonder that Drew is madly in love with Sydney. Of course, he's never actually said this to me before, but I've known the guy since we were in diapers.

You'd have to be blind to miss the way he looks at her and the way he acts around her.

Drew and I grew up together, from the moment we were in diapers when Lucy was already stealing the spotlight. I have no memory of this but apparently Drew handed me his favorite baseball and well, we've been friends ever since. Sydney moved to Izzy when we were sophomores. Drew and I were smack in the middle of the only time we've ever considered being more than friends. This basically consisted of us making out in the back stockroom of his parents' bookstore when we were supposed to be working.

As soon as Sydney moved across the street from us though, all bets were off, not that I minded much. Sydney came into our world like an out of control wildfire. She was from Los Angeles and immediately needed to spice up life here in Isabella. She decided I needed an actual girlfriend in my life—Lucy didn't always count—and she turned our little twosome into a threesome. Suddenly, our life was a little more than baseball, though it didn't stop us from practicing pitches in the backyard. Sometimes I can hardly remember what it was like when it was just me and Drew.

Of course, there's no way to tell if Sydney has ever returned Drew's feelings or whether he'd ever actually do anything about it. I was content to watch and wait and find out. It was not my job to figure it out for them.

"Are you even paying attention to me?" Sydney cuts into my thoughts, sounding annoyed.

"Of course," I lie.

"What did I say?" She crosses her arms across her chest and juts out her lower lip in a mock pout. I can only shrug in response, giving up my lie immediately, and she huffs impatiently. "You're the worst."

"But you love me," I say, absentmindedly picking at an

invisible thread on my bedspread. My thoughts wander to the firmness of Austin's chest and I cough, loudly, trying to clear my head.

Sydney sighs dramatically. "I do." She pauses. "As I was saying when you were so rudely ignoring me, I'm proud of you." I must look confused because she clarifies. "For what just happened."

"God, really?" I laugh. "*That's* what you're proud of?"

"Look, Evie, come on, of course I am. Austin is hot. Like, tie him to the bed and rip his flannel shirt off. And that accent? Holy Moses. *And* he's a baseball player! Which, I know you like even though you'll sit here and pretend that you don't. It's good for you to get a little action sometimes." She winks at me and I can't help but laugh again. Her expression turns serious. "Really, though, you haven't been with anyone since Jesse. You can't blame me for being excited."

I ignore her mention of Jesse. It's not even worth a response. "You're excited because a random baseball player gave me an orgasm without even taking his pants off?"

Sydney shoots up and looks at me, excited. "He did? *Oh my God*. Evie! Can we *please* just talk about this for a minute?" Her last word is so high pitched, it's practically a squeal.

Shit. I put my foot in my mouth, as usual. "Can we please just *not* talk about this?" I beg. "I'd rather just forget it happened."

"I will not forget it. Not even the Jesse the Jerk gave you an orgasm, Evie. I'm pretty sure the only one you've had before are the ones you've given yourself. Suddenly this guy manages to show up in our town and give you one with all your clothes on in our hallway? I'm impressed beyond belief right now."

"I hate you," I say, lacking a better response. "Seeing as

I really do have class in the morning, I'm going to bed." I push myself off the bed and grab my bath caddy from its stored place underneath my bed.

Sydney's voice stops me as I'm walking out of the room. "Evie? Just…just don't do anything stupid, okay?"

My fingers grip the doorway tightly and I close my eyes briefly. "I'm the queen of not doing stupid things, Sydney."

"Evie, stop playing with your shirt. You look like a child," Lucy says, linking her arm through mine as we make our way through the cool sand toward the bonfire.

"I am a child," I respond nervously, dropping my fingers from the hem of my shirt. "We're easily the youngest people here."

Lucy's shoulders are back and she's walking with a confidence I know I'll never be able to master. "Jesse Valdez wanted you to be here, Evie. Isn't that exactly what you wanted?"

"Yes," I answer, hesitantly, as we make our way through the crowd.

"All right then. Stop complaining," she says. She pauses by a keg and smiles at the boy pouring beer into red cups. He smiles down at her and we both have beers in a matter of seconds. She looks around, her eyes searching. "Ah, found him. Come on."

I allow Lucy to drag me down the beach, closer to the bonfire, where Jesse is standing, talking to a couple of girls. He looks up as we walk up and a grin spreads across his face.

"Well, look who decided to show up. The Cordova girls." He excuses himself from the girls and walks over to us. I cross my arms tightly across my chest and look up at him, feeling the nerves bursting in my veins. "How are you ladies doing tonight?"

"Fantastic, now that we found you," Lucy says, smiling flirtatiously.

"You must be Lucy." Jesse's grin grows wider and he looks down at me. "What about you, Evie?"

"I'm…" I clear my throat. "I'm great."

"You look great," he says. "I was going to offer you a drink, but it looks like you're way ahead of me."

There's a long pause of silence as I try to think of something, anything to say. I blush harder and Lucy just shakes her head at me.

"Well, we can't just sit around and hope that one of you grabs a drink for us, now can we?" Lucy's voice is sweet, and I always wonder if that's how I sound. "Oh! I just saw someone I know. I'll be back later." She gives me a knowing look and disappears.

"That was not in the least bit subtle," Jesse remarks, looking down at me.

I laugh, nervously. "I have no idea what you're talking about."

He winks at me before looking around. "I'm sure you don't. Do you want to go for a walk?"

I pause, and nod in agreement. "Sure. I'd love to."

"Great." Jesse grins and holds his hand out to me.

THE WAVES ARE CRASHING ON THE BEACH AND I CAN'T BELIEVE that I'm on a date with Jesse. He's brought a picnic and the moon is shining out over the ocean and everything is perfect. We haven't run out of things to talk about and he can't stop smiling. I can't stop smiling.

"You know…I've only brought one girl here, and that's you."

"Well, I feel pretty special," I say, my face burning.

"Well I think you are," he replies, taking one step closer to me. His hand comes up to my face, brushing the loose strands of my hair behind my ear. We are mere inches apart and my heart is pounding in my chest. The ocean is lapping at our ankles and one powerful wave could knock me over right now. "Have you ever been kissed before, Evie?"

I nod. What kind of question was that? Of course, I had. I wasn't a child, despite what I may have just told my sister. True, I *tended to avoid kissing any of the guys on the team because I wanted them to see me as a teammate. I wanted to be viewed as an equal and not someone they could sneak kisses in the locker room with but geez, I wasn't a nun.*

His lips turn up a bit at that, as he comes even closer to me. "You won't remember any of those," he says, his lips coming down on mine. We stand there, feet in the water, kissing for a moment. One of his hands is lost in my hair and the other is tugging me forward, pulling me up against his hard body. I respond enthusiastically, hardly daring to believe that this is happening right now.

A wave comes rushing in and crashes against my legs, knocking me off balance. We both laugh, his arm still wrapped tightly around my waist. "Do you want to go to the car?" he asks, his voice rough.

I nod, my forehead pressed against his chest. "Yes." He grabs my hand and pulls me away from the water, and we head back up to the blanket. We pack everything up quickly and toss it in the trunk of the car. He comes around the side, opening the door for me, before climbing back in himself.

He doesn't waste any time. He's leaning over the center console, his lips back on mine. I'm gasping when his hand plays with the hem of my shirt and goosebumps erupt all up and down my back. I can barely breathe but I don't want him to stop. His hand inches closer to my bra and I pull back.

"I'm sorry. Is that too much?" Jesse asks, breathing quickly.

I laugh, out of breath. "Um, no?"

"That doesn't sound like you're sure," he says, sitting back. "We can stop if you want."

"No—I mean, it's fine," I say, afraid that I pushed him away too much. "I like it!"

He laughs. "I like it too." Heat runs through me and I want to pull him back over to my side of the car. "But we won't go any faster than you want to, Evie. It's your choice."

"You're not mad?" I ask nervously.

He looks over at me. "Of course not," he says, sounding confused.

"We'll take it slow. It's not a problem." He hesitates. "There's just one thing…"

"What?" I say, fear shooting through me. It's been a fun night and I am enjoying myself. The fact is, I know I'm already madly in love with the image that is Jesse Valdez and I'm pretty sure I was falling in love with the actual person.

"The thing is…" he says, his fingertips tapping a nervous beat on his knees. "I had a great time tonight and I don't want you to have to deal with the shit that comes along with dating a baseball player, especially here in Izzy. Your dad is the coach and I'm pretty sure that means you are off limits. Not to mention that you're underage."

"Okay…" I say.

"I just think…" Jesse says, leaning over the console, his lips just above mine. "I just think it would be better if we keep this between us right now. Just between us."

I consider it for a moment. "I think that's a good idea. I don't think it's a good idea for people to know I'm dating a player on my dad's team. Not when I want to be taken seriously as a ball player. We'll be teammates."

He laughs a little. "Sure, Evie."

There is something about his laugh that grates at me but then he's kissing me again and I forget all about it. His kisses are distracting and leave me completely breathless.

"It's our little secret," he whispers to me.

I nod. "Our little secret."

CHAPTER FOUR

I sleep fine, cozy and curled up in my bed with a fan blowing to combat the heat. It's not until my alarm begins to go off and the memories from the night before surface that the regret begins to pool in the pit of my stomach. *What on earth did I do last night?* I pull my pillow over my face. I let out a loud scream, so loud that the pillow barely muffles it. I'd worry about waking Sydney up, but she could sleep through a tsunami, an earthquake, *and* a tornado simultaneously. My scream isn't going to even get close to waking her up. I throw the pillow off to the side and turn my head to see her sound asleep with an arm dangling off the side of the bed. I laugh at the sight of my best friend, but it doesn't change the budding nausea and feeling that I might throw up.

I get through my two classes in the morning with no problem, but then it's time for Art History again and I feel the panic begin set in.

Last night, the hook up with Austin…my brain refused to accept the fact that it happened, even while it was happening. It all felt like a dream. Last night, I felt like I was imagining it all. It was easy to fall asleep with that mindset, but waking up this morning, it hit me like a freight train. The butterflies in my stomach multiply at the simple thought of Austin and what we did. Last-night-me was stupid, unthinking, irresponsible. Today-me is totally embarrassed at her actions. I have to see Austin twice today. *Oh god.* Yup, this is pure panic.

I had hooked up with a baseball player, in a hallway where anyone could have caught us. I don't do things like that. I am careful and I don't just hook up with anyone and I did everything I could to stay away from baseball players, especially those on my dad's team.

The trick now was to avoid Austin. Of course, this was completely and totally impossible. There is no way to avoid him, not with a shared class and me working for his stupid baseball team.

The only way to deal with this is to face it head on.

Gripping my green tea tighter and letting the cold condensation bring me out of my thoughts, I shake my head and begin to mentally prepare myself for seeing him again.

"Get your head out of the clouds, Evangeline. I've been calling your name for, like, an hour now."

I look up, startled, and see Lucy, matching my stride. She looks fabulous but then again, she rarely doesn't. I haven't seen her for a few days, and I feel that immediate comfort of having her near. It's completely uncontrollable. We're nearly identical—most people even think that we are but there's a slight difference if you pay enough attention. From far away though, people have a hard time telling us apart. We're a mix of our Spanish dad and our Mexican mother, with our brown skin that gets even darker in the summer, our dirty blonde hair, and dark eyes, except for my one blue eye, of course.

My parents have made jokes for years that we checked

off all the qualities of a true Californian girl—blonde *and* Mexican. It makes me laugh now, but it took me ages to get used to that. Lucy always takes things in stride; it seems like nothing ever worries her. She's never worried about fitting in because she's never given fitting in a thought. Lucy walked out of my mother's womb with the confidence of a woman walking down the red carpet on the night she knows she's winning an Oscar.

I, on the other hand, struggled with being biracial for most of my life. I'd spend time with my mom's family and would always feel like I was different. Even as I was speaking Spanish with my grandmother and making tamales with my tías, I felt like my blonde hair, no matter how dark or "dirty" blonde it was, was a beacon, none-theless. I stood out too much. When we went to Boston during Thanksgiving break to see my dad's parents, I felt like my brown skin stood out amongst my small, very white family. I didn't feel Mexican enough and I didn't feel white enough. Even looking in the mirror didn't help me feel any better; Lucy and I were really a perfect mix of both of our cultures.

While Lucy spends most of the time looking in the mirror and figuring out new ways to cut her hair and taking my mom's old clothes from the eighties and refash-ioning them to be current and fun, I spend most of my time looking in the mirror and wishing that I looked differ-ent, more like Mom or more like Dad or even less like Lucy.

I'm proud now to be biracial. I was lucky enough to have parents that taught me the best parts of both of my cultures, and I was lucky enough to absorb the best of both worlds. Blonde hair. Brown eyes. Speaking English and Spanish. Having a small intimate family along the eastern seaboard and a large, always growing family just miles away from home. It's a blessing, even if it doesn't feel like it at times.

I'm proud, now, of being a twin and having a built-in best friend for life. She's the most important person in the world to me and I wouldn't want to look like anyone else but her. I've tried to embrace her fearless personality more over the years. She drives me insane sometimes, but I do occasionally wish I were a little more like her.

Lucy has no idea what happened between Jesse and I a couple years ago. She's never known, and I never want to tell her. Sydney and Drew have been begging me to tell her ever since it happened, but I can't. She's happy and I can't be the one to take it from her. Just because I had my heart broken doesn't mean that Lucy needs to have hers broken as well. Let alone by the same guy. They've been together for so long now…

But I would be lying if I said that it doesn't put a strain on our relationship—a strain that I'm not even sure Lucy is aware of. We've never been the kind of twins that were attached at the hip, but we've always been close. We weren't just sisters, we were each other's very first friend—each other's best friend at that. When Jesse…when everything happened, I couldn't be around her anymore. She was always around him.

It was too much. It was too *hard*.

"You disappeared again," Lucy points out, her voice flat.

I shake my head, trying to clear away my thoughts. "Sorry, Luce, I'm distracted."

"Yeah, I can tell," she laughs. "Where are you headed?"

"Social sciences," I answer, nodding my head in the direction of the building as she smiles.

"Perfect. I'm in the building next door." She falls into step with me and we stay in silence as we both head to class. We garner a few stares as we walk. Since baseball is everything in this town and that rates Dad as somewhat of a celebrity, people know who we are. I can't begin to count how many guys showed interest in me simply to get a moment with my dad. But we're also twins, so it tends to turn heads in our direction anyway, even though Lucy looks like an Instagram model and I barely managed to throw on a pair of jeans and t-shirt this morning. Lucy always prided herself on how she looked though, and I spent high school not bothering to wear anything else besides jeans, with my hair pulled up in a ponytail. Lucy was pledging to a sorority this year and they were strict on wardrobe. Somehow, I don't think she minded that much. She thrived on being a pledge. I was very much in the "*no, thank you*" category in any of the sorority's eyes. Not that I wanted to be a pledge anyway.

"Are you going—" Lucy starts to ask as we approach the courtyard between our two buildings. She's interrupted, however, by a voice that immediately causes a flurry of butterflies in my stomach.

"Well, holy shit, you two really do look exactly alike, don't you?" There's a smile across his face and my mind flashes to the way he was pressed up against me the night before. My body remembers the way he felt against me, and I almost longed for his touch again. I know my face is bright red and I take a sip of my green tea to keep from replying.

Lucy's eyebrows raise and she looks annoyed. "Yeah, that happens sometimes with twins," she replies, sarcastically. "And who are you?"

"Sorry," Austin apologizes, holding a hand out for her to shake. Lucy just stares at it. "I'm Austin. Austin Young."

Lucy's entire demeanor changes and she smiles. It lights up her entire face and pretty much everything around us and I wonder if that's the way I look when I smile. "Oh!

You're Austin, the new shortstop. Jesse told me all about you, *duh*!"

I choke a little on my iced tea at the mention of Jesse. The two of them look at me and I force a smile. "I'm fine…"

"You know, when I met Evie, I thought it was unfair that a girl this beautiful existed but the fact that there are two of you is just cruel." His charm is overwhelming, and my stupid mouth betrays me and curves into a smile before I can stop it. "You two are like little clones of each other."

Lucy laughs. "Well, I guess it's a little easier to bear since only one of us is single. I am very taken." I roll my eyes at this and thankfully it goes unnoticed, at least by Lucy. Austin might have caught it but I'm not entirely sure.

"Besides," Lucy continues, "we aren't totally identical. Evie has those freaky eyes of hers." I resisted the urge to roll my *'freaky eyes'* right back at her.

Austin's eyes meet mine and there's a devilish grin on his face, a smile very unlike the one he gave Lucy. "I like her freaky eyes."

"Okay," I say, loudly, willing this conversation to come to an end. "I think we better get to class now." His words send a thrill through me and I don't like how my body is already reacting to his being so close to mine.

"Wait, I had to talk to you," Lucy pouts.

I start to reply but Austin interrupts, yet again. "It's fine. I'll save you a seat, Evie." He flashes another smile and walks away from us.

Lucy watches him, an appreciative look on her face. "That boy is *gorgeous*!"

"Lucy." Her name comes out sharply; the anger I feel is sudden and immediate. "Boyfriend, remember?"

She sighs impatiently. "I can look, can't I? Jealous much? He did see you first after all."

"What do you want to talk about?" I ask, ignoring her.

"Oh, right. Are you going to Sunday brunch?"

I close my eyes, briefly, before shooting her an incredulous look. *This* was the all-important thing she wanted to talk to me about? "Of course, I am." It was my mom's number one rule. Every Sunday, the whole family—and I mean, the *entire* family—got together at our house for Sunday brunch. My mom makes enough food to feed an army, and that's usually how many people show up. My mom's only requirement for when she and my dad bought a house was a big backyard so she could host these weekly breakfast parties. It has just enough room for maybe three hundred people.

I'm not exaggerating. Sometimes that many people genuinely show up.

Basically, it was a familial requirement to be there.

"Fantastic. Do you want to ride with Jesse and I?" Lucy asks, waving enthusiastically at someone walking by. Out of the two of us, she has always been the popular one. It's probably one of her sorority sisters.

I sigh. The thought of being in the car with them, even for the very short ten-minute ride to our house, sounds awful. It kind of gives me a strong urge to hurl up the contents of my last meal. "I think I'll just go in my own car."

"That makes no sense," she says, sounding annoyed. "Unless you're bringing a date." Her eyes flicked in the direction Austin had disappeared to. "Are you bringing the cowboy?"

"Austin and I are just friends." I assured.

An amused look crosses her face as she turns back to me. "Yeah, well, maybe that's a good thing. He does look like he might be too much to handle."

I want to correct her, to tell her that I handled him *just* fine the night before, but I don't. I really don't need the entire school aware of that and knowing my sister, it'll get back to…*everyone*. I definitely did not want to have to answer any of the questions that Dad might ask if he found out that I hooked up with a player on his team. "I'm going to class. I'll see you Sunday."

"Okay," she agrees brightly as if she weren't just annoyed with me five seconds ago. *Sisters*, I resisted rolling my eyes back at her. "Love you!"

A lot of my own irritation dissipates at this. She doesn't deserve this. She never has. She just…doesn't *know*. "I love you too."

Most of the classroom is already full when I finally enter it but sure enough, there's an empty seat right in front of Austin. I flush and make my way to the desk, sliding in.

"Hi beautiful," he whispers, leaning forward. His breath tickles the back of my neck and sends shivers down my spine that has little to do with the air conditioning pumping through the vents.

"Hi," I manage to whisper back. My pen is clutched tightly in my hand, tapping against my notebook as my whole body fidgets in tandem.

"So last night…" I inhale sharply and he chuckles under his breath. How can a chuckle be so damn sexy? "I can't stop thinking about it."

I tense up, already knowing where he was going with this. "Austin…"

I can feel him pull away; the heat radiating off his body is suddenly gone. "What? What's wrong?" I turn around and there's a frown on his face. "You're about to say something that's not fun, am I right?"

I'm aware that everyone around us can probably hear every word of what we are saying and I lower my voice. "Last night was a mistake."

"A mistake," he repeats, flatly, his expression unreadable.

I blush as I admit, "I mean, it was fun." I lower my voice even more. "*Really* fun, but it just can't happen again. I wasn't lying when I said I have a steadfast rule against dating baseball players."

A corner of his mouth quirks up a little at this. "I'll say it again, it's a weird rule."

I sigh. "It's really not. You're on my dad's team and it's just easier this way. It makes life so much easier, for me *and* you."

"Lucy doesn't seem to have an issue dating Jesse, and he's on your dad's team."

I do my best to ignore him. I don't really have a response to this. I swallow hard and meet his eyes. They're such a deep, dark brown and they reveal absolutely nothing to me. As the professor walked in and sat their briefcase on the desk, I turn back to Austin, wanting to end the conversation before any teaching began. The last thing I wanted was to get called out in front of the entire class for talking. "I just think it would be better if we were friends. *Just* friends."

"Just friends?"

God, I wish I could tell what he was thinking. I bite my lip. "Yeah." Was I being stupid? Maybe I should take it a step further and tell him that acquaintances would be a better idea. I had no interest in dating him or…anything else but how does anyone with a normal sex drive ignore someone as seriously hot as this guy? There's a desk in between us and my body is still tingling with want.

Stupid biological responses.

He still hasn't responded and I start to turn back around, feeling embarrassed.

His hand reaches out for me, grabbing my arm, preventing me from turning around. My eyes watch the way his fingers flex around my bicep before I raise them and meet his. I take a breath and it comes out shaky. I hope he doesn't hear it.

Finally, Austin smirks and it shocks me because this is not the response I had expected. "If you want to be just friends, princess, well then that's okay."

I am taken aback by his response and it takes me a moment to think of something to say back. My eyebrows raise. "Really?"

He winks at me. "Of course. My mama taught me to respect a lady's words and I stick to that."

I can't help it. I laugh. "Your mama?"

Austin leans back and his smirk becomes a full-fledged grin. "Yes, my mama. Maybe I'll tell you about her some-time. Seeing as we're friends and all."

CHAPTER FIVE

"Tell me about Austin."

I'm holding my phone precariously between my shoulder and ear and I nearly drop it. Instead I drop the clipboard I have in my hands and reach for my phone. The clipboard makes a loud clattering noise as it hits the locker room floor but there's no one here to hear it. "Drew, what are you talking about?"

Drew laughs on the other end of the phone and, like always, I want to laugh too, even though there's nothing remotely funny about this conversation. His laugh is just that infectious. "Well, I was talking to Sydney…"

"Damn Sydney and her big mouth…" I cut him off with a sigh, sitting down in a chair and scooping the clipboard off the ground, smoothing out the pages that were crumpled in the fall.

Drew laughs again. "Calm down, Evie. All Syd did was ask if Austin was the new guy on the team and I asked her why and all she said was that she was concerned about you." There's a long pause and I bite my lip, waiting for him to continue. "Should I be worried?"

"Of course not," I say, quickly. The door to the locker room opens and first baseman, Owen Wilcox, comes in. He notices me and nods before heading toward the last row of lockers. I check the clock and realize there's only about ten minutes until practice starts.

"So then tell me about Austin, Evie."

I sigh again and the locker room door opens to let a few more guys in, including Jesse. He smiles at me, but I ignore him, pretending to be fully engrossed in the conversation. "He's just a friend, Drew."

"That's not what I've heard." His voice is light and teasing, playful even. He's enjoying this and I want to punch him.

"What did you hear, hmm?" I ask, sharply. My eyes are firmly on the ground. Jesse's undressing to change into practice clothes with no qualms that I'm still in the room, mere feet away from him.

"That you kissed him. Is that true?"

I lower my voice. "Yeah. Yes. I did."

"You did what, Evie? Say it."

"I kissed him, okay?" I hiss, frustrated. "I kissed him!"

"*Hallelujah*!" Drew yells and I'm suddenly very, very aware that Jesse is listening in on our conversation.

"We are just friends," I repeat. Loudly. Firmly. "That's it. *Period*."

"Jesus, Evie, I'm not asking you to marry the guy but maybe joining him in bed a couple times would do you some good…"

"No," I cut him off. "Not even that. He's just a friend. That's it."

There's silence on the other end and when Drew does finally speak again, his voice is low. All pretense of joking is gone. "Don't be mad, Evie, but does this have anything to do with…"

"No!" I say again, louder, and a couple of the players turn my way, including Jesse. "You know why, Drew. No baseball players. No Quakes. *Ever*."

"You're being ridiculous."

I decided it was the perfect time to change the subject. "Practice starts in ten minutes. Shouldn't you be here?"

"Shit," he answers, and I laugh, happy I was able to distract him. "Gotta go."

"Bye Drew."

Practice goes by quickly and, for the first time in ages, I don't feel like my entire soul hurts to be on that baseball field. Maybe I just need more exposure to baseball, and I'll stop feeling like my heart is broken every time I think of it. I set up room arrangements for the first real away game, spend way too much time wiping down sweaty helmets, and avoid the eye contact of anyone who looks my way, especially Drew, who seems determined to continue the conversation about Austin.

I'm cleaning up the locker room, stashing things into the equipment closet, when Austin comes up behind me.

"Hello there, princess."

I sigh, walking around him, gathering the towels all the players left behind. It kills me that none of them can manage to put them in the laundry basket even though, you know, most of them were legally adults. It wasn't exactly hard. "You really have to stop calling me princess," I say.

He laughs. "I like calling you princess. Especially since you squirm so much when I do it."

"I don't squirm," I mumble. I glance up at the clock and then back at him. He's still in workout gear and he's sweaty as hell. "Why are you still here? Practice ended an hour ago."

His smile fades a little. "I was just doing some additional workouts and did some sprints."

Of course he was. I stare at him, incredulously. Dad has gone rough on them in practice, getting them ready for the first real game of the season. Playtime is over, and all that. I can't imagine why anyone would want to continue to work out after he ran them ragged. "Okay, crazy pants…"

He stays quiet and I wonder if I've said the wrong thing or something. "We have a game tomorrow, so I was wondering if you wanted to do something on Sunday. Go out."

"Austin…" I start to say.

"She'd love to." Drew pops up out of nowhere and we both jump, startled.

"God, Drew, you scared the bejesus out of me!" I say, my hand pressed against my chest as I try to calm my racing heart.

"*Bejesus?*" Austin mouths at me and I stick my tongue out at him. He grins.

"Sorry," Drew apologizes, sounding not the least bit sorry. "I was talking to Coach and overheard you guys." He slings an arm around my shoulder. "Evie would love to hang out with you on Sunday."

I wrap my own arm around Drew's waist and pinch the skin right at his hip, which I know he hates. Sure enough, he winces. I turn to Austin, trying to look as apologetic as possible. "Unfortunately, I can't. I'm busy with brunch on Sunday. Brunch is a big deal with my mom. Which Drew knows." I shoot him a dark, pointed glare.

Drew is frowning and rubbing the side where I pinched him. He ponders this for a moment and then his face lights up as he turns to Austin. "You should come. He should come." Drew quickly looks back at me, nodding his head. "You should totally come, Austin." He sounds a little crazy and I wonder if a stray baseball has made contact with his head lately.

"No, he really shouldn't," I say at the same time Austin asks, "what's brunch?"

"Oh, you know, brunch," Drew says, easily. He takes the towel slung over his shoulders and tosses it toward the laundry basket, where it lands perfectly, on the top of the ones I just dropped in there. I forgive him a little bit. "A full meal that's not quite breakfast, but not quite lunch."

"Your sarcasm is completely unnecessary, Drew." I sigh, turning to address Austin. "Really, it's just my family eating brunch. You'll be super bored."

"I'd love to come," Austin replies quickly. "I like brunch. Who doesn't like brunch?"

Drew smiles widely. "You should really come, man. Lots of food and Evie's family is awesome. You can catch a ride with me."

"Sounds good," Austin agrees. "As long as it's okay with Evie, though."

They both turn to me, smiles on their faces, and I feel cornered. I don't want Austin there. I really don't want him there, in *my* safe space, but we both agreed we'd be friends and I invited friends to brunch all the time. But all the unwanted questions of bringing home a baseball player, and a good-looking baseball player at that…

"Um…" It comes out as a squeak and I clear my throat before continuing. "Just as friends, right?"

Austin looks like he wants to laugh but he holds it in. "Of course, princess. As friends."

"I'll see you on Sunday, then," I say, quickly, both thrilled and horrified by the idea of it. "Now can you guys get out of my locker room so I can finish cleaning and go home?"

They both laugh, as if I've said the funniest thing in the world. "Do you need someone to walk you back to the dorm?" Drew asks.

I shake my head. "No, it's fine." They both start to leave, and I hesitate before saying, "Drew, can I talk to you for a second?"

The two of them exchange quick looks, and they seem to have a conversation without words in a matter of seconds, like an old married couple or something. How did they manage that? Austin nods and leaves and Drew turns to me.

"I hate you so much," I say without preamble, tossing one of the dirty towels at him. "Why the hell did you do that?"

He looks genuinely confused as the towel hits him. I want to laugh as he quickly smacks it away with a grimace. Drew is my best friend for so many reasons. He makes me laugh and he has always been at my side, pushing me to be better. He also could be totally clueless sometimes though and even though I'm frustrated with him, I also just shake my head because there is nothing more *Drew* than him being overly helpful.

"I told you, Austin is just my friend. Why would you invite him to brunch?"

"You always invite me and Sydney," he points out, helping me to grab the remaining things lying on the ground. "Half the team shows up in your backyard for brunch on any given Sunday anyway. How is Austin any different?"

"You guys are like family. The *team* is like family." Drew opens his mouth to interrupt my flawed logic, but I glare at him and continue before he can get a single word out. "It's just not the same thing."

"It's just brunch, Evie," Drew says, shrugging his shoulders. "What are you so worried about? Dare I point out that Austin is part of the team, which based on your logic means—"

"I'm not," I say, sharply to cut him off. I take a deep breath and my next words are calmer than before. "You're right. We're friends. It's just brunch."

Just brunch. With Drew and Sydney and Jesse and Lucy and Austin. *All in one place.* At my home, where I had left so many of my secrets behind.

"Evangeline!"

I wince, hand frozen in midair as I scoop beans to pile on my plate. I put the spoon back in the pan before turning, preparing as believable a smile as I'm capable of before I am fully facing her.

"Hi *Mamá.*" Without second thought I slip back into the easy, second natured accent that I developed at a young age. I guess that's what happens growing up bilingual. I can't help but to always speak with my mom with a sort of resigned patience. I love her, but she's a whirlwind person-ality that requires a certain amount of love to deal with. Lucy definitely got more of her personality.

"*Mija,* I haven't seen you in ages." She reaches for me, as if she hasn't seen me in months, and smothers me in a huge hug, lifting me off the ground as if I'm not four inches taller than her or anything.

I roll my eyes, moving down the line and piling some eggs on top of my beans. I look around for the salsa and my face lights up when I spot the huge container at the end of the table. "Ma, you saw me last week. At brunch, remember?"

"I know," she says, sourly. Even though my mother moved to California when she was fourteen, making her time in the United States longer than her time in Mexico, she still fully retains her accent. It's normal to me, as familiar to me as my own voice, but living away from home…even if only down the street, has made it more pronounced and obvious to me when I see her for Sunday brunch. Like my mother herself, it's comforting. It's the smell of homemade tortillas being warmed on the stove. It's my mamá dancing through the living room, singing Selena songs at the top of her lungs—badly, I might add. Hearing her voice is my mom helping me put a pad on for the first time, simultaneously being supportive and laughing at me the first time I ever got my period. Hearing her accent, it was *home*. No matter where we were. "But I am used to having my girls home. The house is so empty all the time now that the season has started, and your father is never home."

I highly doubt this. My cousins live not too far away, in San Jose and Oakland, they come by to visit all the time. Considering Mom cooks as if she's expecting the entire Quakes baseball team every single day, I don't blame them. I'd take the free food too.

"Okay, Mamá. Well, I'm home now." I move away from her to continue filling my plate and she follows me.

"Well, don't just walk away from me. *¿Cómo es la escuela? ¿Y tus clases?*"

"School is fine. Classes are fine," I reply in English, trying to step around her.

I love my mom. She's pushy and overprotective and by far the nosiest person I've ever met in my life—even more so than Sydney—but at the end of the day, her main concern is taking care of Lucy, Dad, and I. She doesn't stop there; she takes care of *everyone*. She started Sunday brunches in the early days of her marriage to keep her family close. It's grown into something so much bigger over the years, especially once Dad became the coach of the Quakes. Our backyard is constantly open and full of people. My family is here—tías, tíos, cousins, and my abuela, sitting on a lounge chair in the corner, already totally passed out for a late morning nap. There are several recognizable Izzy faces too, including the mayor.

The whole ordeal has grown so large over the past few years that Mom usually spends the entire weekend preparing so that she has enough food. She doesn't need to host these brunches every week, no one asks her to, but she wants to and loves to. She loves to feed people. It's exactly how she shows her love.

It's especially true now that Lucy is living with Jesse and I'm in the dorms with Sydney. She gets lonely. I try to remember this when she gets on my nerves.

"Did you get enough to eat, *querida*?" she asks. She's followed me to the other side of the yard, where Sydney is sitting. I take a seat across for her.

"Yes, Mamá," I laugh, picking up my fork. "I think I grabbed enough food to last me a week."

"You're too skinny," she complains. "You should come home to eat more often."

I am not skinny. Lucy and I both take after our mom, large breasts, wide hips, thick thighs. We aren't fat, not really, but there's more of us to love. There was a point in time where my body was muscled and strong rather than anything else but…well, I haven't kept that up in a long time. When I quit baseball, I pretty much quit working out.

"Sure," I answer vaguely, winking at Sydney. She laughs and then immediately frowns at something she's looking at from over my shoulder.

I turn and my stomach sinks as Lucy and Jesse join us at the table. Jesse loves Sunday brunch; he has two over-filled plates just for himself.

Mom loves Jesse, despite the way that he and Lucy's relationship came to light. I sometimes think it is simply because he's able to throw such a wicked curveball, but I don't know. It also could do with the fact that he's a good and handsome Catholic boy, as well. My mom definitely has her priorities and sometimes it's easier to accept the not-so-good parts of a person when the good parts are so good.

She swoops in on him, placing a red lipstick kiss on his cheek and praising him on his healthy appetite. I'm close to throwing up all over the table in front of me and I haven't even eaten anything yet.

"Your pitching was so good yesterday," my mom is saying. "We are all so proud of you."

"Yes, yes, we're all *so* proud of you," Sydney says, sarcasm coming off her in obvious waves. Lucy shoots her a glare but no one else catches it. She opens her mouth to continue but she cuts off abruptly. A smirk appears on her face and she looks at me, pointedly. "Your date is here, Evie."

Everyone's heads turn in the direction to the open gate leading from the driveway to the backyard where brunch is always held. Drew and Austin were chatting; with a raised hand Drew waved to Sydney and I before practically making a bee-line straight to the food. Drew nods for Austin to follow. Looking sleepy, with his hair sticking up in different directions, Austin begins to load up a plate. I turn back around and start shoveling food in my mouth. The sooner I finish eating, the sooner that I can get the hell out of here.

"Is this why you didn't want to drive here with me and Jesse?" Lucy asks, excitedly.

Jesse's head suddenly lifts from his plate and his eyes flick in Austin's direction before meeting mine. "Who invited Young?"

I start to answer but Sydney gets there first. "Evie did. Is there a problem with that?"

I kick her leg under the table, but she doesn't even

flinch. Jesse hardly looks disturbed by her attitude and merely shrugs.

"Evie told me she didn't like him, didn't you?" Jesse asks. "Why would she invite him if she didn't like him?"

Sydney is staring at me pointedly and I can barely get the words out. "He's a *friend*. He's on the team. Why wouldn't he come?"

"Poor thing is brand new from Texas, honey! He probably doesn't know anyone," Lucy pipes up, playfully smacking Jesse on the chest. She quickly turns back to me with a smile. "You're so good to invite him, Evie."

"There are plenty of people to show him around and be his friend," Jesse says. His eyes are burning as he stares at me and I can't look away. "Why should it be Evie?"

"Why *shouldn't* it be Evie?" Sydney asks loudly and a few heads turn in our direction.

"I don't like the guy," is Jesse's only response.

I put down my fork at this statement and stare at him. "Why not?"

"He just gives me a weird vibe." He shrugs.

Lucy is practically cooing as she runs her fingers through the thick black hair at the base of Jesse's neck. "Babe! You're so sweet and protective of Evie. It's so cute!"

Sydney mimes vomiting into her food and luckily no one sees it but me. The silence seems deafening for a few minutes until the subject of our conversation walks up.

He looks incredible, that stupid, sexy grin stretched across his face, but his eyes show how nervous he really is. He shuffles for a moment while Drew takes a seat next to Sydney, of course. I sigh and stare at the seat next to me, pointedly. Austin looks relieved and he collapses onto the chair.

Jesse is glaring at Austin and I'm not the only person who has noticed this. Sydney is glaring at Jesse and Austin has noticed this. His eyebrow is cocked in confusion and he looks at me questioningly. I shake my head, turning back to my food.

"Great win yesterday, Valdez," Austin finally says to break the awkward silence.

Jesse doesn't say anything right away and Austin's statement hangs in the air. Things begin to feel uncomfortable and I'm ready to cut in, to say something, *anything*. The two of them sitting at the same table is a terrible idea, it's too much for me and I'm ready to burst out into song if that makes all the tension just go away.

Jesse, however, finally answers. "Thanks, Young." He pauses for a moment, a barely concealed smile on his face. "I'm sure you'll get a hit next game."

Austin's face pales but his expression doesn't change. "Well, we have one of the best batting coaches in the entire college system so if he can't whip my ass into shape, no one can." He laughs and I almost believe it. *Almost.*

"I guess we'll have to wait and see then."

I want to punch Jesse Valdez in the face. This is not the first time I've wanted to do this in the past few years but the frustration, the anger, roars up inside me and I'm so glad that Austin is next to me. His presence is weirdly calming, even though, at the same time, he makes me so nervous too.

"Yeah, you're right. Plenty of games left in the season," Austin says, easily. His arm brushes against mine as he lifts his fork and I gasp at how much that one little touch affects me. It's unreal. We're surrounded by people but that brief moment of contact always makes me forget that. Throwing him on one of the tables scattered across the yard wouldn't be too obviously, would it?

There's a smile resting easily on his lips and is so much more genuine this time. "If it doesn't work out, I could always go in for a career as a male model. I heard my abs are pretty awesome." He casually flips up the bottom of his shirt and I catch an eyeful of those admittedly fantastic abs. I have a sudden thought that my childhood bedroom is right there, and I've never, *ever* had a boy in there before…

Sydney laughs, dragging me from my impure thoughts, and the sound echoes across the yard. Drew looks up at the sound and smiles. "You are not wrong about that, Austin. Not at all." She lets out a low whistle.

Even Lucy looks impressed. "You're definitely on the right path for that." She pretends to fan herself. "We get such good ones here, don't we, girls?"

Sydney and I look at each other and try hard not to laugh. Jesse shoots a look that can only be described as one that could kill, and the smile slips off Lucy's face. She sits back in her seat, her eyes uneasy, as she continues to eat her food.

Jesse's eyes meet mine from across the table and I forget for a moment that Austin is sitting next to me. I can't breathe and I can't even remember where I am. "What about you, Evie? Do you think we get good ones here?"

I swallow hard and drag my eyes away from Jesse's unblinking gaze. Austin is right next to me and I don't even have to look at him to be so enveloped in his presence. He smells so good and he has such a profound effect on me, even if I don't want him too. His brown eyes lock on mine and though he's obviously noticing the two different colors, I don't feel like I'm on display.

"Yeah, I think we get some good ones," I finally answer, faintly. There's a heat coursing between the two of us and I want to reach across the small distance between us and pull him against me and I hate it. I hate this feeling.

Someone coughs loudly and I blink, realizing how far I've leaned toward Austin. I yank myself back and there's a burst of laughter coming from Sydney and Drew. I clear my throat and I pick up my fork again.

I'm helping wash what feels like a million dishes when Mom comes to join me. She rolls up her sleeves and grabs a towel from underneath the sink and starts drying. I smile at her and continue to run my hands through the hot, soapy water. We stay in companionable silence but I'm not stupid. I know my mother, and this is not going to last for long.

Sure enough, she speaks up after a few minutes. "So, Austin Young, hmm?"

I sigh and my hands drop, splashing in the hot water. "*Mamá*…" I warn her. "He's part of Dad's team. Half the people out there are Quakes players."

"Marcella told me you were the one who invited him," he says, and her voice is so loud that I automatically look out the kitchen window to see if anyone has heard her. I can see Drew, Austin and Sydney chatting together and it makes me nervous that my best friends are alone with him, without me to keep them in check.

"How on earth did *Tía* even find out?" I groan. "I mean, seriously?"

"Marcella heard it from Carlos, who apparently heard it from your cousin, Linda, who said that Lucy apparently told," she explains. She waves the plate she's holding around, and I back up before I get knocked out. "That's not even important, *mija*. You invited a boy to brunch and I want to know why."

"It's not what you think," I say, slowly. "He's new and he doesn't know anyone except the guys on the team." I turn to her, planting my hands on my hips. "And if we're being technical here, Drew invited him, actually and I just agreed that he should come."

"He's incredibly handsome," she points out.

Outside, Drew is waving his arms around wildly, telling

some kind of joke or story, and Austin and Sydney are laughing. Austin is actually bent over; he's laughing so hard. I can't help but smile a little.

"Yes, *Mamá*. I know."

She huffs impatiently. "*Sí, sí,* you know. You know, but are you going to do something about it?"

"This is a really weird conversation to have with my mother. Can we just not do this?" I say, handing her a stack of plates. She takes them from me, frowning. Her gaze holds me in place for a moment and I squirm. Sometimes it seems as if my mother has magic powers and can see right through all my bullshit.

"*Querida*, I'm not saying you have to fall in love with that boy. You are young and in college and you should be having fun," she finally says, turning around to put the plates away in the cabinet.

"I have fun," I grumble.

She laughs and I can't help but laugh with her. Her laugh is that infectious. "Go." She began to shoo me away, a towel gripped in her hand before she flicked it onto her shoulder. "Be with your friends. I can finish the rest of this."

I step away from the sink, wiping my hands on another dish towel, before kissing her on the forehead and jogging out of the house. Drew, Sydney, and Austin are still hanging out together, laughing. They all look up when I come back out to the backyard.

"Evie! Over here!" Drew calls. Sydney is laughing. My eye's meet Austin's and there is a wide grin on his face, wider than the one I witnessed through the window just moments before. This grin is just for me and I feel giddy at the thought.

I glance around the yard. Most people have left but there's still quite a few people mingling around. Lucy and Jesse are still sitting at the table, talking. Almost as if on cue, Jesse looks up at me and then over at Austin who is waving me over. His eyes narrow and he shakes his head, almost imperceptibly.

Oh hell no.

I spin on my heel and walk toward my friends. I don't give Jesse the pleasure of looking back.

So how was your date?" Lucy asks, crawling out of her bed and into mine. There's barely enough room for the two of us but she's been doing this since we were kids and it's comforting to have her there.

I pause. "It was…it was awful," I lied. "Well, not awful. Just not that good. There will not be a repeat."

There's a long bout of silence and I think for a moment that she's fallen asleep. "I'm sorry, Evie bear." Her arms come out and wrap around me, comforting me. "I really thought that you two would hit it off."

I swallow hard. "Maybe it just sounded better on paper. Besides, it was just a silly crush. There are other boys." It actually physically hurts to lie to my sister. I never lie to her. I'm a pretty bad liar to begin with but lying to the person who knows me better than anyone else? Pretty much impossible. I'm grateful that it's dark in our room, the shutters closed tightly, and Lucy can't see me.

"There's going to be an absolutely amazing boy out there that's worth every bit of your time, Evie, and he's going to be more than just a crush. I know it." Lucy yawns loudly and snuggles in closer to me.

I have no right to be comforted, having just lied to her, but it feels good to have her around. Just us twins wrapped back in each other's arms, falling asleep in the same bed just like we had as kids.

CHAPTER SIX

"We should go grab lunch."

The words are loud, an almost echo through the quiet, empty hallway outside the classroom door. We just had a pop quiz and I was in the middle of going over all the answers in my head, so the deep voice startles me. "What?"

"I'm hungry. Let's go get food. You know, to eat," Austin speaks slower, but there's a smile on his face and I know he's teasing me.

"We have practice," I remind him.

"In two hours, Evie," Austin whines playfully. "I'm hungry and I'm so tired of eating in the dining hall. Show me where the good stuff is."

"Austin, you've been here for months," I point out, walking down the hallway, hoping he'll follow me. Sure enough, he soon falls into step with me. "You haven't explored Izzy at all?"

"No. I don't really know anyone else aside from the guys on the team and a lot of them have been playing for years. I'm the new guy. Besides, between practice, games, and classes, when do I have the time?" he asks. "I mean really princess, I go to class, I study, I practice, I work out."

I consider this. Austin does keep himself busy. He's a full-time student and he spends most of his time outside of class on baseball, more so than any guy on the team. He's at every practice early and he leaves after everyone else. He's in the weight room all the time and I've spotted him running around campus a few times. Shirtless. Of course. Always. *Damn him*.

"Evie?"

I shake my head, trying to clear my head of a shirtless Austin. "Alright, we'll go to lunch."

"Damn." A smile breaks out across his face. "Well, I didn't expect you to actually say *yes*."

I roll my eyes. "Are you hungry or not?"

"Hungry, Coach," he answers, snapping to attention and saluting him. "Lead the way."

"Don't call me '*Coach*,'" I laugh. "Let's stop at the dorms so I can drop off this stupidly heavy backpack before we go."

He laughs and grabs my hand, leading the way. "I remember the way." His hand squeezes mine tightly.

"You're completely irritating, you know that?" I say, letting myself be dragged through campus.

He shrugs and throws a smile over his shoulder at me. "Yet you still made out with me."

I feel my cheeks warm and redden at this memory. "A momentary lapse of judgement on my part."

We make it back to the dorm and I slip the key in the lock. I'm ready to just dump my stuff on my bed and leave but Austin follows me in. I glance around in case Sydney has left underwear sitting in plain sight, as she's been known to do. I know it wouldn't bother her, but it would bother me. Her side of the room is an absolute disaster as always, but I don't see any unmentionables at least.

Austin doesn't say anything as I dump my school stuff on my bed and grab a cardigan from the trunk that sits at the end of my bed. Without a second thought, I know exactly where I want to take him—the boardwalk, and it gets colder toward the beach. A cardigan or sweater was pretty much a necessity. Pushing Austin back out of the door, I lock the door behind me and we walk out of the dorm hall.

"Where are we going? Are we walking?" Austin asks, perplexed.

I nod. "There won't be any parking, so we might as well just walk. Think of it as your warmup."

We stay in a comfortable silence as we walk through the streets of Santa Isabella. The streets were narrow, with just enough room for bicyclists to go rushing past the cars cruising down toward the beach. Most of the shops are small and family owned, full of handmade goods and souvenirs and weird little trinkets. The other business are restaurants that have been here for decades, serving everything from Italian food to hot dogs to ice cream in homemade waffle cones that you can smell from a mile away. There is a banner strung between two street-lights, advertising the weekly farmer's market. Izzy looks like a town perpetually stuck in summer and I love this place. Part beach town, part small town, *all* baseball. A few people wave to me as we walk and Austin laughs.

"What?"

"Do you know *everyone* here?"

I shake my head but there's a smile on my face. "It's a small town, Austin. I'm the coach's daughter. The Quakes are gods here, remember?" The last part is said a little more sarcastically.

"Really."

I glance over at him, but his expression reveals nothing. "They're looking at you, too. You're a Quake now, even if you're new."

Austin frowns a little, but he doesn't say anything. We pass by Copper Books, Drew's family's bookstore. My face flushes at the thought of Drew and I making out in the back stockroom. Austin replaces Drew in my memory, and I clear my throat loudly, if only to bring myself out of my own thoughts.

"Where are we going?" Austin asks.

"Gomez's," I reply.

"Gomez's?" he asks, raising an eyebrow at me.

"Mhm," I answer, without elaborating. I turn into a small restaurant, tucked in between a tattoo parlor and a vintage clothing store. I open the door for Austin, who immediately grabs it and motions me forward. I smile and walk in.

The restaurant is filled to the brim, as I knew it would be because it always is. I'm standing on my tip toes, looking for a place to sit, when a loud booming voice comes out from behind the counter.

"*Evangeline Maria Cordova*!"

I wince a little at hearing my full name yelled across the small restaurant, the name '*Cordova*' really does turn heads in this town, but a full grin is forming easily on my face. "Hola, Tío. *¿Como estas?*"

My uncle is a big, beefy man, sort of resembling Santa Claus, if Santa was Mexican and spoke in broken Spanish. He always smells like a combination of beans, rice, and cilantro. He comes out from behind the counter and wraps me in a large hug. I try to ignore the overpowering smell coming from him and that was now probably all over my clothes. "*Bien, bien.* I haven't seen you in my place in a while, mija. *¿Que pasa?*"

I shrug, waving a hand dismissively. "Yeah, well, been busy, you know. College life." I look over at Austin, who is surveying the place with some interest. Like most of the businesses in Izzy, it's decorated from floor to ceiling, all four walls, with Quakes memorabilia, including some signed jerseys. I spot Dad's and Jesse's and turn away. It's an explosion of black and dark green. If you're not used to Izzy, it's a lot to take in. "Tío, this is Austin Young. He's the new shortstop."

My uncle's eyes grow wide and he comes over to Austin, sticking a large hand out for Austin to shake. "Fantastic. You're the transfer from Texas?"

"Yes, sir," Austin answers, his accent more prominent than ever. He looks surprised. "I'm a junior this year."

"Well, welcome to Quake town," Tío says, sounding pleased. Everyone treats the Quakes like this, whether they're a completely green freshman or a seasoned senior. "What're you kids having? Want a burrito?"

My stomach grumbles happily in response to that. "That sounds perfect. Two, please." Austin opens his mouth to say something, but I cut him off with a glare. "*Two* burritos." The restaurant is filling even more, and someone bumps into me from behind. "Better make it to go."

"I can clear a table…"

I shake my head. "It's fine. We'll go eat on the boardwalk."

My uncle winks at me while writing our order down and spinning it around to the cooks. "Sure, sure. The view is much nicer out there anyhow…" He looks over at my shoulder at Austin. "Your mamá told me about this kid."

I bury my face in my hands and resist the urge to groan. "Whatever Mamá told you is a lie."

"Sure, sure," he repeats, and turns away to help another customer. He reappears not much later, a white paper bag in his hands. He holds it out and Austin grabs it before I can. Tío hands me a couple of cans of Coke and waves me away when I try to pay. I smile in thanks and turn to leave the restaurant.

Austin stops, a curious look on his face as he stares at something right behind the cash register.

Oh, god. I forgot. How could I forget? Hanging on the wall, in sixteen-by-twenty-framed glory, was a photo of me in the black and white baseball uniform of my high school team, the Santa Isabella High School Storm. I was barely sixteen in that photo and it had been taken right before I…

"Is that…" Austin trails off, squinting at the photo on the wall. My heart is beating wildly in my chest, wishing I could make the photo disappear from the wall with sheer will. It's nearly four years old and you might not be able to tell that is me but…*oh god*, I didn't want to take that chance.

"We should get going," I cut in, quickly, steering him as best as I can out of the restaurant. "We don't want the burritos to get cold."

We walk quietly down toward the boardwalk. I can tell Austin is still thinking about what he might have seen in the restaurant, and I only hoped that he couldn't tell that it was me in the photo. I really didn't want to have to explain that I used to play, not to him and most definitely not right now. I suppress a sigh and begin to look around me. The sun casts an orange glowing hue over everything. The weather was nice, warm despite the breeze coming straight from the water. We walk down the pathway, keeping out of the way of cyclists and even a few people on rollerblades. Parents were beginning to shoo their children back in the direction of tables and benches, ready to eat their own lunches. I turn to look at him, but he is watching everything with fascination and it suddenly hits me. If nobody has shown him around, he had never seen any of this before.

"You really haven't been down here yet, have you?" I ask, leading him onto the actual boardwalk.

He shakes his head, taking it all in. "Did you think I was lying? I just haven't had a chance to." His eyes dart around and I nearly laugh. The boardwalk can be overwhelming the first time. I don't know if Austin's even seen the ocean before.

Hearing him say something and then actually watching him experience something for the first time is really an awe-filled moment. I can't believe he hasn't been here yet. Besides baseball, the boardwalk is the only reason to even come to Santa Isabella. It has everything you need on a beach boardwalk: Food, rides, street performers, games. There's not a lot of people out here now, but you can hear the satisfying creak of the ancient roller coaster and kids laughing down by the cotton candy stand. The boardwalk isn't much compared to the massive one in Santa Cruz, which is north of us, but it holds its own. There's an ancient Ferris wheel that creaks enough to give you nightmares while you're at the top, but nearly every kid in Izzy had their first kiss in those hot, plastic buckets. It was almost like a rite-of-passage here in Santa Isabella. There's also a roller coaster, swings, bumper cars, and a tilt-a-whirl. There are people of all ages set up in camping chairs along the edge of the boardwalk, overlooking the ocean, hoping they'll get a bite on their fishing poles.

Past that, though, is the ocean and yes, I've grown up down the street from the ocean my entire life, but the sight of the sun glistening against the deep blue water never gets old. The sun is beginning to go down and the sky is a water-color of pale pinks and purples. The beach below us is empty but there are a few late afternoon surfers far out, bobbing up and down as the tide comes in. I tear my gaze away from the view and look back over at Austin, who looks truly mesmerized at the sight in front of him. I guess that answers my question about him seeing the ocean before. He looks incredibly attractive right now and I need a distraction, *now.*

"Here, let's go say hi to Maggie," I said, veering to the right and heading toward the ticket booth.

"Maggie?" Austin asks, sounding confused. His eyes are still on the endless ocean in front of us.

"She works in the ticket booth. I swear, I don't know if she lives here or what because she's literally always here and I never see here anywhere else in town." Sure enough, when I peek in the window, Maggie is sitting there, her wild red hair pinned back in a butterfly clip. "If you're a pretty good flirt, she'll give you a ride wristband for free."

"Oh really?" Austin asks, sounding amused.

"Maggie is on a constant search for her future ex-husband," I inform him. The kids in front of us finish with their purchase and run off toward the roller coaster. "She's been married seven times. I've been a flower girl twice." I say matter-of-factly as we step up to the window.

"Wow." Austin looks a little taken aback.

"Hey Maggie," I said, sticking my head inside the window.

"Well, hello, darling." Maggie squints for a moment— she refuses to admit that she needs glasses—and then smiles. "Sorry, honey, couldn't tell who it was right away. Thought you might have been Lucy."

"Nope, not Lucy," I quip. "I wanted to introduce you to someone." I step aside so that she can see Austin through the window.

"Well, if it isn't Austin Young," she answers, excitedly,

and Austin jumps in surprise. I laugh. "That was quite a catch you had that first game."

Austin looks down at me, as if waiting for an explanation. I throw him a bone. "You're in Izzy, Austin. Everyone here watches baseball. *Everyone*."

"Thank you, ma'am," Austin says. He sounds nervous but the Southern charm is there, oozing out of him effortlessly, even when he's not trying.

"Ma'am!" Maggie laughs loudly. "What a charmer. You better watch out, Evangeline. I just might steal this one away from you."

"He's all yours," I say, holding my hands up in surrender. "I couldn't possibly compete."

Maggie looks Austin up and down, admiring him. A blush spreads across his cheeks, showing off freckles I hadn't noticed before. "Well, he certainly is a looker." She sighs. "You kids want a wristband?"

I shake my head. "Nope. We're going to go eat at the end of the boardwalk. Maybe we'll come back later." I look over my shoulder at Austin. "Come on."

We head further down the boardwalk to where it curves, heading toward the ocean. It ends in a small pier, hanging over the water. It's normally a popular spot so I'm relieved to find it empty. I flop down, throwing my legs over the edge and motion Austin to sit next to me. He sits next to me, handing over a burrito, and pops the top of both sodas, setting them in between us.

"Be prepared to be amazed," I say, unwrapping my burrito and taking a bite. *Oh, yes*. That's the stuff. I don't know what kind of cooking gene runs in my family but damn, do they make great food.

Austin hesitates for a moment before taking a bite. He chews slowly, carefully, before swallowing. "Damn. That's good." He takes another bite. "Yeah, that's seriously great."

I smile and continue to demolish my burrito. "Are you in the starting line-up tomorrow?"

"Yup," he answers, working his way through the burrito. It nearly disappeared and I know for a fact that he'd have no issue finishing mine if I don't.

"Nervous?" I ask.

"Yup."

Okay, well, this conversation is going super well. I swing my legs back and forth, enjoying the cool breeze on my bare skin. I can hear the surfers' laughter as it reaches across the waves and echoes back toward them. I'm not sure what to say and the silence is deafening and when I'm left alone in my thoughts, all I can think of is him and the warmth I feel when he's right next to me and how I kind of want to throw our burritos into the ocean and press his back against the hard surface of the pier and…

"So why Izzy?" I say, desperate for conversation, for anything to stop the X-rated visuals in my head.

"What?" he looks surprised at the question. His hand crumples up the foil and he tosses it back in the bag.

I clear my throat and turn to him. "What made you come here to Santa Isabella? I mean, you're a junior and you were already at Texas, which has one of the best baseball programs in the country. Why leave?"

He's quiet for a long time and I don't think he's going to answer. I turn my attention back to my burrito, taking small bites. My heart pounds in my ears as I begin to feel anxious, like I overstepped or something but I only asked a question —the first question that popped into my head and now I'm freaking out and eating this stupid burrito and how on earth do I get through the day as a functional human being because I'm forgetting at this moment.

"Have you ever wanted something so badly that you were basically willing to do anything for it?"

I'm startled at his question and our eyes meet. I swallow hard. My thoughts flit somewhere else, to another time, to a completely different dream—before I can stop it, the image of me in a Quakes jersey overwhelms me. There's a sharp pain in my stomach at the thought. "Sure," I answer, trying to keep my voice steady.

"That's how I feel about baseball," he answers softly. There's something in the way he says baseball. It's the way a mother says the name of her child, the way some people say their prayers. He sounds happy and reverent and sad all at the same time. Without a second thought, I know what he means. I know how he feels. He's like Annie from one of my favorite movies, *Bull Durham*. Austin is a member of the Church of Baseball.

"What do you mean?" I ask, but I feel like I already know. I get it. But I can't say it, so I need him to say it.

He leans back on his palms. His shirt lifts a little and I can see the tanned skin of his abs and I look away, ignoring the heat that spreads through my cheeks. He affects me so easily. "Baseball is really the only thing I've ever been good at. I've always gotten decent grades. I played basketball too and football because it's basically the law to play football back in Kentucky, where I grew up." He laughs a little. "But baseball...baseball is everything."

I want to tell him to stop talking. Why did I ask him about baseball? Why did I do this to myself? This is self-torture at this point. God, sometimes I truly am a masochist. "I'm sure you were good at other things," I say, lamely. Is this my attempt at changing the conversation? What on earth am I doing?

He shrugs. "Maybe, but that's not what was important. As soon as I started playing baseball, that was all that was in the cards for me. It was the one thing that was going to save us." He rolls his eyes at this, but his tone doesn't match that. He sounds…disappointed.

"Save you?"

He sits up and props up his head in his hands, his burrito wrapper sitting on his lap as he stares out at the ocean in front of us. I'm grateful for him looking away. I don't want to look at him right now, and I don't want him seeing me. To see the pain I was feeling. "We own a ranch out in Kentucky, a horse ranch. It used to be amazing. Beautiful, even. We used to raise the best horses in the state. The ranch has been in my mama's family for years. But it's fallen apart, and, over the years, we've had to sell bits and pieces of the land off to other ranches around us. Mostly to pay off my dad's gambling debts."

Austin pauses for a moment and then continues. "It was never enough for my dad, you know. We have…*had* one of the most successful ranches in the entire state of Kentucky but it wasn't enough. He always wanted more, until he got more and then he wanted even more and lost it all."

I swallow hard, the burrito forgotten in my hand. "And baseball?"

"Baseball was our ticket out. It always has been. I've been playing since I was little. I played well through middle school and high school, enough to get a scholarship to a good school, and the end goal has always been the major leagues. The ranch is falling apart, and my mom really needs the money. It's the only thing I'm good at. It's the only thing I've ever been good at. It's really the only way I can help my mom."

"It's more than that though. I love baseball. I love everything about baseball, and I don't have anything else. There's nothing else I can do. Someone put a baseball in my hand when I was a kid and it was obvious right away that I was good at it." He sighs. "Dad left a couple years ago, not long after I went to UT. I actually was offered a full scholarship to play for Rusk, but they're more of a football school and my daddy said it wouldn't be enough to get me noticed by the scouts so, I took the partial at Texas."

He shakes his head and his next words come out with a bite. He's angry. "Such a stupid mistake. Sure, it's one of the best baseball programs in the country but it's that way because all the players there are amazing. I didn't play. I was better off going to other colleges where I could at least get some playing time. I sat on the bench for two years at Texas. What good does that do me? I need to play. Nothing else is important, Evie. I *need* baseball."

The intensity of his voice startles me. He sounds determined, passionate and ambitious but he also sounds scared, nervous and…*desperate* even. The extra hours in the weight room and the constant running around campus…it all seems to make more sense now. "So, you came to Izzy?"

Austin sighs again. "It's far from home. I almost didn't do it for that very reason. I hate to leave my mom alone. I almost didn't do it, but you guys won the world series two years in a row. I'd heard of the Quakes and the program. I'd heard about your dad. Everyone is constantly talking about the guys on your team, though there's mostly talk about Jesse and how he's likely to get drafted at the end of this season."

I suck in a breath at the sound of Jesse's name, but Austin doesn't notice.

"I spoke with your dad and the other coaches. I spoke with the dean of admissions at Texas and here at Izzy. It took some time, but I finally managed to get a transfer. I really had to show them I wanted to play, that I could play, and it seems to be working out so far. I'm finally getting some playing time." He groans, frustrated. "Except my batting average, obviously."

I want to tell him he needs to raise his elbow but somehow, I know that right now is probably not the best time to tell him that. He doesn't say anything else for a while and I assume he's finished. I feel sort of terrible. I should have talked about the weather or asked him about his favorite movie, a much lighter conversation than the one we just dove into. There was something seriously wrong with me that I managed to pick the touchiest subject. Now we're both sitting here, miserable. Stupid baseball.

And yet…

He interrupts my thoughts. "You know," he says quietly, "I don't really talk about this with anyone. I don't really tell anyone that. I hate talking about my dad and the ranch and all of that." The corner of his mouth quirks up a little bit and I have the sudden urge to kiss that very spot.

I cough and look out at the ocean. "Well, I'm glad you can tell me." They're just words but they're true. I *am* glad he could tell him. It's not easy to tell someone your secrets. I should know.

"Hey Evie?"

"Yeah?" My heart is beating wildly in my chest. How is it that conversation makes me want him more? It should send me sprinting in the other direction, but it doesn't. It just makes me understand him more. I'm even more aware of how close we are, and I just want to close the distance and press myself up against him. I raise my eyes to meet his. His dark hair is windswept and falling in his face and my fingers twitch, wanting to brush it out of the way.

"Are you going to eat the rest of your burrito?"

I can't help it but laugh. "No, go ahead." I hand it over and our fingers brush lightly. Warmth spreads from the contact and shoots up my arm and colors my face. I know he feels it too, but he simply turns away.

"So, what's your story, Evangeline?"

I groan. "Please don't call me that. Evie is just fine."

He laughs at that. "Seriously, though. I just basically opened myself up and spread all my chips on the table for me. Which, you know, I normally don't do. So, what's your story?"

My chest tightened as his words played over in my head. *What's your story?* It's not that I didn't want to tell him...okay well that was part of it. But how was I supposed to explain any of it? Jesse...Lucy...the—*no*, I couldn't. He wouldn't understand. I could feel panic slowly setting in as Jesse's voice slowly filled my head. *"I want to know everything about you," Jesse whispers in my ear. I look around but everyone is laughing, drinking, enjoying the celebratory bonfire. No one notices us together and I'm glad I get to have him like this. I'm glad he's talking to me. "Tell me everything."*

I shake my head, pulling myself back to the present. "I don't have a story."

His eyebrows are raised, and I swear that Southern accent is almost exaggerated when he speaks next. "Now, I think a princess like you would have a lot of stories."

"Really, I don't." I swallowed hard, trying to keep my composure. "I grew up here in Santa Isabella my entire life, I graduated from Santa Isabella High School last summer and now I'm a freshman at CS Santa Isabella. Where we met. Nothing super exciting here."

I haven't known him long and yet I already feel as if I can read the expression on his face. He's thinking about the photo he saw at Gomez's. He opens his mouth to say something and I immediately cut him off. We are not having that conversation. Not now. Not ever, if I have my way. "Come on, let's go ride the roller coaster or something. We have time before practice." I stand up, brushing crumbs off my shorts.

He looks disappointed but he only says, "Okay. Let's go."

"You're coming to the game?" Drew asks, surprised.

"Yeah, so?"

There's a pause on the other side of the phone. "You're not even supposed to be at this game," he points out. "You're off tonight. You haven't voluntarily showed up at a baseball game since we played…"

"Yeah, I get it," I say, shortly, tucking my phone between my ear and shoulder as I search my purse for some money. The student behind the ticket window looks irritated and I smile apologetically at her. Why does everyone seem intent on having a conversation about the past when all I wanted to do was leave it there, in the past? "I'll be fine. It's just a baseball game."

"*It's just a baseball game*? Who are you and what have you done with my best friend? Are you feeling okay?" Drew sounds wary but it's hard to tell. There's a lot of noise in the background, the sounds of laughter and lockers slamming and players getting ready for the game.

"I'm fine Drew," I repeat. "It's no different sitting in the stands than when I'm sitting in the dugout."

"When you're in the dugout, you can turn it all off and treat it like a job. Evie, this is most definitely not the same thing…"

"I am *fine*." I repeat for the third time. "It's not as if I'm going to pl—" I stop talking and take a deep breath. What on earth was going on with me today?

"Does this have to do with Austin?"

I pause in the process of handing a twenty-dollar bill to the girl in the window. "Excuse me?"

There's a shift in Drew's tone, as he switches from disbelief to teasing. "I heard you spent some time with Austin yesterday, took him down to your uncle's restaurant and everything."

"Wow," I say, taking my ticket and walking toward the entrance. "Is that what the locker room talk is today? How the coach's daughter took the transfer kid to lunch yesterday? We share a class together, he was hungry, and we grabbed some food. That's all."

"Whoa, defensive much?" He laughs. "He mentioned that he had tried Gomez's and Tripp asked how he even knew where it was, and he said you guys went after class."

"Oh," is all I manage to say as I make my way into the stadium. The stadium is large for a college baseball stadium and there aren't any assigned seats, except for those behind home plate. The rest are just benches. Everyone liked it that way; you could move around, talk to your friends, that sort of thing. I spot an empty seat near the dugout and make my way down, grateful that there's a seat down at the end.

"Yeah, *oh*." Drew says. "I was just surprised that you were even hanging out with a baseball player. You tend to avoid us, you know?"

"Not you," I point out, but Drew continues.

"I just find it very interesting that you had lunch with Austin, who is a baseball player. A good looking, *Quakes* baseball player at that. Now you're at the game, voluntarily, when you don't need to be. So, I gotta wonder if it has to do with Austin."

"It doesn't," I lie.

There's a long pause and I can practically hear the wheels turning in his brain as he considers how to say what I know he wants to say. "He said you guys talked a lot about baseball and I just…I wondered if you told him. About high school."

Dad's booming voice echoes through my phone's speaker. I feel the familiar wave of anxiety and pain at the mention of high school. "No. I didn't. You shouldn't be on the phone anymore. Good luck."

"I'm probably not going to play," is the only response I get.

"Goodbye Drew."

"This conversation is not over," Drew says before ending the call.

I shake my head, shoving my phone in my back pocket and leaning back against the cool metal bench, ready to watch the game. The players come running onto the field and I can see the back of Dad's head from where I sit. I whistle loudly, just the way he taught me when I was a kid, and he turns, surprised. I wave and he grins at me before turning his attention back to the game and his players.

Austin is having a bad game.

It's the bottom of the fifth inning and we are winning, up by three runs. Gary Cobb, one of our senior pitchers, is pitching a great game, as per usual, and has only allowed Cal State Long Beach one run. Austin, however, has not contributed on offense in the slightest. His first at-bat was okay; he managed to get on base but only because of an error on the part of the opposing team's second baseman. His second and third times up to the plate were just terrible. He's swinging at wild pitches, striking out each time with ease. His elbow is too low when he's up to bat and it's giving him an incredibly awkward swing. I can't stop staring at it. How has no one fixed this yet? He's up for the fourth time and I'm hoping he can change luck.

"Nervous much, Evie?" a voice comes up from above me as Austin steps up to the plate. I look up, into a face so much like my own. "Calm down, little sis."

"You're only seven minutes older than me," I say,

quietly. "Also, what are you doing here? Jesse isn't even pitching tonight."

Lucy shrugs. "And that means I can't come and watch the game anyway? My dad is the coach of the team too, you know." She teases before looking me up and down. "I just felt like getting out of the apartment and I'm still supporting Jesse this way. I feel like it's been ages since I've seen you in Quakes colors."

I run my sweaty hands over my dark green shirt and turn my eyes back to the game. "Well, Drew does play now. Gotta support my best friend."

"Fair enough," Lucy laughs. "Well, he warms the bench anyway. Budge up."

I move over as much as I can and Lucy slides into the seat next to me. Her arm comes up and links through mine. "You nervous for your boy out there?" I look up at her, surprised. She raises her eyebrow, looking so much like our dad in that moment. "You're kind of attacking your cup."

I look down at the Styrofoam cup that's in my lap, one that I've literally been tearing to shreds without even realizing. Why am I here? This is exactly as awful as I could have imagined it. I feel way too much when I'm here. Drew was right; it's just too painful for me to be here as a spectator and not out there…

Lucy reaches for the cup and takes it from me. "He's not *my boy*," I say, tersely, as a strike goes flying down the middle, landing perfectly in the catcher's mitt.

Strike one.

"I heard you took him to Tío's restaurant," Lucy says. She cranes her neck, looking for Jesse but he's nowhere to be seen. *Thank god*. She gives up and looks back at me. "What was that about?"

"Was there a newsbreak about that or something?" I mumble, focused on Austin. He lets a pitch fly past him and it's the right decision this time. It's low and outside and the umpire calls it a ball. I let out a breath.

"This is Izzy, my dear sister. Everyone knows everything about everyone, remember? Tío told Mamá, who called me in a frenzy. She wants to know if you have a boyfriend."

"I don't have a boyfriend," I say, hotly. "He's my *friend*. Like Drew is my *friend*. Can't a girl just have a friend without getting the whole inquisition?"

"Okay, for one thing, you and Drew used to make out in the stockroom at Copper's, so you guys weren't always just friends. Also, it was so gross," Lucy says, laughing. Her eyes are fixated on Austin. He's stepped out of the batter's box for a moment, adjusting his batting gloves. "And two, Drew does not look like that."

She is not wrong about that, so I don't bother answering. Another pitch goes sailing from the pitcher's hand toward Austin and he swings and misses. I sigh. He keeps making the same damn mistake.

"Evie?"

"What?" I ask, tearing my eyes away from Austin and looking at Lucy. She has an expectant look on her face and I know I've missed something. "What is it?"

She grins. "I wish twins really could read minds or something. I would love to know what's going on in that pretty little head of yours."

"You can't call me pretty," I answer drily. "We're twins. It makes you sound conceited."

"Or confident," Lucy answers smoothly. "We are a pretty pair, Evie, wear it proudly." I shoot her a look and she continues. "Your boy just struck out."

I whirl around and, sure enough, Austin is walking back toward the dugout. He looks disappointed. No. Scratch that. He looks *furious*. The bat is gripped tightly in his hand

and he looks like he wants to throw it. He could get ejected or penalized for doing something like that and I know it's the only thing keeping him from doing it. His eyes meet mine as he walks by and he looks surprised. I give him a small wave and mouth '*sorry*.' He shrugs and disappears into the dugout.

The next inning, there is someone else at shortstop and there's a large pit in my stomach. Dad pulled Austin for the rest of the game. I can't see him from where I'm sitting but I'm sure he has to be angry that the freshman shortstop took over for him. I sigh and sit back against the bench.

"Looks like your boy is out," Lucy says, sympathetically. She finally spots Jesse, who is leaning up against the fence in the dugout, and waves enthusiastically at him. He blows her a kiss and she pretends to catch it. I want to gag but her face is practically glowing. It's almost painful to look at it and I nearly flinch when she turns back to me. "If Austin isn't careful, he just might stay in that dugout for the rest of the season."

I'm angry. I'm hurt and frustrated. None of this is her fault but being here is too emotional and everything is piling on top of me and I can't control it. "Not if I can help it," I bark out at her. She looks startled but doesn't respond.

That stupid swing is not going to hold Austin back. It's not.

I won't let it.

CHAPTER SEVEN

I can't believe that I'm doing this.

I have an iced green tea dripping condensation in my hand as I make down the hallway of Austin's dorm hall. I snuck into Dad's office the night before, after the game, and pulled up Austin's records to see exactly which dorm he was in.

Creepy, I know, but it was under good pretenses.

At least, that's what I had told myself last night, and I had believed it at the time. Walking toward his door this morning, I feel more like I'm making a huge mistake. What am I even doing here? Why am I even getting involved with this? It's early and he's probably in the weight room or running around campus and, besides, I shouldn't even care about this.

I knock on Austin's door, waiting a couple of moments for a sign of life on the other side. He doesn't answer so I knock again, louder. The sound echoes throughout the hallway, a loud and resonating sound that startles even me. I remember that I'm in a damn residence hall and there are other people on this floor, people that will probably crucify me for waking them up so early on a Saturday morning. My hand is raised and I'm about to knock a third time when the door finally swings open.

Austin peeks out. His eyes are heavy with sleep and he looks thoroughly confused. He rubs his eyes, tiredly, and I try very hard to not stare at his bare chest that is at perfect eye level. Does this guy wear a shirt? Ever? "Evie? What's going on?"

"Come on. Let's go." My voice is a little higher pitched than normal and I blame it completely on him being shirtless. Who can even function normally around this? It's not normal to look the way he does, not even for a baseball player.

"Go where?" he asks, looking more confused.

I shake my head. "Just trust me, will you? Let's go."

"Can I at least put some clothes on first?" he asks, running a hand through his hair.

"Yeah, fine, whatever, just hurry up," I answer. "Wear something comfortable."

"Unless you'd rather me just stay like this," he teases, leaning toward me. I take a step backward, fighting the urge to grab him. I've had the pleasure of feeling those rock-hard abs pressed against me through a t-shirt but to feel them bare would be a whole new adventure.

I shake my head, hoping that the heat flowing through me doesn't reach my cheeks. I'm so tired of constantly blushing around him. "You wish."

"Oh, but I do," Austin says, opening the door wider. I can see into his room a little bit and I'm curious. Every time we've hung out, it's either been around campus or in the room I share with Sydney. His room is a single, small, and plain, with only a few posters on the wall, including one of Kris Bryant from the Cubs. His room is messy but not in a bad way, just that sort of disorganized mess that seems to be normal for boys, if Drew's room was any way to judge. "Did you want to come in?"

My fingers close into tight fights as I tense. Why does this seem like a terrible idea? The hallway is safe. There are other people in the hallway to keep me from doing something I might regret. His dorm room is private and way too dangerously inviting. I'd rather not go in there, but it would be weird to insist that I remain in the hallway.

I mentally shake it off and nod. "Sure."

He backs up so I can come in and I pass him, stopping just inside, unsure of what to do next. I've been in a boy's room twice. I hardly count Drew because he's my best friend and it never felt like a big deal, not when you're both looking at baseball cards and you're completely unaware that being in a boy's room is supposed to be a big deal. The other time, well, that was a big deal and I didn't want to think about that right now, not with Austin shirtless behind me.

I can feel the heat of his bare chest just a breath away from my back. "You can sit down, you know," he says.

I laugh nervously and go to his desk, lifting a stack of books off the chair and placing them on the desk before sitting down. I'm perched nervously at the edge of it, my knees bouncing. I look up at Austin and immediately cover my eyes. "What are you doing?" I shriek.

He pauses in the middle of taking his blue and red flannel pants off. "Changing?"

"While I'm in the room? Jesus, Austin!" I say averting and suddenly becoming very interested in the *Intro to Broadcasting* textbook laying on the desk.

"Haven't you already seen pretty much all of us naked in the locker room?" he laughs. "I'm wearing underwear. Calm down, Evie, I'm just putting pants on. Don't get too excited over there."

I sputter, unable to get the words out. I huff in silence, looking out the window. My arms are crossed tightly across my chest and I try desperately to ignore the heat that's pooling in my stomach and spreading down my legs. There's just something about this guy that's nearly impossible to deal with. I hated that I wanted him. "Are you ready?"

"Yeah," he answers, amusement coloring his voice. "I'm ready. Are you going to tell me where we're going?"

"Come on," I reply, standing up and heading toward the door. "You'll see when we get there."

He shrugs, grabbing a hoodie and yanking it over his head and locking the door behind us.

AUSTIN LOOKS AT ME SKEPTICALLY WHEN WE ARRIVE. "Batting cages? Really?" He sounds disappointed.

"What did you expect?" I turn the car off.

"A romantic date at the beach, maybe," he answers, vaguely, staring at the entrance to the batting cages. I know this place well; I've been coming here since I was a child. I have both good and bad memories here and I've avoided this place for years. "Maybe a ride on the Ferris wheel where I can hold you close at the top, keep you from being scared."

I scoff. "I'm not afraid of the Ferris wheel."

"Well, I am. Maybe you can hold me at the top, maybe sneak a little kiss. That sounds like a much better idea than whatever *this* is."

I try to ignore the picture in my head of Austin and I on top of the rickety Ferris wheel. Admittedly that does sound like a better idea than this. I'm on a mission though so I just roll my eyes at him. "Stop being such a baby." I get out of the car, slamming the door behind me. He sits in the car for a moment longer and then gets out, following me into the building.

The sensations hit me as soon as we walk in the door and I falter, temporarily losing my conviction. Memories fill my vision as I look around; it hasn't changed at all in the three years since I've been here. Well, that's not entirely true. I spot the banner on the wall, *CONGRATS TO SANTA ISABELLA HIGH SCHOOL! CIF BASEBALL CHAMPS 2016!* That's definitely new.

I force myself to look away from the banner. *We aren't here for me. We're here for Austin.* I quickly set up for the fastest pitch booth and focus on getting Austin ready to go. "Okay, now get in there."

He looks down at me, looking doubtful. His hands are buried deep in the pockets of his hoodie and he looks like this is the last place that he wants to be. I know he feels and yet, there's a part of me that is envious. "Man, I don't know, Evie."

I sit down in the chair that's conveniently provided for spectators such as myself and look up at him. It's immediately a mistake. He's so goddamn tall and I have to crane my neck to look at him. "Look, Austin, just hear me out. You're having one problem on the field and you're driving yourself insane. Your defense is fantastic. You're truly an amazing shortstop. I'm not just saying that. Here's the thing. You work out every single day, yet you're still having trouble every single time you come up to bat. You lift weights and you bulk up but it's not just about strength. Strength would matter if you were connecting with the ball, but you're not. Austin, you're not hitting the ball."

"Yeah, I'm kind of aware of that," Austin barks out sharply, clearly irritated. "You don't have to remind me."

I roll my eyes. "I don't remember anyone telling me that cowboys were so damn sensitive. Stop being a baby," I repeat. "Get in there and hit the ball, okay? Away from the game and the lights and the other players and the pressure. Just go in there and it'll just be you and the bat and the ball. You work out every single day, Austin. *Every. Single. Day.* You work your ass off and it's just not working. You're not hitting anything. Just…listen to me, okay?"

He hesitates for a moment, his eyes traveling back and forth between the batting cage and me. "I guess it couldn't hurt. I slept in today instead of heading down to the weight room like I meant to. I might as well get some kind of workout in."

It's like he hasn't even heard a word I just said. If he gave me just half of a listening ear, he'd realize that I know what I'm talking about. He can bulk up as much as he wants, but his elbow is still too damn low. "God forbid you miss a day in the weight room," I mutter sarcastically under my breath. I lean back in the chair as he pulls the helmet over his head and he steps into the cage.

I watch him for a long time, I can't help but watch him. My eyes naturally find him in class or when I spot him walking around campus or when he's on the field and I'm supposed to be concentrating on the batting order. The things that used to be important to me when it came to attractive features in a guy, ones that I had forgotten about, are suddenly incredibly sexy again. His strong arms, bent at the elbow, his large hands gripping the bat tightly, the muscles in his calves tensing up as the ball flies toward him again and again. His hair is so short, and it looks soft. The night in the hall flashes in the back of my mind as I remembered what having my fingers in his hair felt like, and I want to do it again. I shove my hands in my pockets to keep them from fidgeting so much.

Austin makes contact with quite a few of the balls that head his way but they're sloppy, heading up, instead of straight. On the field, they would be easy pop-ups and that's exactly what we're trying to avoid. He needs to learn how to hit straight shots, out into the outfield. He needs to focus on base hits and less on hitting it out of the park. Home runs don't always win championships. They just look pretty.

Though, to be fair, I'd take any kind of hit from him at this point.

The problem boils down to two things. One, his elbow is just too low. I can't understand how it feels comfortable for him to swing with his back elbow that low. The second thing is that he doesn't follow through with any of his swings, pretty much the basic rule of batting. It can't be good for his arms either; he could seriously reinjure his shoulder. Maybe this weird way of batting has worked for him in the past but it's not working now.

The rotation ends and Austin relaxes his arm, the bat held loosely in his grip. "That wasn't too bad," he remarks. He looks more relaxed and I almost feel bad about having to ruin that.

"You're making contact and that's good but…" I hesitate.

"But what?" Austin asks, his eyebrow raised.

I close my eyes and Jesse's voice fills my head again. I feel like I can't breathe. *I think I know a little more about baseball than you, Evie. I'm the one getting scouted by major league teams. I'm the one that takes this sport seriously. Not all of us can just play for fun.*

"Evie?"

"Your elbow is too low," I blurt out, desperate to drown out that voice in my head. "I don't know how you bat like that because it seriously can't be comfortable. It looks weird and it completely hinders your swing."

Austin's eyebrows raise even higher, nearly disappearing under his messy hair. "What are you talking about?"

I open my mouth and shut it. His voice is still in the back of my head. This feels too familiar. I flush. This is déjà vu. I've been in this position, this exact same one, three years ago. "I'm just trying to help you," I say, carefully. "You need to raise your elbow. I know that you had a shoulder injury when you were at Texas and I know that's probably why you have a weird swing but you have to fix it or you're never going to make contact with the ball."

If I was expecting a response, any response at all, I was immediately proven wrong. He turns his back to me. The next rotation is about to start and the counter on the wall is going down in anticipation of the first pitch. Austin gets back into his stance, his elbow too low again and I want to groan. A rush of embarrassment runs through me. Of course, he didn't listen to me. I watch as he goes through the rotation again, missing more of the pitches than hitting them. My arms are crossed tightly across my chest. He finishes out the last few pitches and this time, he looks as frustrated as I feel.

"What's wrong?" he asks, coming out of the cage.

"You didn't listen to me," I say, shortly. I wanted to keep my patience and stay levelheaded, but my frustration was slowly eating at me. "I know I'm a girl and all that but I'm trying to help you, Austin. I know what I'm talking about. I have the experience with this. You didn't listen to me. You just did the same thing you did before, and did it work? Of course, it didn't."

He looks taken aback and his mouth straightens into a very thin line. "If you were to help me, you wouldn't be yelling at me like I'm a child, Evie. You think I like not getting any hits? You think I don't know that I could be benched at any time, just like I was last night?"

"Well, then do it the way I told you to do it!" I snap.

Austin yanks the helmet off his head and holds it and the bat out to me.

"You do it," he says, firmly. "You get in there, and hit the ball, then. If you're so knowledgeable and experienced, you do it." He drops them at my feet with a loud clang and I jump. I can feel the gazes of the other patrons looking in our direction and I resist the urge to stick my tongue out at them or tell them to just mind their own business.

I pick up the bat slowly, testing the weight of it in my hands as my fingers curl around the grip. All too familiar, but it felt like part of me. Just a mere extension of my arm. Jesse's voice continues to haunt me as I pick up the helmet.

"Evie," Jesse says, that stupid cocky smirk on his face. I hate that smirk but he's beautiful, he's here with me and it's all I've ever really wanted. "I appreciate the help, baby, I do. But do you really think you know more about baseball than me?"

My face is bright red. "I just…I just wanted to help you. So, you can get better. I improved my average this last year and I just want to…" I trail off, uncertainty in my voice.

"Just leave baseball to the real baseball players, okay?" he says before turning away and heading back into the cage. I have nothing to say to him. How can he think I'm not real? He knows what I can do. He's seen it. But I can't think of anything to say.

My eyes water for a moment at the memory and I look away from Austin so he doesn't see it. I hesitate to actually step into the cage. It's been way too long since I've done this, and I don't even know if I *can* do this anymore. I used to work so hard so it can't just all be gone. I take a deep breath and stand up, picking up the discarded bat and helmet. I feed money into the machine and look over my shoulder at Austin. He looks like a child throwing a tantrum, slouched in the chair I've just vacated, looking grumpy.

I open the cage door and step through. God, it feels

amazing to be back here. This small box feels like home. My body remembers what to do even if I don't and I can try and deny it all I want, but it's nearly undeniable. I like being here. I like holding the bat in my hands. I get myself into position, falling right into the familiar stance without even thinking about it. I don't have to think about it. Even if I didn't remember, didn't want to remember, my body still remembers.

I'm frustrated and I know I need to calm down and focus if I want to hit anything that comes my way. I was never good at connecting with the ball when I was too emotional. I take another deep breath and let it out slow as the first pitch comes barreling my way.

The bat makes contact, sending the ball flying. If I were on the field, it would be a perfect base hit, provided that the shortstop wasn't into diving catches or anything. Pitch after pitch came out of the machine and I made contact with every single one of them. Not every hit is beautiful but I'm hitting them. It feels good to be back in the cages. It feels *natural*. I hit one last pitch, sending it skittering across the ground. I relax my arms. They feel a little shaky and stiff. They haven't been used for this kind of action in a long time and even though I know I'm probably going to be sore tomorrow, it feels exhilarating. It feels like the first time I ever held a baseball and the emotions I'm feeling right now scare me. I try to focus on the reason I'm here and look over at Austin.

There's an indecipherable look on his face and I can't tell what he's thinking so I wait for him to say something. "You're not left-handed," he finally manages to say. "It's completely different."

My mouth drops open. Is he seriously kidding right now? I know I've just done infinitely better in this cage than he did and he's complaining that I don't bat left-handed like he does. Stupid left-handed…does he know not to anger a girl with a bat in her hand?

I don't answer. Instead I feed more money into the machine, and I switch to the other side, looking more confident than I feel. If it's been a long time since I batted normally, as a right-handed person, it's been even longer than I've done it left-handed.

I don't do as well as I did the first time around. Of course, I don't. That would be a freakin' miracle and I wasn't very good at batting left-handed to begin with. I'm just naturally right-handed. But I do still bat well, much better than Austin during the two rotations he took in the cage and I feel an odd sense of satisfaction at that. I'm not a competitive person—not anymore, anyway—but his words make me feel a deep need to prove myself. I make contact with most of the balls, mostly because I'm pissed off and it's fueling my swing. Each hit is packed with a punch. This feels too good.

I feel a sense of relief when the rotation ends, and I can take off the helmet and get out of this cage that suddenly feels so suffocating. I let myself out and immediately ran smack into Austin. He's stood up and somehow managed to plant himself right in front of me.

"What are you…" I start to say, as the bat and helmet fall to the floor. He grabs my arm and pulls me up against him, his face just a breath away from mine. I remember the last time we were this close and a heat spreads through me. "What are you doing?" I ask, my voice shaky. My hands are gripping his arms tightly, mostly to keep myself from losing my balance and falling over. I'm trying to ignore how good this feels and how incredibly safe I feel with his arm wrapped tightly around my waist.

"What the hell was that?" he asks, under his breath. He's staring at me like he's never seen me before and it's unnerving. I look over his shoulder and see that there's quite a crowd around our spot. People know who he is, people know who I am, and we are attracting way too much attention for my liking. My temperature is rising and the warmth coming from him is not helping. We're both sweaty and disgusting but I am so attracted to him like this that I lean closer, my fingers digging into the skin of his arms. His muscles flex under my grip as he holds me up. I hope he can't feel my heart pounding because it's going a thousand miles a minute right now.

"What the hell was what?" I manage to say and I'm relieved to find that my voice still sounds relatively normal.

"That," he answers, indicating toward the cage. "What you just did in there. What was that?"

His lips are right there. They're right in front of me and I remember so vividly how they taste and how they feel when they're pressed tightly against mine. My eyes are drawn to them. I want so badly to kiss him again and I'm having a hard time convincing myself that being with a baseball player is a terrible idea. *I should not kiss him*, but would it really be that bad? "I was just doing what you couldn't do," I say, hotly.

A smile breaks out on his face and I'm blown away by it. "Yeah. Yeah, you did." His face comes closer and his forehead rests against mine. I gasp quietly. "Who the hell are you?"

I force a laugh, my voice shaking. "I'm Evie."

He pulls back, his eyes meeting mine again. They flash back and forth between mine and I know he's taking in the different colors. It usually irritates me, but it feels different when he does it. His brow is furrowed as he studies my face. "You continue to surprise me, Evie Cordova." He leans closer to me.

His lips are just brushing mine when I feel myself go

cold and I yank myself backward. "No," I say, suddenly. His eyes widen and he drops his hands. I stumble, nearly falling to the ground. Every thought about those lips on mine from only a minute ago were long gone now. "No, don't do that."

"Evie…"

I shake my head, running my hands over my clothes, straightening them out. How did I get so flustered so quickly? "I told you. I don't date baseball players. I don't date Quakes players, especially. I told you that we should just be friends." I grab the bat and helmet from the floor and walk around him, heading toward the counter.

Austin's hand comes out to grab my arm and he whirls me around to face him. He tends to do this and there's a part of me that's thrilled by it and another, larger, part that is terrified by it. I hate the way I immediately react to him. I hate it. "Evie, seriously. You're giving me mixed signals here, princess. I get that you have this rule. I get it, okay? But this is me. You *know* me. Let me take you out. Please."

It's the '*please*' that nearly gets me. I don't want to look up, so I keep my eyes glued to the floor. I'm afraid to look at him and into those deep, dark brown eyes. I can't date him. He's a Quake, for god's sake, and he's fully immersed in it. He's obsessed with baseball and he spends most of his time playing and when he's not playing, he's thinking and talking about it. I can't do that. I can't get that close to baseball again. I can't. "I've told you, Austin. No. No means no. You said we could be friends. I just want to be friends with you."

His hands reach for my chin, tipping my face up so that my eyes are forced to meet his. There is no trace of a smile on his face now. Instead he looks curious and concerned. "What happened? What happened that you won't even try to give this a chance, Evie? I don't do this. I don't…I don't care like this and I think you care too so please, just talk to me."

"Austin!" I grab his arm and push it away from me. "You're relentless. No means I don't want to tell you. No means I'm not going to change my mind. No means that it's none of your damn business."

He looks at me in shock and I blush when I realize what I've said and how loudly I've said it. "So, something did happen," he says, softly, trying to reach for me again.

"Just stop." I feel tired. There is so much about Austin that is so different from Jesse but their obsession with baseball and the Quakes is just too similar. I just can't have that much baseball in my life. It's too painful. It's too hard. "It's none of your business. Let's just go, okay?"

He follows me as I return the equipment back to the counter. "Are you mad at me?"

"No."

Corey, the guy behind the counter, is staring at me, eyes a little wide. I'm not entirely sure why but it might be about my unexpected outburst from a few seconds ago. That was more of my sister's type of thing. In fact, I know Corey well from high school, especially since he dated my sister briefly in our freshman year and he was often at the parties that went on after games. He hands back my driver's license and I turn to leave.

"You sound like you're mad," Austin says, falling into step with me.

I sigh, stopping in front of my car and unlocking it. I am mad. I'm mad that he continues to find a way under my skin and that I can't seem to just cut him off. I'm going to have to tell him eventually.

But not now. Not today.

"Let's just go."

. . .

JESSE AND I ARE ON A RARE OUTING IN PUBLIC, BUT IT'S JUST AT the batting cages, so he doesn't think that anyone is going to think anything of it. I have a book open in my lap, watching as he goes through the rounds. I keep frowning. He holds his elbow so weird and it makes his swing so weird and awkward. He's a fantastic pitcher but his swings are all wrong and I'm starting to figure out why.

"Jesse?" My voice cracks with hesitation and I wince. I clear my throat and try it again. "Jesse?"

He turns around and grins at me. "Yes?"

"Um, you should raise your elbow a little. It'll make your swing better."

He stares at me for a moment. "Wait, what?"

I swallow hard and clear my throat. "Your elbow. It's awkward. You should try raising it."

"Evie," Jesse says, that stupid cocky smirk on his face. I hate that smirk but he's beautiful and he's here with me and it's all I've ever wanted. "I appreciate the help, baby, I do. But do you really think you know more about baseball than me?"

"My face is bright red. "I just…I just wanted to help you. So, you can get better."

"Just leave the baseball to the real players, okay?" he says. He turns away and heads back into the cage. I'm speechless and I'm not sure what to say. What do I even say to him? I play baseball. I'm a real player. Does he think that I'm not a real player?

I disappear to the restroom for a moment, splashing cold water on my heated face, and staring at the reflection. I mostly like what I see, except my stupid eyes. Why couldn't I just have normal brown eyes like Lucy? Why did I have to have weird ones? Jesse always calls me Crazy Eyes, and I think he means it as an endearment, but it doesn't always feel that way.

I make my way back out to the cages and I stop in my tracks when I see a girl leaning against the cage, talking to Jesse. She's giggling loudly and the grin on Jesse's face is unmistakable. She's older than me and I feel a swoop of uncertainty go through me. We always have to hide. With a girl like that, he wouldn't have to hide.

"You should definitely come to the party tonight," the girl is saying as I approach them. "It's going to be a great time."

"I'm sure it will be," Jesse agrees, leaning on his crossed arms against the fence.

"I could definitely show you a good time," she flirts. Her shirt lifts a little to reveal a flat stomach and I kind of want to punch her. Instead, my hands fold into tight fists at my side, and I grit my teeth. I can't actually do or say anything. Not without revealing our secret.

"Oh, could you?" he asks, his eyebrows raised. She nods, winking at him, and he laughs. "Well, I hate to break your little heart, but I have a girlfriend. And I like her quite a lot."

Pleasure rushes through me and I have to bite back the smile that's forming on my lips. The girl looks disappointed, muttering "too bad" before disappearing. Jesse's eyes meet mine and I see it. This is the reason we're risking it all, the reason that it's okay to hide. He's worth it. We're both it. Baseball for me and baseball for him is all worth it.

CHAPTER EIGHT

After the day at the batting cages, Austin and I start hanging out a lot more. As friends, of course. At least, for me, we hang out as friends. I'm not too sure about Austin. After classes we've been going on walks back down to the boardwalk and slowly making our way through the small beach town. Someone has to show Austin around anyway.

It's against my better judgement but I don't seem to be listening to my inner conscience as well as I used to before I met this boy at least. There's a huge part of me that knows being with him or dating him is not a good idea—he's too connected to baseball and the world I've been trying so hard to escape. There's also the fact that he's too damn good looking for his own good and I know how easy it could be to just let myself get carried away with him.

However I like Austin. I do, more than I should. He makes me laugh and he reminds me of the person I used to be, not the person that I've become. The past couple of years, I've only really had Sydney and Drew and it feels nice, it feels right, to have another friend. Just a friend.

We spend a lot of time studying for Art History. Neither one of us is particularly good at the course, so we decided maybe we'll learn something if we study together…it's not always as productive as study sessions should be. Austin talks a lot and he makes me laugh. Even when I don't want to, I find the laughter bubbling up in my stomach and it bursts out. I don't want him to make me laugh this much but he does.

He's always looking at me, like he's trying to figure out a puzzle he can't solve, and I'll admit, it makes me uncomfortable. I'm so used to everyone around here knowing about my past and leaving it alone, but Austin doesn't know and I'm sure he wants to. All it would take is asking one person or even a quick Google search to find out, but he doesn't seem like the type of guy to go behind your back to find more. He wants it from the source and I'm not saying anything.

We've made it a habit to make our way to the batting cages at least once a week. Slowly, his swing as gotten better, but he still hasn't changed the position of his elbow, he attributes his success to all the time he is spending in the weight room or running around campus. He's obsessed with baseball. He's obsessed with the team and their progress. He's fixated with his own stats, which he constantly checks. He works hard in school, that's for sure, but he doesn't go out much. He'll sometimes go out with the boys after a game or out to eat at the boardwalk with me but it's mostly just schoolwork and baseball for him.

"Hey, do you want to hang out tonight?" Austin asks, as we exit the locker room. He's leaving at a normal time for once and is there to hold the door open for me as we leave. "I was thinking of maybe heading down to the boardwalk again. I haven't tasted the chocolate covered bacon yet and I feel like it's been calling my name all day."

"I don't really think that chocolate covered bacon is an appropriate item to consume during baseball season. I just might have to tell Coach on you," I tease.

Austin laughs. "I always knew you were a tattle, princess." I pretend to punch him, and he cowers in fake fear. He's a good half foot taller than me so this is just him being silly. Typical Austin behavior. On the field, he's a completely different person. He's quiet, hard, determined, and focused. Nothing is more important than the game. But when he's off the field, he's all smiles and charm. Sometimes, it's hard for me to put the two of them together. "Okay, really, though, do you want to go?"

It's a Friday night, an off day for us. Normally, I wouldn't mind spending time with Austin, but I've kept myself from spending weekends with him. I have this weird idea in my head that if I suddenly start spending Friday or Saturday nights with him, he's going to think it is more of a friendship.

I'm crazy, I know. This is definitely starting to become more than just a friendship.

It doesn't matter anyway. Tonight, I have plans for once. I'm going out with my friends and I'm not going to be thinking of boys, any of them. "Can't."

He frowns. "What do you mean, 'can't'?" he asks.

We've left the stadium and are making our way back to the dorm halls. The air is nice and crisp but cold. The sky is cloudy, and I know that rain is coming soon. I grimace. I hate baseball practice in the rain. I know I'm not the one out there playing and all that, but I do have the memory of what it's like and there's nothing more miserable than sitting with that clipboard in a raincoat, trying not to be soaked through.

"It's Sydney's birthday tonight," I say, shivering a little

against the wind that's blowing right through us. "We're going out."

"Ah. Girls' night?" Austin asks. He reaches for me, his arm wrapped around my waist, when he notices I shiver again. I glare at him and he laughs, taking his arm away. I immediately regret it. It was definitely warmer and now I'm even colder than I was before.

"Yeah, girls' night," I lie. Knowing Sydney, there's probably more guys coming to her party tonight than girls. Sydney loves to go all out for her birthday, but she says it's the only good thing about the month of February. I think she only says that because she absolutely hates Valentine's Day. I don't particularly disagree with her. This year the stupid holiday passed by without a lot of fanfare, thank god.

I was almost afraid that Austin might ask me out.

I was almost disappointed when he didn't.

Despite the fact that I know there will be a lot of guys tonight while we celebrate, I am not going to invite Austin. I really need a break from this kid. He gets into my head and scrambles everything up and I'm tired of feeling confused all the time. I need a break. *Big time.*

"Oh." He sounds disappointed but he doesn't push the issue. "Well, that should be fun. Where are you guys going?"

I eye him warily and his mouth widens into his trademark grin. "I'm not going to crash girls' night, Evie. I'm just making conversation."

I wrapped my arms tightly around me, looking up at the sky. "We're heading to a club called Saints in San Francisco. Can't go to any here because they all know us, so they know we aren't twenty-one."

"Is that a long drive?"

I shrug. "An hour. Maybe an hour and a half. It's not bad, and Sydney is a party animal. This is what she wants."

"Well, have fun." He looks uncomfortable for a moment and I raise my eyebrow at him. "And be careful, okay?"

I laugh. "I'm always careful." I give him a small wave and head upstairs to the room.

Sydney is already getting ready. She looks fabulous, as always. No one rocks a little black dress the way that she does. She's taller than me by a few inches and I'm about not exactly short either, five-foot-seven. She doesn't let that hold her back though. Her heels are at least two to three inches high. She's let her red hair loose for the night and it's falls down her back in ringlets of fire.

She's going to kill Drew. I want to laugh at the thought of it.

"You look amazing, birthday girl," I say, tossing my backpack on my bed. There's a dress on my bed already. "Let me guess, that's for me?"

She smiles. "Of course. My best friend has to look amazing tonight."

I frown. "You know I hate to wear dresses."

"You can't always wear jeans every time we go out, Evie," Sydney says, drily. She's testing different shades of lipstick on her hand. She makes a face and throws one back in her bag and reaches for another.

"But my ass looks so good in jeans," I shoot back, throwing a smirk over my shoulder.

She laughs. "Okay, I won't deny that. But your ass is going to look great in that dress. Especially with the shoes I laid out for you. Just trust me, Evie."

I cross over to the bed to inspect the damage she intends to inflict on me tonight. There's a white dress on the bed, capped sleeves dipping into a sweetheart neckline. It's cut extremely short and backless, dipping into a low v-line at my hips. I'm shivering already just thinking about it. There's a pair of cowboy boots at the end of the bed and I whirl around to look at her. She's barely concealing a smile.

"Cowboy boots? Really?"

"You're going to look incredible." She's finally decided on a lip color and it makes her look fierce. "I figured your cowboy might like it."

"He's not my cowboy! And besides, he's not even coming, Sydney," I said, staring down at the shoes.

She looks over her shoulder at me, her eyes narrowed. "Um, excuse me? Why is he not coming? Did you not invite him?"

I squirm uncomfortably. "I told him it was girls' night."

"Evangeline!"

"Can everyone please stop calling me that…" I complain.

Sydney ignores me. "Why would you tell him that? You know I would love to have him at my party. And I know you would too."

I sigh, flopping down on my bed. "I don't know how I feel about him, okay, Sydney? I don't. And when I'm around him, I can't get my head straight. I just want one night where I'm not dizzy."

"You're being overdramatic. Just get dressed." I nod and start moving toward my dresser. "No, in the clothes I laid out for you. I don't care if he's not coming tonight. You're still wearing it."

"I hate you," I sing at her, grabbing the dress and boots off the bed.

"No, you don't," she sings back.

It takes us roughly an hour to get out to San Francisco and to Saints. The line is short, considering it's a Thursday. Drew is already waiting in line for us, and Lucy and Jesse aren't far behind us. We're expecting a few more people; some of Sydney's friends from cheer, a couple more guys from the team, but for the most part, everyone is already here.

Sydney got me my first fake ID when we were in high school. The idea of using it was the scariest thing in the world to me, especially since pretty much everyone in Izzy knew who I was and knew that I was not over eighteen. The fact that the girl on my ID looked absolutely nothing liked me didn't help either. Soon we were piling in her beat-up Jetta and heading out to San Francisco on the weekend to clubs to dance. I wasn't a huge fan of it, but Sydney loved it and it made me feel grown up.

When we turned eighteen though, Sydney felt it was time for an upgrade and she went out and got us good fake IDs. The one clutched tightly in my hand was my name, my picture, all my information, including my birthday, but just a few years difference. It made me feel a lot more confident when trying to pass myself off as twenty-one years old.

We got through the line quickly and made our way inside. It was much more packed on the inside and we had to fight our way to the bar. I finally made it up to the counter and waved down the bartender. He held up a finger to me, until his eyes met mine. He looked startled and I wanted to roll my eyes, especially as they traveled down to the very ample cleavage I was sporting in this dress.

"What can I get you, sweetheart?"

Ew. Strangers calling me any sort of nickname is an absolute no-go for me.

"Just a jack and coke, please," I said, reaching for my wallet in the small purse I had slung across my body.

"No, I got it," a voice behind me cuts in. Jesse pushes his way to the bar next to me, his hand coming out to touch my waist. It sends shivers up my spine that has everything to do with him.

"Thanks," I manage to say, as the bartender slides the drink toward me.

"You look beautiful." Jesse leans in close, and his lips are breath away from my neck. From far away, it must look like he's kissing me and there's a part of me that wants him to. "I've never seen you look like this."

I take a step back, widening the space between us. Sydney had basically attacked me in our dorm room, forced me into the dress and shoes, and did my hair and make-up. My normally straight hair was wavy, and my make-up was dark and dramatic. I even had red lipstick on, which I knew I would probably chew off from biting my lip all night. "Thanks," I say, my voice shaking. "I'm going to go find Sydney."

"Save me a dance later," he says, turning back to the bar.

I take a deep breath, shaking off the brief encounter, and make my way through the crowd, my drink clenched tightly in my hand. I take a sip while searching for Sydney and Lucy, who seemed to have disappeared as soon as we walked in the door. I shudder. This drink is strong. I take another small sip and sigh. I'm going to be a wreck by the time the night is over if the bartender intends on making my drinks this strong.

"Evie!"

I turn around and see Sydney dancing in the middle of the dance floor. Her arms are above her head as she shimmies her hips back and forth, a drink already clutched in her hand. She looks incredible and I know I'm not the only person who has noticed that. There are a lot of eyes on her. That girl isn't buying any of her own drinks tonight.

Drew comes up next to me. "We should go dance," he says. His eyes aren't on me. They're locked on Sydney, who is laughing and dancing.

"Go ask her to dance," I say to him, elbowing him in the side.

He looks around at me, his eyebrow raised. "I thought I was asking you."

I roll my eyes. "Drew, you may be fooling Sydney, but you don't fool me."

He doesn't answer right away. He just takes a sip of his drink and lets out a breath, his eyes finding their way back to Sydney. "I have no idea what you're talking about."

Right. Of course. I grab his arm and start pulling him toward the dance floor. He laughs and lets me. We push our way through the crowd until we make it to Sydney. She squeals loudly when she sees us and throws her arms around us before letting go and dancing circles around us.

"Dance, guys! It's my birthday!" she yells. She shakes her hair out of her face, and grabs Drew's hand.

"She's only had one beer, right?" I laugh.

Drew holds up his beer. "This is my one and then I'm done. I'll take care of her."

"Okay, Drew." I smirk as I watch him get dragged onto the floor.

We're enjoying the music and drinks and more and more people join us. Sydney's cheerleading friends show up and I see Owen, Tripp, Greg, Sam, and a couple other guys from the team come in. We create our own group in the middle of the dance floor and just as I had anticipated, the boys outnumber the girls, so there's always a fresh drink in my hand. I feel loose and free, happier and less stressed than I have felt in a while.

I'm dancing, my hands above my head, when they finally join us, and I wonder where they've been this whole time. My heart sinks and I don't know why. They've been together for three years now; what do I expect? I smile at Lucy, who waves, and pulls Jesse into her. They dance close and I turn away from them. Owen is behind me; he smiles and opens his arms in question. I laugh and start dancing with him.

"I need a break!" I say when the song ends, and I push my way through the crowd. I've lost count how many drinks I've had tonight and it's making me woozy. I make my way up to the bar and am disappointed to see the same bartender there. He spots me and winks at me before making his way down to me. "Can I just get water?"

"Anything for you, honey," he answers, pouring me a glass of water. I force a smile in thanks and turn away from the bar and am surprised to find Lucy in front of me, with tears in her eyes.

"Lucy, are you okay?" I ask, grabbing her arm and pulling her into the hallway leading to the restrooms, where it is much quieter.

"Yeah, I'm sorry. I just got an email from the—" she says, so softly that I almost don't hear her. A few new tears begin to slip down her cheeks. Without second thought I'm quick to lift my hand, almost as if I'm shielding her face from anybody that might be watching. Lucy deserved privacy.

"Oh, Lucy. Lucy, I'm sorry. Are you okay?"

It feels like a stupid question. Of course, she's not okay. Without even finishing what she was saying, I knew exact what was pulled up on her screen. With a shaky breath she holds out her phone to me and I take it. There's a picture of a beautiful toddler girl on my screen. Her eyes, her face shape, everything, is as familiar to me as my own face. It's painful for even me to look at. I swallow hard and hand the phone back to her.

"I just…I can't right now," she whispers. I can barely hear her over the crowd and all the noise, but I can see it all over her face.

"What do you need me to do?"

She takes a deep breath and when she lets it out, it's shaky. "I'll be okay. I just need a minute and I'll be fine."

"Lucy…"

Lucy shakes her head, wiping her fingers carefully under her eyes. She has some black eyeliner smudges around the corner of her eyes but other than that, she looks fine. Like her puppy got run over, but fine. "No, really. Just do me a favor."

"Anything," I promise.

"Can you go out and dance with Jesse? Tell him I'm in the bathroom or something; I just don't want him to know I'm upset. Not about this," she says, looking past me at the dance floor.

Anything but that. "Lucy…" I start to say.

"Please. Just…distract him." She sniffles and I can feel myself caving in. I never tell Lucy no. It's just so hard to tell her no. "I'm going to freshen up, okay?"

I nod and step away from her. She gives me a watery smile and disappears into the ladies' room. I take a deep breath and turn to the dance floor. Sure enough, Jesse is heading toward the crowd, looking around for Lucy. The two of us collide and he grabs my arm before I can completely fall on my ass in front of everyone here.

"Hey, you okay?"

"Uh, yeah, totally," I answer, brushing my hands off on my dress.

"Have you seen Lucy?"

"Yeah, she went to the restroom," I explain, quickly. "She had to fix her eyeliner or something." I roll my eyes, dramatically. "She instructed me to dance with you until she gets back."

There's a long pause and even though we're surrounded by a ton of people and noise, it's like we're the only two people in the room. My heart is thundering in my chest, and when his hand reaches for mine, I grab it like a lifeline and let him pull back into the crowd.

The song is much slower, and people are pairing up. Drew's eyes meet mine and narrow but I'm not paying attention. Jesse's arms are reaching for me, and it's been so long since they were like this and I'm forgetting everything except for how good this feels, how warm he is, and how amazing he smells. His hands are on the small of my back and his hips are moving against me.

Echoes of our first dance together filled my head. I felt my heart breaking all over again as thoughts of my sister filled my head. She shouldn't have to go through any of what happened, and the fact that she is makes me wish I could hate Jesse even more.

Will you dance with me, Evie?" Jesse asks, holding his hand out to me.

I laugh. "I don't really dance."

His grin widens and his fingers interlace with mine. "You'll dance with me."

The song ends but Jesse doesn't pull away. His movements change speed up to match the tempo of the song, but he doesn't let go of me. I know that I'm drunk at this point and I'm making stupid decisions but I'm so good all the time and for once, I just want to not be good. I want to be bad.

"Mind if I cut in?"

No. *No way.* He's not. He's not here. He *can't* be. Slowly I look down my arm to the fingers that have wrapped themselves loosely around my wrist. He *is* here and he's smiling down at me.

I look up at Jesse. His eyes have darkened, and he looks murderous. I've seen this look before and I take a step back and nearly stumble. The two of them stare at each for a moment, before Jesse finally speaks. "She's dancing with me."

"Well, she can dance with me now," Austin says, easily before nodding behind Jesse. "And look, your girlfriend is coming back."

I flush, feeling guilty, and take another step back from Jesse. He's still staring at Austin, but I know him. I know the kind of control he has. He won't do anything. He turns away, wrapping Lucy in his arms when she reaches him again.

Austin takes me in my arms, and I let him but I'm mad. I'm angry. My thoughts are mixed up and I know I shouldn't want to, but I want to be back in Jesse's arms. "Why did you do that?" I ask Austin.

He raises an eyebrow at me. "I wanted to dance with you."

"What are you even doing here?" I spit out. I try to push him away. "I want a drink."

"I don't think you need another drink." His hands are at my waist, his fingers pressed into mine. "Sydney invited me. Apparently, it wasn't girls' night, was it?"

My lips are pressed tightly together, and I look away from him. It feels amazing to dance with him. Every time I'm close to him, I feel like my body is on fire. I don't like that he's here, but I also love it at the same time. "Still doesn't explain why you interrupted…"

Austin says quiet for a moment and then suddenly spins me around, so my back is pressed tightly against his front. I gasp as his fingers spread across my belly and his hips move back and forth. "Why do you care so much?"

"I don't care," I say quickly.

"Sure." He doesn't say anything again and we continue to dance together. His fingers press tighter against me. His lips find their way to my ear and I shiver when his cool breath washes over the back of my sweaty neck. "You look incredible. Those boots are killing me, princess. One day you're going to wear those again for me and nothing else."

"What?" I think I've heard him correctly, but I don't know.

He laughs lightly and I feel it vibrate through his chest. "Nothing, Evie." He spins me around again and pins me against him. "Are you unhappy that I'm here?"

"I don't know," I answer, honestly. My hands are flat against his chest, and they slowly move up to his shoulders. My fingertips tighten around his hard muscles. I look up at him, licking my lips. The room has gotten hotter. Right? It totally has.

Austin closes his eyes briefly, breathing heavily. "You're killing me," he says under his breath. I can barely hear him, but we're so close. His lips are a searing flame on my jawline and I'm trembling in his grip. His tongue traces a small circle at the corner of my mouth and I'm ready to open for him, when it suddenly hits me, and I yank myself backward.

"No, stop," I say, my hands coming up to cover my face.

"Evie, come on…" Austin says sharply, reaching for me.

"Austin, no," I start pushing through the bodies. The room is spinning and all I can feel is the sweat and heat of all the other people closing in on me. I finally make it out of the crowd and into the cooler air by the restrooms.

I'm about to make a run for the bathroom when a hand closes around my arm and yanks me around. Austin is staring down at me. I hold a hand up, interrupting whatever it is he's about to say. "No. Stop. I don't feel good." He looks at me, disbelieving, but a moment later, I've thrown up all over the floor and he definitely believes me.

Austin finds Sydney and Drew and tells them he's taking me home, after he's parked me in a chair at the bar and instructed the bartender to give me the biggest glass of water they have. The bartender doesn't look so happy to see me this time, but who can blame him with my vomit all over the floor? He hands me the biggest water bottle I've ever seen. Austin comes back to me quickly, his arm wrapping tightly around me.

"Do you think you can stand?" he asks me.

I start to stand up and the room starts spinning again. "No," I whimper. I collapse back in the chair. "I'm just going to stay right here."

He laughs lightly and before I know it, I'm suddenly in his arms. He scoops me up as if I weigh nothing more than a sack of potatoes. My arms go around him. The movement wasn't the best and I feel nauseous all over again.

"Austin, I don't think that helped."

"Close your eyes, princess."

My eyes fall shut, and I lean against his chest. He smells wonderful, even more so than Jesse had. His chest is a little sweaty from when I was pressed against him, but I don't mind at all.

"Go to sleep, Evie. I'll get you home."

"Will you dance with me, Evie?" Jesse asks, holding his hand out to me.

I laugh. "I don't really dance."

His grin widens and his fingers interlace with mine. "You'll dance with me."

I glance around nervously. There are so many people here tonight that know us. His friends and teammates. My friends. My family. Practically everyone in Izzy came to our house tonight to celebrate the fourth of July. They're going to stare; I know it. But when Jesse pulls me in arms to dance, I'm not thinking about it. I'm in love and that's all that matters.

After a few dances, we're both sweaty and we both sneak a couple drinks and head to the backyard. We lean against the shed, where no one can see us and laugh and tell jokes. I love when I have him to myself. He makes me laugh and he doesn't act so serious and so cocky. He doesn't treat me like a child or laugh when I talk about my dreams of playing baseball. He's just…him. This is a Jesse that belongs to only me.

"Come here," he says, softly, pulling me into him. His lips are mine, and I'm drunk, drunk from the alcohol I've been sneaking all night and drunk from the way he makes me feel. Our hands are everywhere, and I can't help fumbling at the belt at his waist.

"What is going on here?" We pull apart quickly. Drew looks at the two of us, surprised. His eyes meet mine and I immediately let go of Jesse.

"Nothing," I blurt out. "I'm just drunk. We're drunk. It's nothing, Drew. Go inside."

"Evie," Drew says. There's wariness in his voice and he looks nervously at Jesse. He looks up to him so much and I don't think he knows what to do with him right there. "Can I talk to you for a moment?"

Jesse looks murderous and I squeeze his hand tightly. "It's fine," I whisper to him. "I'll catch up with you later."

Drew waits until Jesse leaves before exploding. "What are you doing? He's older than you, Evie! I thought you said things didn't work out between you."

"I lied," I admit. "We have to keep it a secret, Drew. He's older than me, and he's on my dad's team. It's the same thing with not dating the guys on the team. People won't take me seriously if they know I'm dating Jesse. It's not forever. Just for right now."

"Evie," Drew says, looking pained. "Is that what he told you?"

"It's fine," I assure Drew, ignoring what has been bothering me for weeks. "I know what I'm doing."

He looks over his shoulder, where Jesse disappeared into the house. "I really hope so. I don't want you to get hurt."

CHAPTER NINE

"Evie."

I don't hear Dad call my name the first time. Owen has thrown a towel in my face and I throw it back to him, laughing. It catches him in the chest, and he immediately whips it around in my direction. I squeal, standing up and running away from him.

"*Evie.*"

The locker room gets quiet and everyone looks in the direction of Dad's office. He's standing just outside the door, his hands planted firmly on his hips and he's looking at me, expectantly. I'm not sure how long he's been trying to get my attention but by the look on my face, I'm probably better off not knowing.

"Sorry," I apologize quickly, wiping my sweaty palms on my jeans. "What's up?"

"Can I see you in my office, please?"

A couple of the boys mutter under their breath and Drew raises his eyebrow at me as I pass him. I shrug and make my way into Dad's office. He shuts the door behind me, and motions for me to take a seat. He remains standing, his arms folded tight across his chest. I've seen this look before. He stares at me for a long moment, as if he's waiting for me to say something.

"What's going on?" I ask. What could he possibly want to talk about? My thoughts began to race as I try to think of anything that I possibly could have done wrong. *He doesn't know that I got wasted on Sydney's birthday, does he?*

He leans back, sighing, and reaches for the keyboard to his computer. He types a few things and then swivels the screen so that I can look at what he's pulled away. I'm confused for a moment until I realize what it is and my heart sinks.

"Why didn't you tell me you were undeclared?" His voice is low, and I can hear the disappointment in his voice.

I shrug. "I don't know." This is not nearly as bad as I had feared…he wasn't yelling or demanding that I go down to admissions and declare myself right this moment, but it's still not great. My knees are bouncing up and down nervously and I grab my thighs, in the hopes of calming myself down.

"Evie, you've wanted to be a sports journalist for as long as I can remember. What happened?" he sounds confused.

Have I? Have I really? I want to yell at him, tell him that he hasn't been paying enough attention, but I don't. Instead I just say, "I just don't know if it's what I want to do, Dad. I'm just not sure anymore."

"Baseball is your life," Dad says, confidently. "You've *always* loved baseball. I just don't understand what changed. This doesn't make sense to me."

I shake my head. "How does it not make sense?"

Come on, Dad, think about it. Really think about it. You know my real dream. You know it. He watched me play for years; I still don't understand how he can be so clueless to think that

I'd rather write about what's happening on the field than actually be on the field.

He leans forward. "This has always been your dream! How can it not be now?"

My frustration is palpable at this point. My dad used to know me better than anyone and now, it's like we're strangers. It feels like he hasn't really paid attention to me in the past few years. I'm starting to wonder if it's my fault though. I haven't exactly been an open book. "Well, maybe it's just not my dream anymore, Dad. Have you thought about that?" I bite back.

Baseball *used* to be my life.

Yet, these days, it seems like it's becoming my life again. How is it after all these years, after all the time we've spent together, he still doesn't see what I *really* want? Baseball was my life and it was my dream but not the way he wanted. He wants me in the baseball world but in the way he thinks is the best.

He pauses. "I just don't understand why you didn't come to talk to me about this."

"I knew this is how you would react. I need to figure out what I want before I completely commit. And I don't know what I want to do anymore. I'm only nineteen years old. Can you at least give me the chance to figure it out? This major is supposed to declare what I'm doing for the rest of my life! I can't—" I cut myself off before my small little outburst turns into something that I can't take back.

He doesn't answer right away, and I wish I could crawl into his brain and figure out what he was thinking. That is one big difference between my parents. My mom wears everything on her sleeve. Even when she's trying to be sneaky and nonchalant about something, you can see right through her. You always know what she's thinking.

Not my dad. He's always under constant pressure and

he always has an even expression. He uses it at home, in the locker room, on the field, in front of the cameras. I wish I could see past it right now because I want to know what he's thinking. He's always loved my dream of being a sports reporter. As much as I didn't think I could wrap my life around baseball, and as much as I knew that I didn't want to be around baseball anymore, I also didn't want to disappoint him.

"Okay," he finally says, "but I think you should sign up for a journalism class next semester. It should still be an option, Evangeline. You don't just give up on a dream you've had since you were a child."

I swallow hard and force a smile. How can he honestly be so, so wrong?

"Sure, Dad."

He dismisses me from the office, and I enter the locker room once more. Most of the guys are gone, but Austin is there, waiting for me.

"What was that all about?" he asks. He takes a step back. "Whoa, you look pissed."

A frustrated noise escapes my lips before I can help it. "My dad just found out that I'm undeclared and he's pretty pissed about it."

Austin frowns. "I thought you were a communications major. Everyone talks about how you're going to be a hot shot sports reporter."

"No. I'm not." I sigh.

He tosses his towels in the laundry bin and turns back to me. He's wearing a gray Quakes sleeveless shirt and it shows off his arms in such a spectacular way. He's always had great arms but all those extra hours he's spending in the weight room are showing. I remember those arms holding me up against the wall and shiver pleasantly. "Well. Why not?"

"It's just not what I want to do, okay, Austin?" I snap. His eyes widen and I immediately regret my tone. "I just don't know what I want to do. And I have to figure that out."

"Makes sense to me," he answers, shrugging. "You're such a baby, you don't have to have your whole life figured out right this minute."

I roll my eyes and laugh. He makes it look so easy to turn my mood around. "You're only two years older than me, cowboy. Don't be ridiculous."

"Hey, I just wanted to make you laugh." Austin laughs. "And I succeeded. Come on, let's go catch a movie or something."

I look around at the locker room. It's not perfect but honestly, at the moment, I couldn't care any less. I'd rather just take the lecture later. "All right, let's go."

I don't know how I get roped into helping Lucy plan Jesse's surprise birthday party. I genuinely don't. Maybe because I'm completely incapable of saying no to my sister? Maybe because I'm a masochist and I love torturing myself? I seem to be proving that repeatedly.

All I know is that suddenly I'm spending nearly every waking minute working on this party. I've sent out the e-vites for the event. I've been on the phone with Mamá for hours, planning the menu for the night. I'm doing all the work, and I'm exhausted. Between school and baseball and this stupid party, I have no time for anything anymore.

I finally can carve away some time in my schedule to spend time with Austin. We haven't talked about Sydney's birthday and I have no desire to. I was drunk. I was acting stupid, with both Jesse and Austin. Sydney and Drew have both tried to bring it up with me, but I've waved them off.

It's done. It's over. I'm ready to move on and forget that night ever happened.

My phone buzzes once, and I ignore it. It buzzes again, and then a few seconds later, a third time. I sigh, shoving it under a pillow. Lucy is texting me a thousand times a day, with ridiculous questions, and I just don't have the patience for it right now.

"Hey, do you want to order a pizza or something?" Austin asks from his position at his desk. His laptop is open, and he's been typing away for about an hour or so, though earlier I caught him looking up stats and things like that when he thought I wasn't looking. He borders on obsessive, but I never say anything. Having a conversation that doesn't involve baseball is hard to do with Austin but I'm not encouraging it.

"Hmm?" I answer, my Art History textbook open on my lap. We have a midterm coming up soon and that, paired with this party Lucy was throwing for Jesse, was taking up all my time.

Austin turns around and faces me. "Do you really have to take up the whole bed?"

I look up from my position at the foot of his bed. My textbook is in my lap, and my laptop is tucked next to me, but I had spread my backpack, notebooks, highlighter, a few index cards, and my phone all over the rest of the small bed. I smile sheepishly up at him and am rewarded with a wide grin. "Well, someone took the desk, so I have to utilize the space that I was given."

"You could always study in your own dorm room, which, as I recall, is much bigger than mine," he suggests, crossing his arms and leaning back in his desk chair.

"And is also shared between two people," I remind him. "I could, but someone asked me to study with him tonight so…"

Austin shrugs. "I guess I shouldn't be that upset that there's a pretty girl in my bed." I roll my eyes and he laughs. "So, pizza? Thoughts?"

I search around for my phone and find it hiding beneath my pack of highlighters. I grimace when I notice the time. I also have seven missed texts from Lucy. *Damn.* "No, I should probably get going. Lucy wants to meet at seven and she hates when I'm late. Never mind that she is always late."

"Oh, you're hanging out with Lucy tonight?" Austin asks.

"Sort of," I answered, packing my stuff back into my backpack. "You know that she's planning that huge party for Jesse's birthday and she's freaking out over all the details because it was to be perfect. I don't know why she seems to think that since she threw an incredible party for his twenty-first last year. Long story short, she's in panic mode and she asked me to help."

"Oh."

I pause in the middle of stuffing my laptop into my backpack and look up at him. "Oh? What does that mean?"

"Nothing," he says, shrugging again, and turning back to his laptop.

"You use ten words when you could use three, Austin. You talk *a lot*. More than anyone I've ever met, and that's including Lucy, who can seriously talk your ear off. You just said '*oh*,' so what's up?" I point out.

He turns back around. "You've been really busy lately. I hardly even see you anymore. You're always helping Lucy with this party. With her boyfriend's party."

"What's your point?" I bite my lip. I don't understand right away.

"I'm just saying. We're supposed to be friends. We're

supposed to spend time together, but you've been really busy lately."

I scoff at this. "We're in college, Austin. We get busy. Are you really going to start that? How about the insane amount of time you put into the weight room and batting cages outside of practice? Hmm?"

He chooses to ignore this. "I'm just saying, you're putting in a lot of time and effort into your *sister's* boyfriend's party," he says, raising his eyebrow at me.

"You're just saying?" I ask, my heart sinking into my stomach. The realization hits me and my memory flashes to the way I acted after he interrupted my dance with Jesse. This is exactly the kind of thing I was actively trying to avoid. "Doesn't really seem like you're saying anything. What are you getting at?"

"He's your *sister's* boyfriend, Evie, not yours. That's all I'm saying."

I can feel the burning in my stomach. "I know he's my sister's boyfriend. God, who do you think I am? What kind of sister do you think I am?"

I had him first though. I did. He was mine until everything happened. Until everything exploded and he made the choice and he wasn't mine anymore.

"I'm not saying that, Evie. You're overreacting." His voice is flat, indifferent but the look in his eyes tells me different and I try to focus on that. He's studying me closely, waiting for a response and he's absolutely getting one from me. It makes me want to punch the calm expression off his face. I hate that he can read me so well.

"Overreacting?" I question, firmly. I don't want to yell. He has a single and the walls here are so paper-thin. "You're accusing me of spending too much time planning my sister's boyfriend's party. Like it's inappropriate or something. My *sister* asked me to help—I'm just helping my *sister*."

"You're putting words into my mouth," he replies. "All I said is that you're spending an awful lot of time on this party, when it's not really your responsibility."

"You're insinuating things and I really don't appreciate that," I point out.

He closes his laptop, and the sound is obvious and loud in the palpable tension between us. He shoves his hands deep in his pockets, something he always does when he's uncomfortable. It amazes me how much I've learned about him in the short amount of time we've spent together. "Forget I said anything. You're obviously in a mood."

That was it. I was in a mood? He might as well have asked if I was on my period, for how rude he was being. Why did guys act like this? *Ugh.* "You know what? Fine. If you want to make barely veiled accusations at me, then fine. I'll go now." I pick up my backpack and start to cross the room.

"Wait, Evie, stop," Austin says, sounding resigned. He stands up and blocks my exit.

"Can you move, please?" I ask, my voice high and polite.

"I'm sorry. I didn't mean to make you mad." He steps closer to me.

"I'm not mad. I have plans with my sister tonight and I don't want to hang out around someone who is making unfounded accusations about me," I say, trying to move past him.

"I was...Evie!" He runs his hands over his hair, looking frustrated. "I just...I think...I don't really know what to say, okay? You don't tell me anything."

"Anything about what?" I'm confused, but there's a part of me that does know. This friendship is incredibly one sided. He has poured his heart out to me; telling me about baseball and what it means to him, telling me about his dad, telling me about his insecurities and his dreams. I have listened but I have not shared. But how can I share this secret with him? How can I share all my secrets with them?

The moment he knows, it'll change everything and I don't know if it'll be for better or worse.

"About…about *anything*, Evie! I have told you *everything*. I've told you things that I've never told anyone before. You—you don't say *anything*! You just come here, and study with me. Or we watch a movie, or we go out and get food, but you don't say anything. You're not my friend, really, but you won't let me be anything more than a friend. Something happened and I don't know what or when, but something happened, and you won't tell me. It's frustrating as hell!" his voice rises as he speaks, and the last part is a full-blown shout. He's stepped even closer to me.

My lips have thinned, and I can feel my entire body shaking at his words. I'm terrified. I can't admit this to him, but I can at least admit it to myself. I'm terrified. Terrified to tell him, terrified of what he'll do or what he'll think if he knows and terrified of the way he makes me feel. "One, I told you, that is none of your business. What happened or didn't happen is just none of your business. And two, I fail to see how this has anything to do with my helping my sister plan this party."

He scoffs loudly and I visibly flinch at the sound. "You know exactly what it has to do with it, Evie. I'm not stupid. I'm not blind."

No, you're not, I think. "I'm leaving," I say, softly, walking around him to the door.

He reaches for me, whirling me around and pushing me up against the door. I gasp and my backpack slips out of my hands and falls to the floor. His hands are holding my arms in place, firmly against the door, and his face is there, right in front of me. "What are you doing to me, Evie?"

Before I can answer, he's pressing his lips against mine and for a moment, I forget where I am, I forget who he is. I forget that I'm not supposed to want this, because *god* it feels so good.

"What the hell was that?" I screech loudly when he pulls away. He isn't kissing me anymore, but his body is pressed right up against mine. How is he so solid? There's not an ounce of softness on him. The feel of him, every hard muscle, pushing against me, keeping me trapped against that door, is incredible and my mind is spinning.

"Evie," Austin says, sounding out of breath. He drops his arms. "Shit, I'm sorry…I didn't…"

It's like my brain has temporarily shut off. This is what I want, what I've been wanting for a very long time and I don't care that I'm not supposed to. I don't care that he's a stupid baseball player. No, that's wrong. I care too much *because* he's a baseball player. "Shut up," I interrupt him. I reach up, my hands wrapping around his neck and dragging him down to me. Our lips meet again and this time, I'm responding. No, this time, I'm controlling it. His lips move soft and slow against mine but it's not enough and I slide my tongue on along the smoothness of his bottom lip. He groans and picks me up, my legs wrapping around his waist.

Our kisses grow deeper, more passionate. There's nothing smooth about it anymore; we've both been wanting for this for too long. I know I'm being sloppy; I know it's like I'm trying to devour him, but he tastes so good and I'm not thinking, I don't want to stop. My hands reach for the bottom of his shirt and I yank it over his head before pulling him back to me. I run my fingertips all over his chest and into the dips of his abs.

He laughs under his breath. "You've been wanting to do that for a while now, haven't you?"

Hell yeah, I have. It's not my fault he never seems to wear a shirt. It's like he's been practically begging me to touch him. "I said, shut up." A smile spreads across my face as he starts kissing me again, biting my lip, one of his hands lost in my hair as he carries me over to the bed. We fall into it, bouncing a little, before his body covers mine and I pull him closer, closer, closer. I reach for my own shirt and it's over my head and thrown in an unknown direction in a matter of seconds. His hands come up to my skin, raising goosebumps, and I whimper. He reaches for my bra, and yanks down the cups. The air in his room is cold and I pull back for a second.

"No. Don't move," he says roughly. His fingers are tracing light circles around my nipples and my back arches at the sensation. Our eyes meet once before he lowers his mouth and sucks, hard. I gasp and my fingers go to his soft hair, pulling him tighter against me.

Austin's tongue flicks back and forth and my breaths come out shallow and quick. Another whimper escapes my lips and I pull him back to me, sucking on his bottom lip before running my tongue against his. He's pressed hard against me and his hips are rocking into me. One of his hands travels lightly between my breasts, across my stomach, down to the button on my jeans. He pops it open easily and for a moment, I tense up.

"Relax, baby," he whispers to me, his tongue tracing circles right behind my ear. A shudder goes through me. "Doesn't it feel good?" I moan a little in response and I feel his smile against my throat. His teeth nip at the sensitive skin there before his lips return to mine. His fingers are slipping under my waistband. He tugs lightly on my jeans and I lift my hips, letting him drag them down to my ankles.

I kick them off and gasp happily when his body covers mine again.

His hand is wrapped tightly around the back of my knee, and his fingers trace the skin up my thigh. He teases me for a moment, tracing circles just above where I want him to touch me. My hips raise automatically, and he laughs lightly. His fingers yank my underwear aside, and he groans, as his fingers slid against me. "Jesus, princess. You're so wet." He swipes his fingers again, gentle and I cry out. "You're so sensitive. Every little touch gets you. I love it."

A moan escapes my lips and my fingernails are digging into the skin of his shoulders. My teeth find the firm skin of his shoulder and he shivers against me. "Austin," I whisper.

"Evie," he says, and he raises himself up, so his eyes meet mine. His hands are fumbling with the button of his own pants. "Evie, I…" There's something in his eyes, something more than just lust and desire, though those are there, obviously. It's deeper, and I'm getting lost in it and it's scaring me. The heat between us suddenly doesn't feel right and I freeze.

I can't breathe despite the air I'm sucking into my lungs. My chest feels tight and I can't stop the shaking that has overcome my body as he gets into my head again.

Jesse's body covers mine and I know I'm only sixteen, but I've never seen anything so beautiful in my life. Could he be any more perfect? I'm shaking nervously and trying to hide it, but I know he sees it. I've never been naked in front of anyone like this before, but he makes me feel confident. He makes me feel beautiful.

"Evie," he whispers, his hands in places that have never been touched before. My entire body is on fire, reacting to every single touch. "Evie, I love you."

"Wait. Stop." My hands are reaching up to his chest and

pushing him off me. "Stop. I don't…I don't want to do this. Stop."

"Evie, wait…" Austin says, sitting up. He's looking down at me in confusion, but he looks so beautiful and it physically hurts to look at him. His face is flush, his lips are full from all the kissing. His dark hair is sticking up in different directions from having my fingers run through it. "What…"

"I have to go." I sit up and crawl out from underneath him. I'm basically naked. My bra is tugged down, and my pants are somewhere on his floor. A flush of embarrassment runs through me. How on earth did I let myself lose my head? I yank my bra up and find my jeans on the floor and tug them on, all while avoiding eye contact with him. My shirt is around here somewhere, and I can't find it, and I can feel the tears right in the back of my eyes and I don't want to cry in front of him and where on earth is my damn shirt?

"What is going on?" Austin asks, grabbing my shirt from where it landed on his desk chair. He holds it out to me. "Are you okay?"

I take the shirt from him, my hands shaking, and pull it over my head. "I just need to leave." His hands reach for me, but I push past him, grabbing my backpack and I head out the door, slamming it behind me.

Jesse lives in a shabby apartment with a couple other guys from Izzy, but it's near the beach, so the raggedness is barely noticeable. Together, we spend a lot of time here…in his room, away from where people can see us. Jesse has either told the guys not to say anything or they honestly don't give a shit. I tend to think it's the latter since the house smells like weed most of the time.

We're on his bed making out, and everything feels so right. We haven't gone far but each time I'm with him, I want to. Every touch and every kiss feels like a firework exploding over my skin and I've never felt like this before. It's not long before articles of clothing start to litter the floor and we're naked in each other's arms. It's warm in his room, the sun beating down on us through the window, but I barely feel it. All I feel is him.

His body covers mine on the bed. I know I'm only sixteen, but I've never seen anything so beautiful in my life. Could he be any more perfect? I'm shaking nervously and trying to hide it, but I know he sees it. I've never been naked in front of anyone like this before, but he makes me feel confident. He makes me feel beautiful.

"Evie," he whispers, his hands in places that have never been touched before. My entire body is on fire, reacting to every single touch. "Evie, I love you."

Tears spring at the corners of my eyes and I smile up at him. "Oh Jesse. I love you too."

He's nudged my legs apart and I can feel him right there, ready for me. His eyes met mine, and in that moment, there was nothing else. It was only me and Jesse. "Are you sure you want to…"

I nod again and again and again. "Of course, I am." I hesitate. "Do you have a condom?"

"Right. Yes." He reaches toward his dresser and fumbles a little before fishing one out. His hands are shaking as he rips the package open and rolls it on. "Are you ready?"

I bite my lip. "Yes, baby."

"I love you," he says again, as he slowly slides himself inside of me.

The tears are falling down my cheeks. It hurts, and I'm bracing my hands on his shoulders. "I love you," I say through the pain. He lets me adjust to it before moving slowly above me, sending a new sensation through me. Our eyes are locked and I'm not looking away.

Later, we're wrapped in each other's arms and the fan is blowing a cool breeze across our heated skin. Jesse's lips are pressed tightly

*against my forehead and I'm clutching him tightly. "This is perfect,"
he whispers to me. "Absolutely perfect."*

"YOUR HUMMING IS SERIOUSLY ANNOYING," LUCY REMARKS,
lowering her sunglasses to look at me.

"She's not wrong," Sydney says, on the other side of me. She's
lying out, soaking up the sun and I wince. I know that no matter
how much sunscreen she's slathered on herself, it's not going to help.
That pale, freckled skin is going to be close to resembling a tomato
before the end of the day. "Why do you keep humming?"

I can't help it. I can't stop smiling. I have a secret from the
world, except from Drew and, of course, Sydney, since Drew can't
keep his mouth shut and I'm in love. I feel like I've suddenly stepped
into a Disney movie or something. Now I understand why they want
to sing all the time.

"Are you dating someone?" Lucy asks, interrupting my
thoughts.

"No," I say quickly. "Why would you say that?"

She studies me for a moment. "I don't know. You're just so
happy all the time now. And then there's the humming."

I turn away, hiding a grin. "I have no idea what you're talking
about, Lucy."

CHAPTER TEN

"How was the party?"

I startle and nearly fling my notebook off my desk. I can't help but chance a glance up at Austin.

I haven't seen him in a few days, not since I ran from his dorm room, my clothes disheveled, and my hair looking like I just had sex for hours. I faked being sick just to avoid him for a couple days, hiding in my dorm room, avoiding practice and class. Sooner than I would have liked it was the weekend, which meant I had to leave my dorm. To an extent anyway. Between Jesse's party and Sunday brunch, any time that I wasn't with Lucy and the rest of my family, I was hiding away from everyone. Specifically, a rather hot cowboy baseball player. I was afraid Austin would show up at the party, as the entire team was invited, but he didn't, and I wasn't sure whether to be relieved or disappointed.

I was perfectly content on missing class again on Monday, but Sydney wasn't having it. She had no idea what was going on or why I was perfectly happy to hide under the covers and watch murder documentaries on Netflix, but she knew something wasn't right. She dragged me out of bed, made me put clothes on and walked me to class like I was six years old instead of nineteen.

"It was okay," I finally answer, turning my eyes back to my notebook.

"Good. I'm glad." I look back over at him. Our eyes meet and he turns away. *Great.* Now we can't even look at each other.

I open my mouth to say something, anything, to make this completely awkward silence go away, but out of the corner of my eye I see the professor shuffling in. I'm saved from having to come up with anything. I flip my notebook open and write the date neatly in the corner.

"All right, class, it's that time," the professor says, reaching into his bag. He brings out a stack of papers and starts passing them around.

I take one from the stack and pass it along to the girl behind me. With a deep breath I begin to read over it, by the time I'm finished reading the front page, I'm ready to groan out loud. I'm still smack in the middle of midterms and this guy thinks it's a great idea to assign a term paper? Wonderful. Between all the things going on in my life, I knew I would be hard pressed to fit this into my schedule.

"Yes, yes," the professor says, laughing, as the groans fill the room. "I'm the worst professor ever. I figured you're all doing so well in my class that I had to give you a paper as a reward."

"Thanks!" one guy calls out. "I'll blame you when I can't spend time with my girlfriend." Laughter fills the room.

"Gladly will take the blame, Mr. Ramos," the professor answers easily. "But I'm not a harsh professor. You'll be working as partners for the paper, which I have already pre-assigned to you."

More groans fill the room and our professor begins to speak loudly over them, calling out the names of the partners. Desks scrape across the carpeted floor and people start standing up, moving to meet up with their partners.

"Evangeline Cordova and Austin Young."

Of course. I look over at Austin, and he smiles hesitantly at me. I smile back, just as unsure as him, and look back down at the paper in my hand. There's a blank space at the top for my partner's name and I write Austin Young on the line.

The rest of class is spent with each pair of partners, while we all try to figure out what the paper was going to be on based from the provided topics. Austin scoots his desk closer to me and clears his throat a few times but neither one of us says anything. Just a few days ago, I was basically naked on his bed, with his fingers inside me, and now I can't look at him without a blush spreading across my face. What is wrong with me?

I finally take a deep breath and start talking. "We have to write this paper on a particular piece of artwork. What did you want to write about?"

"Um," his voice cracks. "Do you think we should talk about the other night?"

A brilliant red blush fills my cheeks and I turn away. "I don't think that's a good idea."

"Princess," he says softly. His fingers reach for me, and grab my chin gently, turning me so I'm looking at him again. I'm falling into those stupid deep brown eyes of his and I swallow hard.

"Don't call me that," I whisper back.

"Okay, fine, *Evie*."

I take a shaky breath, as his eyes flick back and forth between mine. He always looks at them separately but not like he's thrown off by them. It's almost like he sees something different in each of them. "Austin, we're friends, right? That's what you said?"

He pauses and he doesn't answer for a while. He looks disappointed but he forces a smile. "We are always friends, princess. That never changes." He lets go of my chin and grabs the assignment paper. He scans the list before pointing to one. "Is that one okay?"

I lean over him, and I can feel the heat radiating off him. It was just a few days ago that I had that warmth pushing me into the soft covers of his bed. Despite the heat, I shiver and nod. "Yeah, that's fine."

Maybe being *just friends* with Austin was going to be much harder than I thought. I'm falling for Austin. I know I am, and I know I have to stop it. He is not what I want for myself. He's a baseball player and I just can't do that to myself. I can't sit here and support his dream when our dreams aren't that too far apart from each other.

We don't see each other much over the next few days unless it's at practice, a game or class. We smile, make small talk but it's not like it was before. Our friendship seems broken and I don't know if we can fix it anymore. We broke a barrier that night and while part of me wants to go back and stop everything from happening to begin with. The other part of me wants to keep going, to finish what we started.

I'm late for the Thursday night game. I got caught up in studying in the dorm and didn't realize that the game was about to start until Sydney came home and started changing to go to the game. I ran all the way from the dorm hall to the stadium, through the hallways to the locker room, and burst into the dugout.

Dad looks pissed but he just wordlessly passes the clipboard to me and I sink into the chair sitting right outside the dugout. I glance down and then back up, just in time to see Austin strike out, swinging. The pitch is perfectly down the middle, but his swing is still awkward, and the ball goes sailing past him. He stalks back to the dugout.

I hesitate and then his eyes latch onto mine. I have such a visceral reaction to him. My entire body lights up, inside and out, when I see him. I can't help the smile that stretches across my face when I see him and even though I know he's pissed off as hell, he still manages to smile at me. "Austin?"

He looks over his shoulder as he descends into the dugout. "Yeah?"

"Um…" I pause and my eyes automatically search for Jesse, who, sure enough, is staring right back at us. "Elbow. Remember?"

Austin stares at me for a long moment and then nods, continuing into the dugout and taking a seat. I let out the breath I've been holding in and turn my attention back to the game.

The next time Austin gets up to bat, he raises his elbow. He doesn't manage to get a hit, but he walks and when he takes his base, he winks at me. I duck my head, blushing, pretending to make notes on my clipboard.

We're trailing by one run in the bottom of the ninth when Austin comes up for a third time. We need to score in this inning, or we lose, and I hate to be those guys whenever they lose. We play roughly fifty games a season, so losses happen but Dad hates to lose, and he lets them know.

Austin looks good out there. His elbow is low for a moment before he seems to remember, and he raises it. I sit up straight. He swings at a pitch and gets a good hold of it, but it flies foul, into the stands.

"Come on, Austin," I whisper to myself. "Come on." For someone who is trying not to care about this boy and how well he does on the field, I'm doing a very poor job at it. I do care. I care a lot and I want to see him hit the ball, and not just because I've spent a significant amount of time in the batting cages with him. I want him to hit the ball because it'll make him happy. I want Austin to be happy.

The next two pitches are way outside and low and Austin lets them pass. He steps out of the batter's box for a moment, taking a few practice swings before stepping back in.

The next pitch is another foul, this time heading in our direction. I dodge out of the way as it goes flying past me, barely missing me by about a foot. Austin mouths '*sorry*' and winks at me. I laugh, shaking my head.

The next pitch is a little outside, but Austin reaches for it, and makes contact with it. My heart leaps into my throat and I watch as it skitters across the ground at good speed and goes speeding into center field.

Austin is fast. I haven't had a chance to see him run, not like this, and I'm not surprised when he easily turns the base hit into a double. He slides into second base before the center fielder can get the ball back in, and pops up, a huge smile on his face. He removes his batting gloves and tucks them into his pockets. The crowd is going wild, and my hands are clapping hard.

"Way to go, Austin!" I call loudly. He hears me and winks again.

Owen goes past me and heads for the plate. He's one of our strongest batters and, sure enough, a few pitches in, the ball goes flying, sailing above everyone's heads and out of the stands. The stadium erupts as Austin and Owen go running around the bases. The team goes sprinting out of the dugout.

We've won.

The team goes out to celebrate at Mitch's. I decline the invitation and return to the dorm room after making sure that the locker room was all back in order. Sydney beat me back and is taking off her jersey when I walk in.

She looks miserable when I walk in. She changes into pajamas, grabbing a large bag of Cheetos sitting on the bed in front of her as she scrolls through her phone. Her attention is fully on the screen in front of her and I get the feeling that something is definitely wrong.

I know that I haven't been around much lately, but she's seemed incredibly down since her birthday. I feel like something happened that night after Austin brought me back home, but she won't talk about it and the best thing to do with Sydney is to let her come to you. It doesn't stop me from trying though.

"What's wrong?" we both ask to each other at the same time. Dry, humorless laughter soon echoes throughout our small, shared space.

"Nothing," Sydney says first, shaking her head. I raise my eyebrow at her and she shakes her head. "Really. It's fine."

It's not fine.

I know her well enough to know it's definitely not fine, but I remind myself that she'll come to me when she's good and ready. "What about you? Not celebrating with the team?"

I shake my head. "I need a break." I yank my sweatshirt over my head and toss it into our laundry bag. I sigh and flop onto my bed, headfirst.

"A break?" she asks. I feel my mattress dip as she joins me, and her hands go to my hair. We've been in this position before, a million times at a million different sleepovers, and I feel a sudden comfort in the familiarity. We take care of each other. She put me back together again three years ago, and I'm her partner in crime for all her wild adventures. I'll never stop being grateful that she came into my life in high school.

It's the reason why I find myself suddenly overwhelmed

by everything that I've been keeping inside for the past few weeks. I take a deep breath and then suddenly everything is all just spilling out. I can't stop. I'm telling her everything, all the times Austin and I have talked and all the times we've spent together, and what happened between us in Austin's dorm. I even told her about what happened on her birthday and the dance we shared, and what he said to me. Sydney stays quiet the whole time that I talk, letting me get it all out. I finish and the room fills with silence. She doesn't say anything.

I roll over on my back to look at her. There's a small smile on her face and I frown. "What?"

"God, Evie, you're so stupid. I mean that in the best way possible because I'm your best friend and I love you," she says, her smile growing wider. "Isn't it obvious? You're falling for him."

It's my turn to get quiet. I stop and think for a moment and I know that's she right. I *am* falling for him. Despite all my best efforts, I'm falling pretty damn hard for Austin. If I admit it, and I won't, I'm probably already there. It's more than just his looks, though that *is* part of it. He's an incredible person. He works hard, and he's smart and he has more passion than I've ever seen in a baseball player before. I shouldn't want him, but I know that I do. "I am, aren't I?" I finally answer, my voice no louder than a whisper.

"Of course, you are, dummy," she laughs. "What are you going to do about it?"

I open my mouth and close it. Thinking over every option that I could think of. Really, there were only two: Try my best to keep him in the friendzone, or actually give into my feelings. "I don't know that I should do anything about it."

Sydney rolls her eyes. "And how the hell does that even make sense?"

"Sydney, you were there three years ago. Jesse tore me apart. You saw me after what happened. I don't want to go through that again. I *can't* do it again."

She speaks softly, her hand going back to my hair. "Evangeline Cordova, you are not the same girl you were three years ago. And Austin isn't Jesse. You know that."

There's a lump in my throat when I speak next. "And I'm just supposed to watch him and support him as he plays here? What about when he plays in the minors? Or when he makes it big and goes to the majors? Am I just supposed to act like it doesn't hurt me every single day because I wish it were me out there on that field?"

Sydney pauses. "It doesn't have to be like that though. You know that. You gave it up, Evie. *You* did. No one else. You can make the decision to go back."

I don't answer. I rip my eyes away from her knowing gaze and stare up at our ceiling.

"You're being ridiculous, and you know it. When you have something that is amazing standing right in front of your face, you go for it, Evie. You don't run from it. You should be running to Austin, running to baseball, instead of doing everything you can to stay away from it."

I sit up suddenly, and she yanks her hand back from my hair. I'm so tired of talking about me all the time. I was tired of every conversation being filled with Austin or Jesse. "What about you, Sydney? What about what is right in front of *your* face?"

She looks confused. "I have no idea what you're talking about." Her forehead wrinkles as she thinks. "Aren't we talking about you?"

A sigh escapes my lips. We are talking about me, but I'd really prefer we didn't. I don't want to push the issue today; it's not worth starting a fight with Syd tonight. But we are going to have to talk about Drew sometime. It's just too much for me to handle as an outsider anymore. I'm about to speak again when my phone buzzes. I stare at it, face down on my bed, afraid to pick it up.

Sydney sighs dramatically and grabs it for me and holds it out to me. I press my fingertip to the keypad to unlock it and she opens the text. She loses her frown and a gigantic grin breaks out across her face.

"What? What is it?" I ask, reaching for my phone. She tosses it to me, and I glance down. There's a text message from Austin that reads:

You better be at every game from now on, princess. You're my good luck charm. Sweet dreams.

My heart is pounding in my chest and I can't tell whether I love the feeling or whether I need to run to the bathroom to throw up. "I am in so much trouble."

She grabs my slim phone from my hands and reads the message for herself.

"You *are* in so much trouble," Sydney agrees, giggling.

I groan, frustrated, and throw myself back on my bed. My phone falls out of my hand and lands on the floor and I make no move to pick it up. I need to figure out what the hell I'm going to do about Austin Young.

I *HATE* AWAY GAMES.

I hate making sure that all the boys are bunked accordingly, and I hate having to room with Jane, the team's athletic trainer and the only other woman who is involved with the team. When the team heads out of state to play, I don't go, mostly because I can't afford to miss school and Mama might have a heart attack if I miss Sunday brunch.

But if the game is only a handful of hours away in Santa Barbara? I'm on board and heading out.

I'm sitting in the front of the bus, next to Dad, who is

putting together the lineup for this weekend's game against UCSB. They're not a huge competition for us, but we're heading toward the end of the season and every win counts if we want to make it back to the playoffs. We won the college world series twice in a row, but we lost last year, against Vanderbilt and Dad is still super pissed about it.

I have my headphones out to drone out the noise of the guys behind me on the bus. We've already been on the road for two hours and they're still loud as hell. Even though they all range between the ages of eighteen and twenty-two, they act like sixteen-year-old boys in the high school locker room and I've had enough fart noises and dirty jokes to last me a lifetime.

When we finally arrive at the hotel room, I jump off the bus, shouting out the names of the guys rooming together as they get off. My dad originally had Jesse and Austin rooming together but everything about that sounded like a disaster waiting to happen and I hastily changed it, so Austin was rooming with Drew instead.

"Remember guys, no going out tonight!" I called as they followed my dad inside. "You have a game tomorrow!"

They all laugh and clap me on the back as they pass me. I know that quite a few of them are going to disobey the rules tonight but hopefully they think enough with their head that they don't wake up tomorrow completely hungover or they'll be running laps when we get back to Izzy.

Austin smiles at me as we enter the hotel. "You should come up to the room later." I raise my eyebrow and he laughs. It's so loud and it echoes in the large lobby. "I'm just saying, hanging out with me and Drew has to be a lot better than hanging out with Jane all night."

I look over my shoulder at the team's athletic trainer and laugh. She's a nice enough lady but she's going to be lights-out by about eight tonight, and I can't handle that kind of bedtime. "You're not wrong about that."

"Yeah, so come join us later." He ruffles my hair, hitching his bag back on his shoulder. He and Drew grab their room keys and disappear into the hotel room.

I've been in the room with Jane for merely an hour and a half and I'm about ready to kill someone, and I'm leaning toward her three kids. She's shown me about a million pictures and videos of them on her phone. I like kids and all, but I'm about ready to lose my mind.

My phone buzzes and I know who it is before I even look. Austin. I hadn't planned to take him up on his offer but true to form, Jane was already tucked into her comforter, with her sleep mask over her eyes. I sigh, and head to the bathroom. I'm already changed into my paja-mas, just a tank top and yoga pants but it works well enough. I inspect myself in the mirror a few times before sighing and deciding that yes, it works well enough.

Jane is asleep when I head back into the room, so I grab the room key and make my way down the hallway, running a hand nervously through my hair. It's just Austin. It's just Drew. It's fine.

Drew immediately answers the door when I knock softly on it. He stands aside to let me in, a knowing smirk on his face and I wonder how much Sydney has told him this time.

Austin is sprawled on the bed and I'm about ready to punch him in the face because seriously, I know I've said it about a million times, but I can't handle how he is completely incapable of wearing a shirt. It's hard to keep my head on straight with him looking like that all the time.

"What's going on?" I ask, standing nervously in the doorway. Drew shuts the door behind me and shoves me further into the room and I stumble. I turn to glare at him, but he just shrugs. He gives me a look, and I've known him so long that I can read it easily. *Do you want me to leave?* I shake my head fervently and he smirks again.

"We figured we would just watch a movie or something. I brought a few drinks with me," Austin said, sitting up and reaching into the mini fridge sitting underneath the TV. He pulls out a bottle and hands it to me, our fingers brushing. "You might want to take it easy tonight, princess."

"Ha ha." My voice is sarcastic, but even I can hear the tremble in it. "What are we watching?"

"They're showing the newest Marvel movie on HBO, so I figured I'd turn that on," Drew said, grabbing the remote and flipping the channels, flopping on the bed. I hover for a moment, wondering if I should just take the desk chair.

"Come here," Austin said, patting the spot next to him on his bed. I squirm in place for a moment before heading toward him. I sit as close to the edge of the bed as possible, trying to ignore the heat that is coursing between Austin and me.

Drew looks up at me sympathetically and pats my knee, before taking a seat on his own bed. I am immediately comforted by it, and some of the butterflies that have been threatening to burst out of my stomach calm down a bit. I cross my legs and take a gulp from the bottle. I grimace a little. I hate beer but I could use some liquid courage right now.

We're about halfway through the movie when Austin notices how close I am to the edge. One wrong move and I'm going to topple to the floor and admittedly, this is uncomfortable. His eyes narrow and he looks up at me, a question in his eyes. I shake my head, and suddenly his arm is snatching me up, and my hip is pressed against his side. I squeak loudly.

"What are you doing?" I ask him.

"This part is scary," Austin answers, winking at me. His hand is resting gently against my knee now and I have to force myself not to knock him over the head with the pillow.

"You're ridiculous," I tell him.

"You love it, princess," he remarks back, looking completely at ease. My hip is burning through the fabric, pressed so closely to his chest.

"Seriously, should I leave? I can leave…" Drew mutters under his breath, tipping his beer back.

"No," I say quickly, at the same time as Austin says, "sure."

Drew looks up at me and I shake my head. He seems to have a permanent smirk across his face, and he turns back to the movie, shaking his head. "Then both of you shut up."

Austin squeezes my knee gently but doesn't say anything else, except to ask if I want another beer when I finish my first one. He takes a swig of it before passing it to me and there's something incredibly intimate about wrapping my lips around the mouth of the bottle after his lips have been there. I'm having a hard time concentrating on the movie and I'm wondering if it was just a better idea to stay in the room with boring 'ol Jane.

His arm curls around me almost instinctively, his fingers spread across my stomach and the heat of it burns through my shirt. I take another shaky sip. I'm grateful for Drew's presence because I just might do something stupid right now. The beer is making me loose and sleepy and that is exactly when bad decisions happen. I grab a pillow from behind me and squeeze it tightly as I can, hoping that it'll keep my hands occupied and away from Austin. The last thing I want is to stay in Austin's bed…

When I wake up the next morning, I realize that I did nearly exactly what I didn't want to do and accidentally fell asleep in their hotel room. The heat is nearly unbearable.

I'm practically being smothered by Austin, whose arm is slung around my waist and my legs are tangled with his. I'm afraid to move but I manage to extract myself from his grip without waking him up. I look back at both, my best friend and...the boy that I can't quite figure out. I sigh and slip out the door and back to my room, crawling into my own bed before Jane can realize I never came back.

THE SUN BEATS DOWN ON ME DURING THE GAME AGAINST UC Santa Barbara. It's so hot and I am missing the cooler weather of Santa Isabella. I can tell it's having an effect on the guys as well, but they keep playing as if they aren't losing ten pounds just by sweating.

We're up three to two in the bottom of the third and I'm seriously proud of Austin. He's holding his elbow at exactly the right height, and its showing. He's been up once and managed to get a good hold of the ball. He's improving, and Dad's watching him.

I'm watching him too.

He continues to have a good game. He gets a hit every time he's up at bat. We're closing out the game in the ninth when the center fielder for the other team gets a hold of our closer's pitch and it goes flying out toward the outfield. Austin dives and catches it smoothly in his glove, rolling onto his side before throwing the ball to Carlos at second base. Carlos steps on the base before shooting it to first. *Double play*. We've won another game.

The team comes rushing into the dugout, laughing and cheering. Dad claps Austin hard on the back and there's no missing the pride that is on Austin's face.

"Great game," I tell him, as we pack everything up in the dugout. "I'm impressed, cowboy."

"Well, thank you, good luck charm," he said, dipping

into that Southern charm that always gets to me. I laugh and push him away from me.

"Just repeat it tonight, okay?"

We have a double header against UCSB today and the guys get a couple hours to shower, relax and then head back onto the field.

"Anything for you, princess," Austin whispers to me, and when no one is looking, he brushes his lips quickly against my forehead. I pull away, feeling a shock go through me. He raises his eyebrows at me in question and I just smirk at him, turning away from him and heading back into the visitors' locker room.

We lose the night game and the team heads back to the hotel. It doesn't feel good to get a loss right after such a great win, but the team is pretty happy, and they're laughing and joking as they head back to their rooms. Austin ruffles my head once before disappearing into his own room. He had another great game, even though we lost. He hit four for four, threw for two double plays *and* managed to stop a line drive that could have made the loss that much worse. He looks incredibly happy and it's rubbing off on me. I smile at him when he ruffles my hair and walk down the hallway to my own room.

I'm sliding my room key in the slot when I hear my name. Thinking it's Austin, I turn, a smile already on my face. It falls when I see that Jesse is coming toward me. My heart is pounding in my chest and I can't help it. My body reacts to him of its own accord.

"What's up?" I ask him, suddenly aware that this is the first time we've been relatively alone in ages. I take a step away from him and my back hits the wall.

"I wanted to talk to you about something," he says, an easy smile on his face. Everything has always been about charm with Jesse and it works. It should come off sleazy or cheesy, but it doesn't. He's just that charming and it's what keeps this invisible cord between us from breaking. I am brought under those eyes and those lips and that stupid smile every single time.

I swallow hard, hoping that he can't see that my heart is beating a fast rhythm in my throat. "Talk to me? About what?"

"Austin," he answers simply. He waits, as if waiting for me to say something but I don't know what he expects me to say. "What's going on there?"

"I — I have no idea what you're talking — what you're talking about," I stammer out.

"Evie," Jesse says, his voice smooth. He comes closer to me, and my breath gets caught in my throat. "I'm not blind. I see something. And I'm just wondering what's going on there." I don't answer and he continues, his voice a little firmer. "I don't like him. I told you that. I care about you and I don't want you to get hurt."

I'm immediately angry and I push him away from me. "I don't think that's your business, Jesse. It stopped being your business years ago."

He looks surprised. "I care about you, Evie," he repeats. "You know that."

His words are like a stab to the chest. They're both what I want to hear and what I never want to hear again. "I know that," I whisper back, looking away from him.

"I'll always care about you," Jesse says, his eyes pleading with me. "You know that, Evie. Don't forget that."

"I just don't want you to get mixed up with the wrong guy," he pleads with me now.

I shoot a glare at him. "It's none of your business, Jesse. It's not. Not anymore. Whatever is or isn't happening between me and Austin has nothing to do with you." I turn away from him to go into my room, but he reaches out and grabs my arm, holding me back.

"Wait, Evie…" he starts to say but his phone rings and we both know exactly who is on the other line. He lets go of my arm like it's burned him and reaches for his phone.

"Exactly," I say, escaping into my room before he can say anything else.

CHAPTER ELEVEN

I t feels good to be back in Izzy after having been gone all weekend. I liked the occasional get away, but Izzy was home; being gone for more than a day was too much. I love the way Austin's performing—he's only improving, and it's getting harder and harder to deny how much I want him, but the confrontation with Jesse the night before is fresh in my mind and I know myself well enough to admit that I have no idea what I'm doing.

Most of the team is heading to their cars or making their way onto campus to head back to their dorms. It's late and they look beat. The team's record is pretty damn good so far this season and I'm proud of them. Slowly, I've gone from just thinking of this as a job to caring about the Quakes again. I *want* them to win, I want Austin to win.

With a sigh, I lean over and pick up my bags. There are only a couple of things that I need to drop off in Dad's office for the following week's practice before I head back to my own room and I'm exhausted. Thankfully, the walk is short and quiet, and I really need the solitude right now. Being surrounded by thirty rambunctious and victorious baseball boys gives me a headache sometimes and the quiet makes it easier to think.

I've just dumped Dad's stuff in his office when I feel my phone begin to buzz. Thinking it's just Sydney wondering where I am, I ignore it and lock the office up. My phone buzzes again and a bit irritably, I fish it out of my pocket. There are two text messages there for me and my breath catches in my throat. The first one reads, *"I'm on the field."* The second one says, *"Come find me."*

Austin.

I can't find him at first. The halls are large and empty, and the stands are silent and yet he's here somewhere. He said to come find him and I have no idea where he is. He's on the field? There's no one there, and there's no way to miss him.

I walk down the steps to the small wall that separates the stands from the field. I spend so many of my days and nights here and yet it's been so long that I've just stopped and looked. It's been so long that I've taken it in. This used to be my favorite place in the world and now? Now I'm not sure I know what it is, but I know that I miss it. I want to be out there.

I know that everything that I used to love about it is still there and that I'm not sure what to do about it. I want to let it all go. I don't want Jesse to taint everything that I used to love but how can I stop it?

I take a deep breath and I feel calm, at peace even. I appreciate the quiet. It's been a few days since we've had a home game here, but I can smell the freshly mown grass and popcorn and I can almost hear the cheers and that satisfying crack when a bat makes contact with a ball. There's a huge part of me that wants to run onto the grass, barefoot and press my face against the dirt of the pitcher's mound. How is it possible that a simple game can do this to me?

I swing a leg over the wall and hop over in one swoop. If there was a crowd here, I would've flashed them all in my dress and I know I could have walked around, through the dugout or something like that, but what's the fun in that? I have a half mind to just start running around when a voice calls out to me.

"Nice dismount."

I jump and turn around, and Austin is sitting there, in the relative darkness of the dugout. He's dressed in the same clothes that he was wearing on the bus, so it would appear that he came straight here to the field rather than back to his dorm. I never used to understand why Dad felt the need to make the boys dress so impeccably when not in uniform but I'm appreciating it now. He's in dark jeans and a tan button up shirt, the sleeves rolled up to his elbows. His hair is a mess, like usual.

"Hey there, beautiful."

I continue to stare at him. He calls me beautiful but standing at the top of the stairs, looking down at him, I know I've never seen anyone as beautiful as him. "What are you doing here?" I ask, softly.

"Come here."

I hesitate for a moment, before coming down the steps and into the dugout. "What's going on, Austin?"

He doesn't answer right away, and I wonder for a moment whether he even heard the question. He just stares at me and I feel a flush fill my cheeks. I'm not in anything fancy, just a loose sundress, but he makes me feel naked, like I'm back in his bed. I'm ready to turn away when he finally speaks. "Don't run."

"I'm not running," I say quickly.

"Then where are you going?" he asks, the corner of his mouth tilting up. "I want you here. I'm happy."

I let that sink in for a moment. "You're…happy?"

He nods. "Yeah. I'm really happy."

"You brought me down here…because you wanted to tell me you were…*happy*?" I ask slowly.

"Yeah. Yeah, definitely. I haven't felt like this in so long." He pauses and takes a deep breath. "Evie, last night was incredible. I had the hits and I had it on the field and it felt good. It finally felt like I was doing exactly what I needed to do. All I could think was…I need to share this with you. You're the only person I want to share it with."

I take a step back. The words make me feel incredible. They make me feel special. They wash over me like a cool breeze on a hot summer's day and the goosebumps on my arms are not in my imagination. He makes me feel this way. He makes me feel important. Needed. *Wanted*. I want him to say more, but I also don't want him to. I'd given my heart to a Quake before and he stomped all over it. There is just so much more that Austin doesn't know — all the secrets I've kept hidden away. "Austin, I don't know…"

"You don't know what?" Austin says, his voice getting sharp for a moment. I start to speak but he continues, not even hearing me. "No, listen to me. You don't know if I should share this with you? Why shouldn't I? I'm not trying to sound cocky, but I was fantastic last night. I did everything I was supposed to do. And the only reason I did everything I was supposed to is…is you. It's all because of you, Evie."

I shake my head, repeatedly. "No. No way, Austin. You're talented, and you're incredible on the field. That has nothing to do with me."

He stands up and walks over to me, grabbing my hands. His hands are so much larger than mine and they nearly swallow both of mine up. "Yes. It does. Can't you just accept a compliment? I wish you knew how hard it was to give it. I've spent most of my life focused on baseball, working out, pushing myself over and over again. Who would have thought I would get better just by letting someone believe in me? You take me out to the batting cages all the time and you're calling me out on my shit all the time." He pauses and laughs a little at that. His accent gets more prominent when he talks so fast and I can't help but smile back at him. It's small but it's there. "You make me want to be better, Evie. You make me believe in myself more than I ever have before."

My hand is firmly in his and when I try to take a step back, he follows. "Austin, you can't say that. You can't do that."

"Why not?" he says, his voice softer. His eyes are on mine and I feel suddenly like I can't breathe. He's too close. I can't think when he's this close and I don't like it. I need to think. I can't lose control for a moment. "It's just the truth. I'm just honest. You said you hate lies."

"Because…because…" I can't get the words out. I can feel the heat of him, his skin so close and all I want to do is bring him closer. My mind flashes to the kisses we shared in his dorm room and I want more. And I hate myself for wanting more. "Because you can't, Austin! I can't handle how I feel about you. It's too much, and I can't do anything about it. I won't let baseball break my heart again."

I've said too much.

He pushes away from me, looking angry, and I stumble in surprise. I already miss his warmth. "Break your heart, *again*? Evie, I don't know what happened. I don't know. But you're here right now and you feel something. Doesn't that mean anything to you? Why do you keep pushing me away?"

I don't answer and he comes back over me. "I'm tired of arguing with you. I'm tired of telling you the same things again and again and I'm tired of you coming up with the same excuses. You know there's something here. You *know* there is. That's why you're so afraid."

He's right. He's so right. I'm falling harder and harder every minute, every second we're together and I don't care that he's a baseball player. He's just Austin to me, and baseball player is just one of the parts that makes him this incredible man. I *love* baseball. I miss baseball. He reminds me why I love it so much.

Austin is right—all of this scares me. The way he makes me feel is incredible and intense and I haven't felt like this in three years. I don't even know if I felt this way three years ago. Standing next to Austin, it feels huge and overwhelming and I feel like I'm drowning in all of it.

I try to push him away from me, but he brings his mouth down to mine and I forget everything. I'm responding enthusiastically, before I can stop myself, I feel my arms wrap themselves around his neck and I can't help pull him closer. The feel of him pressed tightly against me wipes my mind blank and I want him closer. Even if there were just a couple of layers of clothes between us—it was too far. My mouth is fast and feverish against his, but he keeps pulling back. He's taking it slow, each kiss like a breath of fresh air against my lips. He stops for a moment, his lips hovering over mine, and I can feel the frustration building at having to wait. I'm impatient. I want him closer. I want to kiss him again. I want to lose myself in the feel of his mouth and his tongue against mine. I lean closer to him and he pulls away, his lips just a whisper against my jawline. I'm shaking. He makes me want him so badly.

"Don't tease," I say, hotly. He laughs but it comes out shaky and I know he's feeling it too. Feeling all of *this*, too big to even describe.

"I've waited too long for this moment to rush this," he whispers to me. His hands are soft on my back, his fingers tracing my spine lightly. He lowers his head, and I shudder as his lips trace a slow pattern on my neck. It's simple, sweet, but it feels amazing. I'm literally panting. I feel the wetness between my thighs and it just increases my desire even more. I want him. I've wanted him for a while and god, I'm so tired of saying no. His hand is running up and down my spine until it reaches my neck and he tugs lightly on my hair. I gasp and he covers my mouth again.

This time, he lets me control and I feel like I'm swallowing him up, with how fast I'm kissing him. Every touch feels like a spark against my skin, like it's going to set my entire body on fire. I've been denying him for so long that it both feels amazing and completely forbidden. I want him so badly and I'm finally saying yes. My fingers grab at the buttons of his shirt, nearly tearing them off as I tug his shirt off. He has another one underneath, a simple white tank, and I sigh, frustrated. Austin laughs and helps me lift that one over as well. Every bit of him is so hard, so warm against me.

"Your turn." He reaches for the zipper on my dress and it falls to the ground, a pool at my feet. The straps of my bra are falling down my shoulders and the cool breeze feels incredible on my bare skin. I feel so hot; every inch of me feels like I'm burned. His hands are light on my arms as he runs his fingers up and down my skin.

He lifts me and my legs immediately go around his waist. I'm flexing against him and now he's the one to shudder, now he's letting out small groans. My tongue slides against his and my moan echoes in the quiet of the empty stadium. My hands are at his belt, but we're pressed too close together. I can't reach it with my legs wrapped so tightly around him. I growl, frustrated, and he laughs again.

"Calm down, princess," he says, softly. "I want you to be naked first."

The words send shivers down my spine, and he's carrying me over to the bench. When he puts me down, it's so careful and so gentle. I feel so taken care of. When my bare skin presses against the cold metal, it's a shock against my warm skin. His fingers fumble for the clasp of my bra, and it soon joins my dress on the floor of the dugout. His hands are at my waist, pushing me back against the bench as he leans down, his lips tracing circles between my breasts. My breaths are escaping in little moans and I cry out when his mouth wraps around a nipple. My fingers are lost in the softness of his dark hair and I pull him tighter against me. Just when I don't think I can handle it anymore, he switches to the other side.

His fingers are trailing a searing line down my body. There's a roughness when he grabs the inside of my thighs and I buck under him. He laughs a little and holds me in place, as he continues to tease me. Everything about this is slow and deliberate. I'm wet, my entire body is on fire and I'm ready for him. He's going to make me beg for it at this point. His hand tugs at my panties and they're down my legs and tossed to the side before I can think about it.

"Is this okay, baby?" Austin asks, his fingers hovering just over where I want him to touch me.

"God, don't stop," I beg him. My fingers wrap around his arm, and I pull him toward me again. His fingers trace the soft skin there softly, before sliding to the right spot. I cry out again, my head thrown back. He takes the opportunity to trail light bites across my collarbone. I'm gasping again and again as he rubs his thumb against me, one of his fingers gingerly slide inside me. "Don't stop. It feels so good. Please, don't stop."

After another moment, he does stop and I'm ready to lose my mind when he lowers himself to his knees. I'm confused for a moment until his teeth find the tender soft skin of my thigh and I know exactly what he's doing. I protest faintly, but he ignores me—I don't want him to stop. I just want all of him right here, right now. There is a devilish grin on his face and my protestations die in the back of my throat.

His tongue reaches for me, just one quick movement, and I jerk. It feels incredible and I'm almost surprised I don't come right then and there. His hands are wrapped around my hips and he holds me in place as his tongue and teeth work me over down there. I'm not holding back anymore; my hips move up and down and I'm literally grinding myself over his face.

"Austin," I whimper as I come closer to the edge. "*Oh*!" He doesn't slow down, if anything he works his tongue faster, and the crash hits me before I can even prepare myself for it. My cries are loud, and I know we're in public, but I can't help myself. It feels incredible. His tongue is still moving, and I have to pull him away, as shivers continue to roll through me. "Stop, stop, it's sensitive."

He pauses, and his forehead is pressed against mine. I lift my hands and place them on his chest, feeling the fast thrumming of his heart underneath my palms. I take a moment to catch my breath before I sit up. He stumbles backward a little and I pull him up to a standing position. My hands are at his belt and this time, he's letting me unbuckle it. I unsnap the button of his jeans with my finger-nails and tug his pants down. His underwear goes down with it. I stand up and help him out of them, and then there he is, naked in front of me, fully naked and I'm not turning away. I can barely breathe.

"Are you okay, princess?" Austin asks, his voice full of genuine concern.

I swallow hard, and step toward him, pushing him back-ward until he's sitting on the bench. His eyes grow wide when I fall to my knees in front of him. I have a sense of nervousness suddenly. It's been so long; *what if I do something wrong?* Austin leans forward and catches me in another sweet, lingering kiss and every single one of my doubts go out the window. My hands closed over him and pumps a few times. Austin groans and his hips flex. I smile a little and do it a few more times, watching as Austin leans his head back and his eyes fall closed. *Perfect.* I lean forward and take just the tip in my mouth and suck, hard.

"Fuck," Austin groans, jerking a little. I hum a little in response and move my lips further down, taking in more of him. I can tell he's trying to hold back, but when my tongue drags along the side of his hardness and I swallow once more, his hands reach out for me. His fingers are lost in my hair and he's not sitting still anymore. His hips are flexing again and again, and he has the control now and he's groaning loudly and I'm preparing myself for it when he pulls away. "Ah, Evie…"

"What are you doing?" I ask, confused.

He lifts me up, easily, and in the back of my head, I'm grateful that all those hours in the weight room have been good for *something.* I nearly giggle at the thought but before I can think of anything else, I'm in Austin's lap, and he's pressed against me, sliding in between my completely drenched folds, and his lips are pressed tightly against mine. Nothing has ever felt like this and I'm ready for it. I don't want to wait anymore.

"I want you so bad. Evie, I want you." He's breathing hard, as lips leave a hot trail down my neck. He bites down softly, and my hips press against him. I whimper and press my fingers tightly into his shoulders. My lips find his again, biting his lower softly. "Baby…"

"Take me," I interrupt him. "Please."

Austin doesn't hesitate, reaching for the pants that I've

just discarded moments before. He fumbles around for a second before reaching into a pocket and pulling out a condom. I raise my eyebrows at him, and he laughs a little.

"A little presumptuous, don't you think?" I ask, moving against him.

He closes his eyes, and a deep sound resonates from his chest. I'm smiling. I'm making him feel this way.

"Better safe than sorry," is all he says in response. He rips the wrapper and it's on before I know it. He doesn't wait. He doesn't ask if I'm ready; he knows I am, and he goes for it. He pushes inside me. I gasp, my fingernails digging into the firm skin of his shoulder blade and he stops, letting me adjust. I'm not a virgin but it's been awhile, and I'm not used to it. I finally nod at him and he begins to move, and I gasp again, this time with pleasure.

It feels amazing—*he* feels amazing. It feels exhilarating. It feels like hitting a homerun out of the park. My hands are gripping him tightly and we're moving against each other. We are having sex in the Quakes' dugout and it feels better than anything that I've ever felt before. Sex has never felt like this for me and now I'm starting to finally get what people rave about. I'm panting, I'm moaning out loud as he moves inside me, and I can barely control him.

"You're so beautiful. You're so sexy. *God, Evie.* You're perfect." Each word comes out as a gasp and they fill me with more pleasure.

"Austin..." his name comes out quick and breathy and he pulls me closer to him, moving faster.

"Does that feel good, princess?"

I nod, pressing my forehead against him. Our hips are crashing together, and we aren't even pretending to be gentle anymore. Every move, every thrust is hard and desperate, and I am getting closer and closer to the edge. "Austin?"

"What?"

"Make me come, baby," I whisper in his ear.

A tremor goes through him, and his fingers are spreading against my bare ass and he uses it to anchor me as he pushes inside me again and again. I can feel him pulsing inside me and I know he's about to come. He groans loudly and just before I come apart with him inside me, he says it.

"I love you, Evie. I fucking love you."

Before I can respond, he's coming, the growl low in his throat, as he pumps a few more times inside me. I gasp and am a beat behind him. I whimper loudly as I squeeze my legs around him. My lips form the words "I love you too," but I don't know if I say them out loud. My forehead is pressed tightly against his as my body slowly begins to relax. We both stay silent while we catch our breath.

Now that I've come down from my high, I remember that we are both stark naked in the dugout, where, presumably, anyone could find us. "We should put our clothes back on."

Austin laughs. "Yeah, that might be a good idea," he agrees but he shows no inclination of letting me go. His hands are pressed firmly against my back, his thumbs tracing circles on my sensitive skin.

"You kind of have to let go of me," I remind him.

He groans. "Do I have to?"

I roll my eyes, and carefully extract myself from him. I suddenly feel incredibly exposed and quickly look around the dugout for our clothes. We toss them at each other, laughing, as we manage to get back into our clothes.

As soon as I'm clothed, Austin reaches for me, and pulls me toward him, dipping his head to press a firm kiss against my forehead. My hands grip his waist tightly. "Come home with me?" he asks, softly.

I don't even have to think about it. I nod. "Of course."

"Good," he whispers in my ear. "I want these clothes back off."

I nod eagerly and take his hand, as we hurry out of the dugout.

CHAPTER TWELVE

"Austin, where the hell are we going?" I ask him. He came to my dorm early that morning, pulling me away from the great dreams I was having. Dreams of his warm body pressed back against mine…

I had answered the door in my pajamas, and he laughed before making me change into clothes. He didn't tell me where we were going so I changed into a gray t-shirt and jeans and hoped that would be good enough.

We don't move at a quick pace or anything as we walk through the campus. It's early in the morning, and I don't have class for a few hours, and there aren't a whole lot of people out. Only crazy people take classes before nine in the morning.

Austin's fingers are linked loosely with mine and it feels comfortable, like it's something we've been doing forever instead of just for a couple weeks. Everything about being with him felt easy. There was no sneaking around, no reason to feel like it was forbidden. Yeah, we hadn't told anyone, but we didn't have to hide and it felt freeing as hell.

I was sure that Austin would be taking me off campus

until he turns into a building that I haven't been in before. I haven't had a chance to take any classes in the Humanities building so I'm confused. He leads me up the fifth floor, and we take a left and then a right before heading into a large room.

There are several people already in there. Most of them are working on computers, looking a little stressed out. One guy is standing next to a large table, frowning at whatever is laid out in front of him. He spots us when we walk in and smiles. "Layout is the worst part of my day. I'm glad you guys could make it."

I frown and look up at Austin, who doesn't look surprised at this greeting at all. I look around a little more and it finally hits me. I know exactly where I am. Panic fills me, and I want out now. I don't want to be in this room. "Austin. What the hell? *Why*?"

He looks nervous for the first time than I've ever seen him. He's never nervous. "I just wanted you to check it out. You don't have to do anything. But I know this was your dream once, so you shouldn't completely give it up." He pauses, waiting for me to react.

"I just…" I look around, not sure what to say. According to…well, everyone, it's supposed to be my dream. This is where I'm supposed to be and right now, I can't think of any place I'd rather be less than here.

The guy that had smiled at us sticks his hand to shake mine. "Hey, I'm Jacob. Jacob Rodriguez. I'm editor-in-chief of the Daily Shake. I heard you were interested in being a sportswriter."

I throw another panicked look at Austin, who must not see the panic on my face because he just smiles and busies himself with something else in the room. I look back at Jacob and force a smile. "Sure." The one word is incredibly painful.

"You're Coach Cordova's daughter, right?" he asks. I nod, and he continues. "Is there a reason that you're not considering it now?"

I hesitate and he immediately waves his hands at me. "It's okay. You don't have to tell me. From what Austin told me, you're incredibly passionate about baseball and would make a great writer."

"It's...an option," I answer, vaguely, glancing around the small office. My hands are sweating profusely.

Jacob breaks out into a smile and it literally takes over his entire face. On anyone else, it would be overwhelming, but it works well for him. He calls someone over and a ridiculously tall guy walks over. "This is Caleb Brown. He's the sports editor."

Caleb smiles politely and reaches out to shake my hand. I feel like an adult today, with all the hand shaking and I'm wondering if I look like an adult or a little kid that has absolutely no idea what she's doing. "Austin was telling us about you. You're interested in writing about baseball for the Shake?"

Austin is across the room, talking to a few other people, and his mouth quirks up when he notices me looking at him. Part of me kind of wants to punch him in the face but I think of the way our limbs were tangled up last night and it's hard to stay mad at him. "Yeah. I think so. Maybe?"

The two of them laugh. "It's okay. You don't have to be sure. It's a lot of work, and not a whole of payout. We aren't exactly known for journalism at this school. It's all baseball, baseball, baseball." Jacob winces. "I mean...not that baseball isn't..."

I wave it away. "It's fine." I look around and I feel sick to my stomach. This is not at all what I want. I've never had to face it. I've never had to actually say no, and I don't know how to say it now.

"How about this?" Caleb starts. "The girl that I normally have covering the Quakes games has been out sick with mono all week." He rolls his eyes, and sighs. "Since you're already going to be at the games, you could cover them for me for the rest of the week. See how you feel about it."

"Can I think about it?" I say. *Just say no, Evie. Just say no.* The words won't come out.

Jacob claps me on the back, and smiles. "Yeah, absolutely. There's literally no pressure. I mean, we'd love to replace Crystal. She knows absolutely nothing about baseball."

Caleb shakes his head. "She literally starts her articles with '*So the Quakes won again...*' You can't be any worse than that." I raise my eyebrow at him, and he laughs. "You know what I mean. Come on, follow me and I'll show you what I need from you."

I escape as quickly as I can out of the office once I feel it's polite to do so. We walk through the hallways, down the elevator and back into the courtyard in silence. We make it almost back to the dorm hall before he finally says something.

"You're not mad at me, right?" Austin sounds nervous and I want to laugh. The idea that anyone would be nervous about me being mad at them is completely laughable. But there's nothing about this that is laughable. I still feel sick to my stomach.

He reaches for my hand and I let him take it. "I just didn't think you should just give up on that dream. Everyone says that this is your dream."

I make a face. "Everyone says. Everyone always says. Everyone says this and yet no one ever stops to actually ask *me*, do they?"

Austin looks taken aback. "What are you talking

about?" he says, slowly. He pulls his key out of his pocket and lets us into his dorm room. I follow him inside but I'm too antsy to sit. I stand near the door, my arms folded across my chest. "Evie?"

"I wish you would have asked me before taking me there. You just…you just *assumed*, and you assumed wrong. I didn't want to go there. I didn't want to be there." The words come out stiff and short.

"I…I don't understand," he replies. He sits on the edge of his bed and pats the spot next to him. I pretend not to see it, staring intently on a small stain on the carpet near his desk like it's the most interesting thing in the world. "Don't you want to be a sportswriter?"

I squirm. "Not really," I sigh, covering my face with my hands. "I've never wanted to be a sportswriter. Ever. I've never wanted that. But it was basically forced on me because it was the only appropriate career choice for me. It was better than what I really wanted. What I wanted…my dad wasn't okay with that."

"Okay with what? What did you want, Evie? Tell me." He sounds thoroughly confused but I can hear in his voice that he wants to know; he genuinely cares what I have to say. But I still hesitate. I've been keeping this locked inside for so long and it feels weird to say anything. "Evie. Please. You know you can tell me anything."

"I—I want to be a ball player!" I burst out. "I wanted to be a baseball player. I don't want to be stuck sitting in the dugout watching, Austin! I want to be out on that field. I wanted to play for the Quakes, and I want to go pro! My dream has always been to play, not—not sit on the sidelines and just watch!"

There is a deafening, achingly long moment of silence as he processes this. I lower my hands, afraid of what might be written on his face but there's nothing but curiosity. Finally, he says, "that was you in the picture in your uncle's restaurant."

It isn't a question, but I nod. There's a lump in my throat and I swallow hard. I will not cry. I won't cry. Baseball doesn't deserve anymore of my tears. "I played for the high school team, along with Drew and…we won the CIF championship when I was a junior. I hit a double that game to score the winning run."

"You play baseball?"

Each word comes out slowly, carefully. He's still processing.

"I *played* baseball," I clarify. I'm suddenly very, very tired and I sink into his desk chair.

"Well, that explains why you hit the ball way better than I do." I look up at him and he's grinning. "Why did you stop?"

The words get caught in my throat and it takes me a moment before I say anything. I inhale and let out the deep breath slowly. "I've never loved anything like I love baseball."

Austin doesn't say anything but when his eyes meet mine, I can see nothing but pure understanding in his expression and it gives me the courage to continue.

"My dad loves baseball, you know? He *loves* the Quakes. He played for them and I think he always wanted a son to play on the team. He got me and Lucy instead. Lucy likes baseball, she always has but from the moment I held a baseball, I loved it. He taught me how to play and I played in Little League and I played through middle school and I made my high school team and I played there. I just got better and better and I just loved the game."

I pause and look at Austin. He's watching and listening intently. He doesn't say anything, and I take that as a sign that he wants more.

"I think as I got older and made it clear what my goals were, my dad kind of realized, oh, shit, she's a girl. She can't actually play baseball. That's insane! That's when he stopped showing as much enthusiasm for me playing and started pushing the sportswriter agenda...so it just...yeah, that's where that started."

Austin leans forward. "Why did you quit?"

My mouth drops open. I'm taken aback. "What do you mean? I just told you..."

He shrugs. "You told me part of the story. Something is missing. You love baseball, Evie. I can see it on your face every time we're on that field. You wouldn't quit something you love that much unless there was a reason."

I press my lips tightly together before replying. "I already told you why I quit."

He looks like he doesn't believe me, and I don't blame him. I'm a terrible liar for someone who has been lying for so many years. "Well, then...do you still want to play?"

I consider the question. If he would have asked me this a few months ago, I would have known the answer without a doubt. I surprise even myself when I whisper to him, "every single day."

"What position did you play?"

The corner of my mouth lifts a little. "I played left field. I wouldn't take your spot."

He smiles. "I had to make sure." He sighs. "Why don't you play?" I don't answer and he continues. "Evie, I've seen the way you watch us play and it makes so much more sense now. You want to be out there. So be out there with us. Come play."

"It's not that simple," I tell him, my voice pleading. "It's not like it's normal for girls to play."

He considers this. "I mean, you're not wrong but that doesn't mean it's unheard of. There are women all over the world who play baseball and there are some badass women playing baseball here in the states. You know the names, Evie. I know you do."

Of course, I knew the names. I could practically recite them in my sleep. "Austin, I haven't played baseball in three years. I couldn't do it even if I wanted to."

"You want to," Austin says, confidently. "Besides, if you were that good, all it would take is some good training to get you back in shape and you're on one of the best baseball campuses in the country."

I'm saved from answering when his phone lights up with a phone call. He smiles apologetically and picks it up.

"Sorry, I have to answer this," he says. I wave him off, sinking into the desk chair. "Hi Mama."

I sit straight up in the chair, feeling suddenly like I need to leave the room. My heart is pounding, and I feel both relieved and anxious that I've finally told him. I can't handle a conversation with his mother right now. It was all too much at once.

"No, I'm not busy. I was expecting your call. Yeah, I'm with Evie right now. Yes, she's the girl I was telling you about." Austin winks at me.

I shoot to my feet, suddenly ready to be out of this room. He looks up at me and I motion to the door, mouthing that I had to go. He nods and mouths back at me, "This conversation isn't over."

As I shut his door behind me, I think that it is. It most definitely is.

"I DON'T UNDERSTAND, EVIE." MY COACH LOOKS UP AT ME, concerned. His hands are folded in front of him, elbows resting on the desk. "You're quitting? You're about to be a senior. You and Drew are captains. Why would you quit?"

My voice is hollow when I answer him. "It's just time, Coach. No one is going to take a girl seriously. I need to focus on other things. I can't keep wasting my time with baseball, pretending to be a ball player."

There is a confused look on his face. "Pretending? Evie, you've never been pretending. You're a damn good player. I know that. Your dad knows that. Your team knows that. We need you next season."

"I've made my decision."

Coach sighs, leaning back. "Are you sure? Are you really sure?"

I nod, afraid to say anything more, afraid that if he asks me again that I might burst into tears.

He nods, disappointment written across his face. "Okay, Evie." I start to turn to leave but he speaks again. "You'll always have a place on this team, Evie. If you change your mind, you let me know. You belong on this team."

My lips are pressed tightly, and I dig my fingernail into my palms, focusing on the pain and not the tears that are threatening to spill onto my cheeks. I don't answer him and instead I turn and leave.

I let baseball break my heart one more time.

CHAPTER THIRTEEN

"Tell me the truth. Have you screwed Austin yet?"

"Excuse me?" I ask, nearly choke on the chip that I've just shoved in my mouth as I turn to my sister.

"You heard the question, Evie," she laughs. There's a drink in her hand and I know it's not her first, or even her second. She's been especially upbeat lately, and I know a lot of it has to do with the email she got a few weeks back during Sydney's party. She always throws herself into what I call a "chasing happiness mode" when she gets one of those emails.

"You're drunk," I say, pushing past her and heading to the kitchen to grab another slice of pizza.

"Hey, don't walk away from me. I'm your twin. You should tell me everything." Her voice is loud and everyone that she's invited to this weird *party-that-wasn't-originally-a-party* is looking at us now. She reaches out and pulls Drew over to us, as if by magic. "You tell Drew everything."

"I don't tell Drew everything," I tell her at the same time Drew butts in.

"Jesus, Lucy, she doesn't tell me everything."

Lucy stares at the both of us before she starts tipping to the side. Drew grabs her arm and sets her upright. "Are you drunk?"

"That is *so* beside the point," Lucy says, leaning closer to me. "I asked my twin a question and I want her to answer it."

"Lucy, stop bugging your sister." Jesse appears out of nowhere and wraps his arm around her. I'm surprised at how much it still bothers me. I've hardly thought of him lately; Austin has been the only thing on my mind. Austin and baseball and my sharing the truth for the first time in too long. Yet...it still bothers me. I hate it. Even after everything, I still hate that he's with her and not me. "Come back over here with me, baby."

"No," Lucy's jaw is set, and her stubbornness is even more prominent when she's drunk. "I want to know what's going on between Evie and Austin."

The room falls into silence at this, and I can feel everyone staring at me. Most of the people at this get together are from the team, so everyone knows me. Everyone knows Austin. I can feel Jesse's eyes boring into me.

"What's going on between Austin and I is no one's business," I say, my voice shaking.

"You're my twin," she repeats, "so I think it's *totally* my business." Lucy drawls, tripping over her words. "So, what was it like? Is he good? That boy looks like he'd be a fun time."

"Jesus, Lucy," Drew says again, sounding disgusted, and Lucy just giggles in response.

"You guys do spend a lot of time together," Jesse says, so quietly I almost miss it.

I glare at him. "So? Do you have an issue with that?"

"No one is saying that there's an issue with it, Evie,"

Jesse answers, shrugging. I can tell he's lying though. He absolutely has an issue with it. "Besides, if there was something going on between you and Young, you'd think you would want to tell your sister. Sisters don't keep secrets from one another."

I couldn't keep from glaring at him as his past words played in my head. One of our last conversations before I decided that I would never let a baseball player break my heart again.

Jesse's eyes are turned toward the ground, in this last moment together he can't even give me the decency of looking into my eyes. "You can't tell her, Evie. It'll kill her. I know she's your sister, but you can't tell her."

Then choose me, *I want to scream at him, but he's already standing up. He's already walking away.*

My face flushes and I don't want to be at this stupid party anymore. "It's none of your business," I repeat, my voice firm.

My eyes meet Drew's and there's no mistaking the emotion that is in his eyes. He's disappointed in me.

My phone beeps in my pocket and I pull it out, turning away from everyone. I open the text and a grin immediately spreads across my face.

Miss you, princess. Get your ass over here.

"I'm ready to go," I whisper to Drew.

He nods, knocking back the rest of his soda before tossing the can in the trash. He fishes his keys out of his pocket and says goodbye to everyone.

He's pissed. I can tell.

I say goodbye to everyone and follow Drew out to his car. He unlocks the door for me, and we sit in an uncomfortable silence as he drives us back to campus. We are never like this. Knowing someone since you were a child usually makes any awkward situation null and void.

"Just say it," I finally speak up. "I know you're dying to."

Drew stays silent for a moment. It must be serious. Because Drew never acts like this. He's my goofball. "Why did you lie?"

I open my mouth to answer and close it again. "I didn't lie," I say finally, my voice low.

"That's bullshit, Evie," Drew retorts.

"I did not lie," I repeat back at him. "I told them it was none of their business and it's absolutely none of their business."

"Sure, Evie, it's none of their business" he says, angrily. "Why wouldn't you just tell them? You're obviously happy, happier than I've seen you in a while, and you should share that with everyone. Unless you are still hoping, stupidly, after three years that Jesse was going to suddenly come back to you. Guess what, Evie? He's not. He's with Lucy. That's not changing. He. Chose. Her."

"Believe me, I know that, Drew," I say, my arms folded tightly across my chest. "I know that. I get to see it every single day. Trust me, I know it."

"I don't think you do." Drew sighs. He turns into the parking lot. "I feel like you keep telling yourself that as if you're trying to convince yourself. But it's not working." He stops the car in front of my dorm hall, and sighs again. "I love you, Evie. You're my best friend. I just don't want to see you mess this up. Jesse isn't worth losing Austin over."

What Drew said is on my mind as I make my way to Austin's dorm room. He's not wrong. I am acting like a total idiot. I know how I feel about Austin. I know this. We have fun together. He's bringing back my love for baseball. And the sex is incredible. Sex like this…well, I thought it was only meant for books and movies. I didn't know it was real.

But I can't help the way I get around Jesse. It's like I

forget Austin even exists when Jesse turns his gaze on me. What we had was real. No one can convince me that it wasn't.

I shake my head as I approach Austin's door. This is the boy I'm with. He's the one I want right now and I'm all about the right now.

I'm so lost in my thoughts that I barely notice Austin when I let myself in. When I do, I can't help myself. I laugh loudly. "What would you have done if someone besides me had walked into your room?"

"Who said this was just for you, princess?" Austin says smoothly, winking at me.

He's sprawled out on his bed, naked except for a cowboy hat, strategically placed right over his dick. It's hilarious, but god he is sexy as hell. He's been working out more and you can tell. His arms are more defined and his stomach even tighter. He's been running around campus shirtless and his skin has turned a beautiful golden-brown color. Deep dark brown eyes are on mine, steady and sure. His hair has grown, and I want to brush it out of his eyes and run my fingers through the silky strands. Austin Young is beautiful, and I can't stop myself from staring at him.

I raise my eyebrow at him, trying not to let him see how much he's affected me. "Well, if you're waiting for someone else then, I'll go."

I pretend to walk away but he's suddenly behind me, his firm body pressed against my back. God, he's fast. He's lost the cowboy hat and I can feel him, hard and ready for me.

"The only person I'm ever going to be waiting for like this is you, princess." His lips are right by my ear and it sends shivers up my spine. I spin in his arms, pressing my lips against his bare chest. His eyes fall closed and a rumble goes through his body.

I reach up to drag his face toward mine, but he stops

me. My lower lip juts out in an immediate pout and Austin laughs.

"Last time," he starts to say, his fingers playing at the hem of my shirt. His fingertips are just a whisper on my skin but it's like a thousand volts of electricity. "I couldn't wait to get my hands on you." My arms lift as he pulls the shirt over my head. It gets tossed to the side.

I love the way Austin looks at me. His eyes drink me in like he can never get enough. I feel like I should maybe feel self-conscious or something, but I don't. I like the way he stares at me.

He takes a step closer, his fingers tracing my spine. "God, you're so beautiful, Evie." His hands reach the base of my neck, lost in the hair there. He tugs lightly, his teeth on the gentle skin there. "Today, I'm taking my time with you."

I shiver as his lips latch onto my earlobe. His tongue tickles the skin just below it and my hands reach for him. I can feel the warmth of his body beneath my fingertips and I want to taste him. His teeth are leaving light marks on my collarbone and I crane my neck to give him better access. A breathy moan escapes me. Austin's fingers are at the clasp of my bra and he unhooks it with ease.

His hands come up to cup my breasts and my nipples tighten with need. His thumbs rub across them once and I gasp.

"These are incredible," Austin groans, both of his hands squeezing tightly.

I laugh. "I can tell you think so."

"I just want to keep them all to myself." He lowers himself to his knees, and gives me one sexy, lopsided smirk before wrapping that beautiful mouth around my nipple. I gasp again and my knees buckle at the sensation. Austin catches me before I can fall and keeps me standing. My hands wrap around him pulling him closer, my fingernails lightly scraping against his scalp.

I'm about ready to lose it; his tongue flicking back and forth when he switches to the other side. His fingers are at the button of my jeans, pulling it open and sliding the zipper down. He's talented, his mouth sucking on my breast, teeth teasing the nipple, while his hands pull my pants and my panties down to my ankles. I kick them off, my toes curling against the skin of Austin's knees.

Austin pulls away, his hands reaching for my bare ass. "I love this too." His hands squeeze and I can feel what it does to me between my legs. The moisture is going to start running down my legs. "I just want to bite into it."

I lean down and press my lips tight against his. "Austin, all of this is yours," I whisper. It scares me how much I mean that.

"Good," he says firmly. His hands come up to my waist and he pushes me back a little. "Turn around. Brace your hands on the wall."

"Okay…" I turn around and place my palms against the wall. I'm not sure what's going to happen next until I feel his lips on the back of my neck, at the top of my spine, and I gasp at the sensation. My body tingles and presses closer to the wall as he slowly traces soft, warm kisses down my spine. I can't see him, and the anticipation of each kiss is driving me insane. When he places a kiss at the base of my spine, I actually moan out loud.

He spins me around suddenly and gently pushes me, so my back is against the wall. Austin is on his knees and watching me carefully as he lifts one of my legs and drapes it over his shoulder. I can feel his breath on me, and my hands reach for him, fingers weaving through his thick hair.

Austin's lips are tracing circles on my inner thigh. "Is this okay, princess?"

My eyes squeeze shut as his teeth bite the skin there. "Mhm," I manage to say. My lips are pressed tightly together, and I start humming in anticipation.

His fingers reach for me, sliding through the wetness with ease. He's gentle as he finds the exact right spot. I suck in a breath and he laughs softly. His thumb is tracing rough circles on my clit and I'm finding it hard to breathe.

"Austin," I moan, my leg squeezing tighter around his shoulder.

"Do you want me to stop?" he whispers.

"Please don't," I beg him.

"Too bad. I'm going to." I'm ready to drag his hand back until he spreads my legs a little more and his tongue replaces where his thumb had been only moments ago. He's amazing at this and I know it's not going to take very long for me to come. My moans are loud, and I know the walls are thin, but I don't care. He makes me feel perfect, amazing. He must be drowning in how amazing he is making me feel down there.

"Come for me, princess. I know you're close," he murmurs before he returns to me, his lips sucking at my clit before his tongue plays at my entrance. My ass is gripped tightly in his palms.

"Fuck," I say. It comes out in a gasp. The feeling is washing over me and I'm whimpering loudly as I come on his talented tongue. He stays down there for a moment before raising himself up to me.

I'm shaking when his hands grab my face. He stares at me for a long moment before he kisses me. The kisses are fast, feverish, and aggressive. I can taste myself on his lips and I feel like I should be disgusted but I'm not. Every taste is different and new. I've never wanted anyone like this.

Austin's eyes are wide and on mine and he's breathing heavily. His eyes flicker between my blue eye and unmatching brown eye. He can see me better than anyone. "I love you."

I smile at that. We've been standing here for a few minutes, both of us completely naked. Everything is on display, my curves, my fat, my stretch marks. I'm not perfect but I'm not thinking about that when I'm in front of him. Not when he says that. "I know," I finally answer.

"Are you going to say it back?" he teases.

I shake my head, trying and failing to hide that my smile grows. I'm pretty sure that I do feel the same way. I'm still not even sure if I said it that night in the dugout. It's all such a haze to me. I want to say it to him. But I want to be sure first. Austin deserves that.

"Evie, you know I'm teasing you right?" he asks, softly, his fingertips light on my shoulder blades. "You don't have to say anything."

"No, I don't," I agree with him. I push him away from me and he looks surprised. I push him again and he loses his balance and falls back on the bed. "But I can show you."

Austin's look of surprise changes into one of anticipation. He smiles at me as I crawl onto the bed, my body lying on top of his.

"I like that idea," he admits. His hands go behind his head, leaving his body completely open to me. I lower my head to his and I take my time with him, kissing him again and again.

There's a satisfying noise in his chest as my lips leave his and move across his jaw to his neck. I spend a little extra time there, knowing how much he loves it. He's practically panting when I move to his collarbone. My thumbs play with his nipples and his hips lift. I can feel him poking at me. My hand finds him, and I wrap my fingers tight around him. He groans loudly and I drag my tongue across his abs in response. He tastes wonderful and I moan a little as I do it again.

"Damn, Evie," Austin breathes, his arms flexing.

I make sure my eyes meet his once before my mouth wraps around him. My hand is still pumping at the base as my tongue circles him. He's not holding back anymore, and his hips are lifting again and again. I let him take control and grip his hips tightly as I lower myself over him. His groans are getting louder and I know he's ready for release.

Austin pulls away suddenly and I'm on my back in an instant. "As much as I would love to come in that pretty little mouth, I need to be inside you." He reaches for the box by his bed and the foil wrapper is ripped open and the condom rolled on before I can even see it happening. He spreads my legs and positions himself at my entrance. "Please?"

I nod, reaching for him, pulling him closer to me.

He starts off slowly, his hips rocking into me, but it's not long before he's moving faster and rougher. My hands are gripping his shoulders tightly and my eyes are on his face as he gets closer and closer. His moans get louder and he stills as he comes. He collapses on top of me, his head pressed tightly against my chest. "Jesus, princess. The things you do to me."

A rush of pride and affect and something that feels a lot like love fills me and I wrap my arms tight around him. I clear my throat. "Are you hungry? Should we order a pizza?"

Austin laughs and the sound shakes my entire body. "This is exactly why I keep you around."

I laugh too and reach for my phone. I don't know what's going to happen with the two of us, but I really like what is happening now. And I try really, *really* hard not to think about what Drew said earlier.

CHAPTER FOURTEEN

There is something very different about being under the lights of the stadium tonight. I feel…lighter, better, *happier*. I don't want to think this a product of good sex but maybe it is. I'm happy. Austin makes me happy. Spending time with him makes me happy, and I can see how much happier and confident he is on that field and it makes me even happier. There's just a ton of happiness going on in the dugout and I can barely handle it.

The only thing that would make it better is to be on the field with the guys. I don't know if it's possible; I've never felt like it's been a possibility but even just admitting it to myself feels better. I feel a sense of relief in being honest with myself. I miss baseball. I love baseball. I think I want to play again.

I can feel Jesse watching me. Every time Austin walks past me, every smile we exchange, every holler I give him when he makes a great play, doesn't go unnoticed by him. He's hovering, and I am not a big fan of it. I want him to go away, and this is the first time I've felt this in a long time. I feel like I'm walking on thin ice and I don't know why I wasn't just honest in the first place. I think of what Drew said after the party and I know he's not wrong.

The guys are running back into the dugout and I shake my head to clear my thoughts. "Young, Thompson, Humphrey." Austin winks at me as he slips his batting gloves on and my face flushes and I can't help the grin that stretches across my face. Drew looks at me in shock, and I'm glad. He hasn't gotten much playing time this season and we're up by three runs. His grin is even larger than my own and I know it's worth it to randomly throw him in the line-up. Dad throws me a curious glance and I shrug, and he rolls his eyes.

Austin heads out of the dugout towards home plate and gets into his stance. It's perfect; his elbow is finally at the right level. The lights are bright, and I can hear the cheers coming from the stands. People are cheering his name. There is a scout in the stands tonight from the Royals and, sure, they're here for Jesse but their scout has been watching Austin closely too. It makes me burst with pride and nervousness, but I try to push it away. I'm focused on him. He's the only important thing going on in this stadium.

The first pitch is a strike and I can see the frustration rolling off his shoulders. He steps out of the box for a moment and takes a few practice swings. He looks up and his eyes meet mine for a moment. I smile encouragingly and he smiles in return.

The second pitch is a strike as well, and I swear loudly, earning me a glare from Dad. Jesse is fidgeting next to me but I'm not paying attention to him. My attention is on Austin and Jesse is merely a fly, buzzing around, irritating me.

The third pitch comes flying toward Austin and he reaches for it. The bat makes a connection and it goes flying. The stands are erupting in cheers and I'm jumping to my feet. The clipboard falls to the ground, clattering against the cement of the dugout, and my hands are over my mouth in shock as I watch the ball fly over the heads of the infield, the outfield and out past the fence.

Austin just hit a homerun.

Something like pride fills me as I watch him run around the bases. He has a smile that could cure cancer on his face. I don't think I've ever seen him this happy before. The rest of the team has run out of the dugout, meeting him at home plate. They clap him on the back and jump all over him. I'm still standing, staring at him, and everyone in the stands behind me is yelling in excitement.

The team finally starts walking back to the dugout and Austin is grinning, his eyes on only one thing: Me. He pushes his way out of the crowd that surrounds him and walks straight toward me. He's moving fast and I'm panicked. What on earth is he doing? There's a blazing look in his face. He stops right in front of me. He's breathing heavily and he's sweaty and dirty, but he smells just like he's supposed to.

"Hi," he says, breathless. I can feel all eyes on us. We're blocking the dugout, and essentially, the entire Quake team from resuming their places inside. Everyone is looking at us. I know it.

"Hi," I say back. "What the hell are you doing?"

"I just hit a homerun." *Seriously?* Everyone just *saw* him hit a homerun. I glance around and, sure enough, everyone is staring at us. I can feel the burn of their gazes on me. I can see Drew and Dad out of the corner of my eye; one of them is smiling and the other looks incredibly confused. Join the club, Dad. "You should probably get in the dugout though. You're kind of in the middle of the game."

His answering grin is infectious, and I smile back. "I know. I just wanted to share this with you." He leans forward, grabbing me by the back of my neck and pulls me into a kiss. It's not quick either; he deepens it and my hands are gripping him tightly and everyone's cheers are even louder. He pulls away and smiles again, passing me and taking his seat in the dugout.

People are still watching me. The rest of the team passes by. Most of them are smirking and clap me on the shoulder as they pass. Jesse says nothing, just passes me without a word. I can't move.

I'm pissed. I'm elated. I have no idea how I'm supposed to feel.

I spend the rest of the game in a haze. I can feel the stares and they are incredibly distracting. I forget the line-up twice and I can barely keep track of the game at all. I miss Drew's first at-bat, which I'll probably get shit for later. Eventually, Dad walks over and grabs the clipboard from me. He raises his eyebrow at me, and I just shrug in response. I have no answer for him. I don't know how to feel.

The game finally ends, and I think we win. The entire team disappears into the locker room. I know he'll wait until the rest of the team has left to go home.

The more I think about it, the angrier I get. Behind closed doors was what we decided. No one would really know until the end of the season. I wanted to be sure of Austin before I told the entire world. I didn't want to get hurt again. I had to be sure.

Plus, we'd talked about it. If I was ever going to tell my dad that I wanted to play for the team, that I just even wanted to try out, to see if I could do it, the guys had to take me seriously as a player. How seriously could they take me when he just kissed me in front of a sold-out crowd?

Austin Young just laid a claim on me in front of everyone in Santa Isabella. Practically the whole town turns up for the games and by tomorrow, the rest of the place is going to know too. It might as well be front page news in the *Santa Isabella Journal*. It was definitely going to be the front page of the Shake.

I go into the locker room, ready to rip into Austin. Sure enough, he's the only one left in there. He's sitting in a chair shirtless as he types away on his phone. There's a smile on his face when he sees me, but it fades quickly when he sees the expression on my face.

"Evie? What's wrong?" he asks confused.

I falter a little, finally noticing that he's shirtless. "What the hell was that, Austin?"

"What on earth are you talking about?" He leans forward and his stomach muscles tighten. It's incredibly distracting. Why does he have to look like this?

"You know what I'm talking about!" I screech. "Do you ever wear a shirt?"

Austin breaks out into a smile. "Does me being shirtless bother you, princess?"

"No," I sputter. "And that's also beside the point! Why did you kiss me out there? Everyone saw, Austin. *Everyone*."

Austin's smile slips but he doesn't say anything.

"You know how I feel about you, Austin, but you also know that I wanted to wait. *That* was *not* waiting."

"You're right, Evie," he immediately says, standing up. "I didn't even think. I was just so happy at that moment and I wanted to share it with you." He reaches for my hands. "You're the only person I want to share it with." He sounds sincerely apologetic, and nervous. Definitely nervous.

The fight goes out of me. "Why do you have to be so charming when you're apologizing?"

He smiles slightly. "I wasn't trying to be."

"I know," I answer wryly, "but it's hard to say mad at you when you say things like that."

"So, you're not mad at me anymore?" Austin walks over to me, enveloping me into his arms and placing a firm kiss on the top of my head.

"No, I'm not mad," I grumble.

"You kind of liked it, didn't you?" Austin asks, laughter shaking through his body.

"No!" He doesn't say anything, and I roll my eyes. "Okay, I kind of liked it. It was the kind of fantasy that sixteen-year-old Evie would have dreamt up."

Austin pulls back and looks at me. "Oh, really?"

I laugh. "God, yeah. A sexy star player of the Quakes laying a passionate kiss on me after hitting a home run? That was my dream. If I were in uniform too, it would just be the ultimate fantasy."

"A sexy star player, eh?" Austin asks, a cocky grin on his face.

"I hate you," is all I answer.

His mouth is on mine before I can react, and the kiss nearly brings me to my knees.

"Okay," I admit, breathing heavily. "Maybe I don't hate you."

Austin laughs. "I never doubted that for a moment."

I poke him hard in the shoulder. "You know, I haven't completely forgiven you yet, cowboy."

His arms snake tighter around my waist and he pulls me in closer to him. "Damn. What do I have to do to make it up to you, princess?"

"Hmm," I say, pretending to think about it. I smile up at him and pull his face down to mine.

He's responding enthusiastically and it's not long before my back is pressed against the cool metal lockers. I bite his bottom lip lightly and he hums under his breath.

"I like the noises you make," I tell him.

"I like *you.*" His lips graze mine as he smiles.

"Excuse me."

The two of us jump apart and my hand goes to my mouth, as if I could wipe away the kiss. Jesse is standing there, staring at the both of us. His face is expressionless, but I can see the slight tick in his jaw.

"I thought everyone had left already," I say after a long silence.

"Nope. Coach and I were discussing some things," Jesse says, his arms crossed tightly on his chest. He looks at Austin and his mouth quirks up a little. "He wants to see you now."

I glance up at Austin and see all the color drain from his face. I have no idea what Dad wants to talk to Austin about but judging by the look on Jesse's face, it can't be good. Austin squeezes my hand before walking away. "I'll be out in a second. Wait for me?"

I'm nodding when Jesse butts in. "Don't worry about it, Young. I'll walk her to the dorms."

My mouth has already opened to protest but Austin is shaking his head at me. He looks at Jesse. "Thanks, Valdez. I appreciate it."

Jesse stays quiet the entire time he walks me to the door. He doesn't say a word to me, and he is a safe distance away from me. My arms are wrapped tightly around my waist. We finally reach my building and I turn to thank him but immediately stop. He's glaring at me.

"What?" I ask. "Why are you looking at me like that?"

Jesse stares at me a moment longer before finally speaking. "You lied to me." His voice is low, angry.

"What on earth are you talking about?" I say, my arms falling to my side.

"You lied to me, Evie," he repeats. "I asked you a few weeks ago if there was something going on with you and Austin and you said no."

"No," I said, firmly. "I said it was none of your business."

"At our party…"

"You and Lucy were calling me out in front of a ton of people. It was none of your business and none of their business. It still isn't."

"I told you I didn't like him, Evie," Jesse says, his voice raising. "Now he's kisses you on that field, like he's claiming you, like you belong to him."

"Why are we having this conversation?" My voice is full of emotion. Anger, nerves, anxiety. This is the way he makes me feel way too often. Jesse and I haven't talked like this to each other in years.

"Because I don't like it," Jesse says, running his hands through his hair. "I don't like seeing him with you."

"You have no right to feel like that, Jesse." My voice breaks and I can feel the tears in the corners of my eyes.

"Just tell me that it's not serious," he begs. I take a step back, shaking my head. His voice is low, and it wavers as he speaks. "I can't handle if you tell me…"

"No," I interrupt him. "You can't do this. You have no right!"

"Evie…" he starts to say, taking a step toward me.

I back up again. "No," I repeat. "You know how I feel about you, how I have always felt about you. You know that." I pause, taking a deep breath. I will my tears not to fall. "But I'm not doing this with you. You made your choice. You chose her, remember? Not me."

There is a long bout of silence and my sniffles seem amplified.

"Maybe I should have chosen you," Jesse says, his eyes meeting mine.

I shake my head. "No."

"You wanted that." His voice is steady but there's a push in it. "You still want it."

"None of that matters, Jesse," I say, softly. "You *needed* to choose Lucy. After everything that happened, she needed *you*." I wipe my fingers angrily under my eyes. "Now, I'm going to bed."

"Evie, please…"

"It's none of your business, Jesse."

He grabs my arm. "Just tell me it's not serious. Tell me that you still love me."

"I'm not telling you anything," I say, yanking my arm away from him. "Leave me alone. Leave Austin alone."

Jesse pauses for a moment. "I didn't want to have to do this…"

I step back. "Do what?" I ask, warily.

He pulls his phone out of his pocket and fiddles with it for a moment before turning the screen toward me.

I gasp, knowing immediately what it is. The footage isn't very clear and its obviously from a lesser quality camera, but I know exactly what it is. Its Austin and I in the dugout, having sex. My hand covers my open mouth and I'm horrified. This *cannot* be happening. I was not the type of person to have a sex tape, but there it was, in front of my face, undeniable. How could I forget about the security cameras that were installed last year after an opposing team broke in and vandalized the dugout?

Before I ran into Jesse, I'd been starving, ready to dive into the bag of Doritos that were waiting for me back at the dorm. Now I feel nothing but revulsion. I'm seconds away from throwing up, though there's nothing in my stomach to throw up. I can't stop watching. Fear shoots through at me at the thought of who has seen this and who might see this in the future.

"Where did you get this?" I finally manage to ask.

Jesse is watching me, carefully. "The guy that watches the security tapes passed it along to a couple of guys on the team." I inhale sharply. "No one knows it's you. Or Austin. But I did, immediately. I sleep next to your clone every single night. I know what you look like, even with the bad quality."

I'm barely registering what he's saying. I can't stop watching the video. I have a sex tape. I'm on that screen and it's not ending, when does it end? Can it please just end? My knees grow weak and I sink onto a nearby bench. "Oh my god."

"Hardly anyone has seen it, Evie. I made sure of that. It's okay." His voice is reassuring but his next words aren't. "But…"

I look up at him, sharply. "But what?" I'm horrified to hear the unrestrained sob at the back of my throat escape. There's no taking it back. "But *what*?"

"I might be forced to share this with Coach if you continue your relationship with Austin. I don't think he'd be very happy about one of his players taking advantage of his little girl in his stadium. He might feel compelled to remove Austin from the team. We wouldn't want that, would we?"

My hands are shaking as I process what he's just said. "You wouldn't."

He shrugs. "I just want what's best for you. Why can't you see that? Austin is not good for you. Don't force me to do this to show you."

I think of all the hard work Austin has put in to get where he is now. I think of the Royals scout in the stands tonight. I think of his mother back home and the responsibility he feels to help her and their ranch. I think how all of that can be ruined so quickly if Jesse shows that video to anyone. "Go away, Jesse."

"Do you promise to stay away from him?"

"I said, go away!"

Jesse takes a step back, looking a little shocked, but he doesn't react to my shouting at him. "I know you'll make the right decision. You always do."

I'm not sure how long I remain sitting there. I barely register anything until I feel a warm, large body squeeze in next to me on the bench and I realize that Austin has joined me.

"Hey, are you okay?" he asks, pressing his lips to my temple. The kiss is warm, but I barely feel it. "You're freezing."

"I'm fine," I say in a cheerful voice that sounds forced even to my own ears. "I'm just tired. I just wanted to wait here to say good night to you."

Austin frowns. "Do you want me to come up with you?"

I shake my head, my jaw clenched tightly. I will not cry. "No. I'll just call you tomorrow, okay?"

He smiles at me and I falter in my resolve. "Of course. Call me tomorrow." He kisses me swiftly and I fall into it, holding him tightly before letting him go and practically sprinting into my dorm. When I make it to my room, I notice that Sydney's bed is empty, and I'm relieved as the tears pour down my face.

CHAPTER FIFTEEN

"Who is this girl and why is she in my dorm room? I swear I had a single this semester." Sydney's eyes are wide when she walks in but there's a smile on her face.

"Very funny," I say, flatly, not lifting my eyes from my computer screen.

"I'm just saying, it's been awhile since I've seen my best friend," Sydney points out, collapsing on her bed.

I spin in my chair to face her, immediately feeling ashamed. I've become that girl who completely ditches her best friend because of a boy. Sydney has never done that— no matter who she dates, and there have been quite a few that have come and gone. But no matter what, she never forgets me. She always made it a point to include me. Now I've done the total opposite. I already feel miserable and this only makes me feel worse. "I know. God, I'm sorry, Syd. I've been a terrible best friend lately."

She laughs. "It's okay, Evie. I'm glad you found Austin." She pauses, making a face. "But why are you home? I wasn't expecting you."

I swallow hard, turning back to my computer. The truth

is, I've been ignoring Austin for the past few days, ever since my encounter with Austin. He's texted, emailed, called and I've ignored pretty much all of it. I text him once to tell him I'm busy and I email my part of our Art History project to him but that's it. The team is out of town for a few days and he said he'd call me when he gets back but I didn't respond to that either.

I've cut him out, cold turkey, and it hurts. I'm mad at myself for letting myself get in so deep, for letting myself feel everything I feel for Austin. If I would have just cut it off at the beginning, maybe it wouldn't hurt so badly. I'm having a hard time regretting it though; how can I regret feeling all of the amazing things I've felt with him?

On the other hand, I'm also so angry at Jesse too, for everything he's done to me and everything that he's still doing. He's claimed to love me for the past three years but how is it possible for someone who loves you to treat you like this? He doesn't like Austin; that much is clear, but why do this to him? Why take it that far? Why hurt Austin in a way that would hurt me too?

There's too much going through my head and its making this even more difficult. I can't tell if I've made the right decision. Then I remember the video and Jesse's threat and I tell myself that I'm doing the right thing. Austin's career is more important. It's the most important thing.

"Evie?"

I shake my head. "Sorry. The team is away for the weekend."

"You didn't go with them?" Sydney asks casually.

I shrug, trying to be nonchalant. I can't look at her. I can't make eye contact with her. She'll know something is wrong immediately and I'm not ready for this conversation with her. "I don't need to be there all the time."

"Evie…" Sydney starts to say but her phone interrupts

her. She stares at it for a moment and then frowns. She punches the screen viciously and tosses the phone aside. It lands with a thump against the wall.

"Whoa, what was that all about?" I ask, grabbing onto any excuse to change the subject.

"Nothing," she says shortly. It doesn't sound like nothing, but I know better than to push it. Something has been off about Sydney, ever since her birthday. She's been quieter, and at home, in the dorm, more often. She's been more sober lately. Something is on her mind. I want to ask her if it's about her dad. Her dad is really the other person that can put her in this kind of mood, but he's also the only subject that shut Sydney down faster than anything else.

"How are things with Austin anyway?" she asks, effectively ending the conversation. "You guys looked pretty amazing together at the baseball game the other night."

I feel myself blushing at the memory. "Yeah, well, he shouldn't have done that…"

"You loved every minute of it, Evangeline Cordova," Sydney scoffs. "Seriously, you guys looked amazing out there. Like a couple out of a movie or something. Even I was jealous."

"One day, you're going to fall madly in love with someone, Sydney, I promise that," I say, turning back to my laptop and the stupid paper that is doing nothing to distract me from the fact that Austin has just texted me and I can't answer. I won't answer. It doesn't help that his name is typed just underneath mine on this paper.

She shrugs. "Yeah, maybe." She stays quiet for a moment. "Do you love Austin, Evie?"

I open my mouth to answer her, to say something, though I don't know what. I'll have to tell her eventually that Austin and I just aren't going to work. Before I can say anything though, it's my phone's turn to interrupt. It trills loudly and I grab at it. It's Drew and I can't help my disappointment. I'm a stupid mess. I slide my finger across the screen and answer. "Hey Drew. What's up?"

"I got to pitch today!"

"Yeah I know." I laugh. "Dad said he was going to be throwing you in this weekend. I'm sad that I wasn't there to see it."

"I did pretty well. Not fantastic but there's always room for improvement. Maybe you can check out my pitches when we get home?"

Sydney looks at me curiously and I mouth *Drew* at her. She frowns and picks up her phone, typing something furiously on it. I study her but she refuses to look at me.

"Yeah of course," I answer.

"Why aren't you here this weekend?" Drew asks. There's a lot of noise in the background and it sounds like he's in a bar or something. I recognize most of the voices and I know the team is celebrating their win today.

"Uh…" I hesitate. "I just had a lot of homework and I thought it was better to stay home. Plus, I haven't really spent a lot of time with Sydney lately, so it gives me a good amount of time to do so."

All I can hear for the moment is the sounds of laughter and loud music. Drew finally speaks. "Is Sydney there?"

"Um, yeah, she's here. Why? Did you want to talk to her?" Sydney flashes a panicked look my way and shakes her head, looking like she's ready to bail.

"No," Drew interjects quickly. I look back over at Sydney and shake my head and she loosens a little. "No, it's fine." He pauses again. "So, the scout was at the game today."

"Scout? What scout?" I ask, forgetting all about Sydney.

"The scout from the Astros? Didn't Austin tell you?"

"Tell me what?" I ask, clutching my phone tighter to my ear. "Did something happen?"

"Of course not," Drew laughs. "A scout from the Astros came by to see Coach the other night. He was at the game where Jesse pitched. The one where Austin hit a homerun. He wanted to watch them more, both of them. Apparently, he wanted to look at Cobb too."

Butterflies erupt in my stomach immediately, even though this is exactly what I wanted. This is good. "Wait, is that what Dad talked to Austin about that night?"

"Yeah…" Drew says slowly, immediate relief washed over me. Dad wasn't talking to Austin about the kiss or the video. He was talking to Austin about the scout. "Didn't Austin tell you that?"

"Yeah, of course. Of course, he did. I just forgot," I burst out quickly. I'm becoming a worse and worse liar by the moment. "So, the scout?"

"Right. Well, he came out to our game tonight, which turned out so not well for Jesse. He wasn't pitching, but Austin had a great game. I think the scout really liked him. He even introduced himself after the game."

"Wow," I say softly. "That's amazing. He's probably so excited."

"I'm sure he's going to call you tonight, Evie," he says quietly, and I can barely hear him over the cacophony of noise in the background. "He's just having fun right now."

I laugh lightly and it's pretty good. I almost believe it's real. I take a deep breath as my heart sinks a little but, even if Austin does call me—it's only going to voicemail. "It's fine. He's having fun."

"Are you sure?" Drew sounds hesitant, like he's ready to go searching through the crowd to find Austin and that's the last thing I need right now.

"No!" I laugh again. "No, really, it's completely fine. I'll let you go. Good luck tomorrow okay?"

"Yeah, okay. Good night, Evie."

"Night, Drew." I hang up the phone and toss it on my pillow.

"Austin didn't tell you about a scout coming to see him?" Sydney asks carefully.

"It's not a big deal," I say. I roll my eyes. "He probably just forgot. We're not even really dating, Sydney. He doesn't have to share anything with me."

"Evie…"

"Let's go out," I interrupt her loudly. "Get some food or something. Let's have a girls' night. It's been too long."

Sydney purses her lips for a moment before reaching for her phone and bag. "Okay, let's go, but you're paying for dinner."

I laugh, before glancing down at my phone. No missed texts. No missed calls. I don't think he's going to text me tonight. This is exactly what I should want but it feels awful to see a blank screen. I want to share this with him. I shake my head as I shove my phone in my back pocket. Out of sight, out of mind, is going to be my motto tonight. "Fine. Let's go."

AUSTIN HAS BEEN BACK IN TOWN, WITH THE REST OF THE team, for two days now. I've seen him once in class when we did our presentation and at practice but other than that, he's been pretty MIA. This is exactly what I wanted but it still feels horrible.

I miss him. There's a pure physical feeling to missing him. It's like I'm missing a part of myself. I've somehow made Austin an essential part of my life without even realizing that I was doing it. I miss his teasing smile. I miss him calling me princess. I miss the way he smells and god, I miss the way his body covers mine and how I forget everything when we kiss. I even miss the confident way that he tells me he loves me, as if there's no question about it. I never realized how much of a magnet he was until he was gone and I'm afraid to see him again, afraid that simply being next to him will make this even harder.

I avoid even looking at him during practice. I say hello and smile but dodge any attempts at conversation or affection. He looks confused and hurt but he doesn't push it, not when we haven't had a moment to ourselves since he's gotten back. He won't say anything with everyone around and I do my best to make sure we're always surrounded by people. I know I just need to tell him it's over, but I don't know if I have the strength to tell him that.

I'm cleaning the locker room after practice one day when I realize that we're the only two people left; even my dad has left for the night. I panic when I see him. "I have to go," I say, immediately, turning toward the door.

"Evie, stop," Austin sighs. "We need to talk."

I turn around and look up at him. "Talk? About what?"

He doesn't say anything for a moment, and I can feel the anxiety churning in my stomach. This is the conversation I've been avoiding for the past week.

"Austin?"

"I'm angry," he finally says.

"You're angry?" I repeat.

"Yes."

My heart is beating a firm beat against my rib cage. I'm afraid to continue but I have to know why. I have to do this. I have to have this conversation. "Why?"

He pauses for a moment and then clears his throat. He won't look at me in the eye and I don't like that. He never avoids eye contact with me; he's the one person that never avoids looking at me straight in the eye. "Why am I angry? Evie, you've been avoiding me for a week now. You won't talk to me. You won't be alone in the same room as me. I have no idea what's going on."

"I…" I start to say but I have no idea what I'm trying to say. He's right. I must break up with him to keep his career intact but I'm too big of a coward to do it. "Austin, I…"

He cuts me off. "I just don't want to hear it anymore, Evie. I'm trying so hard but every time I take a step closer, you pull back. I'm tired of it. I'm tired of all the secrets."

You're keeping secrets from me, Evie."

"I'm not…I'm not keeping secrets," I stutter out. I take a few steps back but there are only lockers behind me. I lean against them; they're the only thing keeping me upright.

Austin looks over at me and the expression on his face is one of anger. I've never seen him look like this before. I admit, it scares me a little. "I followed you. That night after I talked to Coach. I knew I could catch up to you and I wanted to share the news about the scout from Houston."

I pull away from him, and I can feel the ice fill my veins. "Okay…"

"I saw you and Jesse. I saw you guys talking." Austin is breathing heavily, and his hands are gripping his knees tightly. "I always had a feeling, you know? You always acted so weird around him, and I kept telling myself I was imagining it."

Our eyes meet and he's not looking at me like he loves me. He is looking at me like he doesn't even know who I am. "But I wasn't, was I? Was I, Evie?"

"Austin," I whisper.

"No," he interrupts calmly. "I was right. I saw you guys and it became so obvious, you know? You had something. You and Jesse had something years ago. That's why you kept pushing me away. Because of what happened with him. And then right after…you ignored me for days. I don't think that's a coincidence."

I open and close my mouth a few times. "Austin, it's not what you think…"

He interrupts me. "You're in love with Jesse Valdez."

"I'm not," I say automatically but I honestly don't know how true that is. I love Austin, oh god I'm in love with Austin. I know this now. I'm looking at him and I know that I love him. But I can't love him. I can't love him if he's going to become a pro ball player. I don't trust Jesse not to ruin baseball for Austin the same way he ruined it for me.

"Why do I feel like you're lying to me?" Austin says, staring at me. "It's so hard to tell. I love you, Evie, but I feel like I don't even know you."

I shake my head. "You do know me," I insist, pleading for him to believe me.

"I thought you were different, Evie. I met you and I thought, who is this incredible, beautiful, funny girl? You're not like anyone I've ever met before. I've never wanted anything more outside the world of baseball. Not until you. The more I got to know you, the more I loved you. And it turns out you're just a girl who is pining after her own sister's boyfriend."

I quickly stand up, running my hands through my hair before looking back at him. "You have no idea what you are talking about."

"Don't I?" he asks, staring up at me. "Jesse and Lucy have been together for years and you've just been sneaking behind her back this whole time. What kind of person does that? And why did you have to drag me into it?"

I inhale sharply. I forget about the video and I forget about Jesse's threat. They don't matter, not if Austin thinks this of me, not if this is the person he thinks I am. "No,

Austin. That is not it at all. You have no idea what you're talking about."

"I know," he whispers, and I barely hear him.

"What?" I'm confused.

"I know…" he takes a deep breath and continues, "I know about the baby."

The world spins for a moment and I lean against the lockers behind me to keep from falling over. "The baby? You know about…the baby?"

Austin nods and I can't handle the look he's giving me. Like he's undressing me; not my clothes but all the layers I've built up over the past few years. "Yeah, I know about the baby."

My hands are shaking as I wipe the sweat off my forehead. "How…" My voice cracks and I clear my throat. "How did you find out?"

He presses his lips tightly together and I swear I see moisture in the corners of his eyes. As soon as I look though, it's gone, and I know I must have imagined it. "When I was gone this weekend, with the team, one of the guys started asking me about you. I told him it was casual, but that hopefully things were moving in a good direction." He stops. "I thought you'd be okay with that. Everyone saw us kiss at the game."

He stops for a moment and his hands drag through his hair. He's frustrated, and his hand hits the wall, hard. The sound echoes in the empty locker room. "And Jesse comes in and tells me how you told everyone at Lucy's party that there was absolutely nothing going on with me. Nothing. After days of you ignoring me, it felt fucking awful, Evie, and I was so angry with you. You kept lying, not to Drew and not to Sydney. But you kept lying to Lucy and…Jesse. Again and again and I had to know why."

I flinched. *Oh god. No. Just…no.* I didn't want to know what was going to come out of his mouth next. "And?"

"And I talked to Drew, who wouldn't tell me."

Drew is an amazing friend. Even after all these years, he has kept my secret. I can't help it. I breathe a sigh of relief.

It doesn't escape Austin's notice and he tosses a glare in my direction. "He told me to ask you. But he would tell me this. He told me that three years ago, Lucy caused a scandal by getting pregnant at the age of sixteen with the town's star baseball player, Jesse Valdez."

I choke on a sob. I don't want to hear this. I don't need to hear this. "Austin, please. Stop."

"I'm not going to stop, Evie. I'm not. I asked you again and again to share with me, to talk to me and you wouldn't. I had to find out from someone else that your sister got pregnant, and she gave up her baby. She was heartbroken. Drew says she acts tough but the pictures and emails she gets from the adoptive parents nearly kill her every time she gets them."

I lose my ability to stand up and slide to the ground, my hip catching on the edge of an open locker door. The pain shoots through me but I barely notice it. I can't take my watery gaze off Austin, who can't stop looking at me as if he doesn't even recognize me.

"I don't know the rest of the story, but I can guess. You've been in love with Jesse for years, and you guys had a thing going on the side. Which is fucked up, Evie. Your sister had a baby and she gave that baby up and you're sitting here, pining after her boyfriend all these years. What is wrong with you?"

I shake my head, back and forth, back and forth. "No, Austin, that's not…" The tears are falling down my cheeks and I can't stop them. I can barely breathe. "That's not at all what happened. If you just let me explain…"

Austin whirls around. "I tried to let you explain, Evie. I tried!" His voice is loud and scary, and I flinch away from him. "And this is the story that comes out? I thought I knew you. I fell in love with you, having no idea that this was the person that you really are."

"You knew exactly who I was when you fell in love with me, Austin," I shot back at him. "And you know I love you."

It's the first time I've said it out loud and Austin looks shocked at the words. "I wish I could believe that, but I don't."

I open my mouth to protest but he cuts me off.

"You should have never fallen in love with me," I shout back at him. "I told you to stay away from me." The words spill out of me before I even have a chance to think of what I'm saying. All I know is that he's hurting me, and I want him to feel the same way.

"Maybe I shouldn't have. You're not the person I thought you were," he replies sharply. "God, Evie, I don't even know you."

Panic fills my veins. This is not at all what I wanted. I don't want to leave. I don't want him to leave. This is exactly what I've wanted to avoid. I don't care about Jesse's threat anymore. It means nothing. He can show the whole world for all I care. I just don't want to see Austin leave. "Austin, wait," I beg.

He shakes his head. "I think I need to leave. I can't...I can't look at you right now."

I stare at him for a long moment but he's not saying anything else. He won't even look at me anymore. I watch him as he gathers his things, quietly, and makes his way to the door. Before he can leave, I say one more thing, one more plea. "You don't know the whole story."

His fists are clenched. "I know enough, Evie."

I nod, resigned. Heartbroken. "Yeah. Apparently, you do."

I sit on the locker room floor for a few minutes before pulling myself up. I walk through the door, shutting it quietly behind me. Somehow, I make it through the hallway, down the elevator and across the quad to my dorm hall. I push the button for the elevator and wait a few moments, jabbing it again when the elevator doesn't appear. I'm angry and hurt and confused and I have no idea what to do. Maybe this is for the best. Maybe I should go back. Maybe I have no idea what I'm doing.

The elevator doors finally open and I'm surprised when I see Sydney and Drew both in there. They look angry, standing at opposite ends of the elevator but their expressions change when they see me.

"What's wrong?" Sydney says, reaching for me.

Drew's eyebrows disappear in his hair and he looks panicked. "Oh god, Evie…"

"He found out about Jesse and…and…Lucy," I say, the words coming out slowly and calmly. I look up at the both of them. "We're over."

Jesse is picking me up in ten minutes, and Lucy has been in our shared bathroom for about twenty minutes. He says he has something important to talk to me about and I look like a total wreck. I wish I could at least drag a brush through my hair.

"Lucy!" I pound on the door again. "Seriously, you've been in there forever."

The door finally swings open and she's standing in the doorway. "Sorry," she mutters.

I take a step back. She's been crying and she's not even trying to hide it. "What's wrong?"

"Nothing," she answers, trying to push past me, something clutched tightly in her hand.

I grab her shoulders and pull her back to me. "Don't do that. What's wrong? You never cry and you're crying right now."

She holds out a plastic baggie to me, wordlessly. I take it from her, confused, before peering into it. My heart stops when I see the thin white plastic stick. There's a bright pink cross on it and I may not have seen these in real life, but I know exactly what it is. "Lucy. Oh my god. Are you pregnant?"

Lucy nods, bursting into another fresh bout of tears. She clutches the wall for support. The pregnancy test is gripped tightly in my hand and I'm not sure what to do. I feel the buzz of my phone in my back pocket, but I don't reach for it. Jesse can wait. He's not important right now. "I can't believe this is happening," she whispers.

She slides against the wall, collapsing against it. Her knees are pulled up to her chest and she looks like a mess. I've never seen her look like this, and it scares me. "Who's the father, Lucy?" She shakes her head and I ask her again.

"Please don't hate me." Her voice is so low that I barely hear her.

"Why would I hate you?" I ask, confused.

"You…you said your date with Jesse went awful," she says, quickly, wiping her tears on her arm. "I didn't mean to…I didn't mean for it to happen. But we kept dancing at the fourth of July party and one thing just led to another and…I figured you guys only went on one date and…"

My eyes are on her, and I can feel her arm underneath my palm, but it suddenly feels like my senses are dulled. Ice is filling my heart and trickling into my veins. This isn't happening. It can't be happening. "Lucy," I whisper, my voice thick. "Is Jesse…" I can't even say the words. Saying the word makes it real and I can't say it. It's not real. It can't be real.

She nods, pressing her cheek into the wall and squeezing her eyes shut, a new wave of tears crashing down her cheeks.

Just then the door opens and Jesse walks. I'm shocked. He never comes in. We always meet a few blocks away. What is he doing here? He glances between Lucy and me and his face falls. He comes over to us, and I want to reach for him but he's already reaching for Lucy. His arms go around her, and she presses her face tightly into his chest. "It's okay, baby. It's going to be okay." His eyes meet mine, pleading, and I'm numb. "You're going to be okay."

"TELL ME IT'S NOT TRUE," I BEG.

"I can't tell you that, Evie," Jesse answers. We're sitting in my backyard, back in trees where no one can see us. I'm sitting on an old stump and he's standing in front of me, too far away for me to touch.

"Why?" I ask, choking on tears. "Just…why?"

"I don't know. There was something about her," he finally says after a moment. "But I love you."

I want to hit him. I want to throw myself at him and tear him apart, but I also want to push him into the ground and take him all for myself. He makes me sick, but I love him. I can't handle these feelings. My hands are lost in my hair and I'm shaking. "You can't do that. You can't."

"I could be with you…"

"You can't, Jesse! You can't. My sister is going to have a baby! Your baby!" I scream at him.

He shoves his hands in his pockets and suddenly he doesn't look twenty anymore. He doesn't look like a confident adult. He looks like a kid; a scared little kid and I don't know how to feel about him when he looks like this. "She's already decided. She's going to give the baby up. She's going for adoption."

I look up at him. "But Jesse…" He cheated on you, Evie, with your own sister. I tell myself. I repeat it over and over again.

"We'll be together, Evie. I promise you. I love you so much." He crosses the space between us and kneels in front of me, pressing his lips to mine. I clutch to him, my tears mixing with his.

. . .

*"EVIE, YOU CAN'T TRUST HIM. WHAT IS WRONG WITH YOU?"
Sydney says, her voice high.*

*"I love him, Sydney," I answer her, my face pressed tightly in my
pillow.*

*"He cheated on you, with your own sister," Drew reminds me.
He's parroting my own words back at me and I don't think I like it.
"He doesn't love you. And even if he does…"*

"What?" I yell at him. "What?"

"You should tell Lucy," Sydney pleads. "You should tell her."

"I can't do that," I whisper. "It'll kill her."

*"It's killing you." Drew looks worried, and his hand is rubbing
my back in small circles. "You don't deserve this."*

*"Neither does she," I shoot back and neither one of them argues
with me.*

*"DO YOU WANT TO HOLD THE BABY?" THE NURSE ASKS. "BEFORE
we hand her over?"*

*I look down at Lucy, who is staring at the ceiling. She hasn't
looked at her baby at all and I'm afraid for her right now. My sister
is strong but she's never been through something like this. After the
blow out from my parents—and the entire town—finding out that
the star pitcher impregnated the coach's teenager daughter, they
made the decision to give the baby up. It was decided that adoption
was the best idea for all parties involved but I often thought that she
only was going with what both our parents and Jesse wanted.
Watching her right now, I still think she's unsure. Her hand is still
clutched tightly in mine and I'm pretty sure all the bones in my
fingers are permanently damaged. I can't bring myself to care. Not
when I can feel my sister's heart breaking. "Lucy?"*

*"No," she whispers. Tears are rolling down her cheeks. "No, I
don't…I can't hold her."*

The nurse nods, knowingly, wrapping the baby tightly in a blanket. She starts to walk out of the room.

"Wait. Evie," Lucy suddenly says, her hand reaching for my arm. "The letter."

"Right," I agree. I reach into my pocket, where a letter is stored. It's addressed to Stacey and Charles Nicholson, the couple adopting Lucy's child, her daughter that was just born moments before. I hand it over to the nurse. "This is for the Nicholson's."

The nurse tucks it into the pocket of her scrubs, smiling sadly. "Of course." She pauses. "Are you sure she wouldn't like to hold the baby?"

I look down at the baby; amazed at how much this tiny little girl looks both incredibly like Lucy and just like Jesse. She's perfect and she's moments away from leaving our lives forever. "I don't think that's a good idea." She nods one more time and leaves the room, taking my niece away. I turn around and Lucy is already turned on her side, curled up in the fetal position.

"Evie," she pleads. "Please."

"Oh Lucy," I sigh, sadly. I cross the room, and quickly climb into the bed with her. I wrap my arms around her and hold her, letting her cry, knowing that my heart is breaking at the same time as hers.

"We can't be together," I tell Jesse. He's sitting in a chair in the waiting room. I want him to argue with me, to tell me that I'm wrong but I'm not surprised when his next words come out.

"I know," he whispers.

I feel like someone has reached into my chest and pulled out my heart and stomped on it. I feel like there's a thousand people pointing at me and laughing at me. I've never felt like this before and I know I never want to feel this again. "You chose her, Jesse. The moment you decided that I wasn't enough for you. The moment that you cheated on me with her and got her pregnant… that's when you chose her. I can't do that to her."

"I can't either. I'm on the team, Evie, and she's my coach's daughter. I can't…I can't leave her. Not when her heart is broken like this. Not when baseball is everything to me. Your dad would ruin me if I…if I…" he can't even finish the sentence.

I'm angry. I'm hurt. Stupid baseball. It's always more important. In this stupid town, that's all anyone can think about. It was the only thing I cared about until Jesse and now he was ruining it, he was ruining everything. "Well, you always did love baseball more than me."

He's staring at the ground. In this last moment, he can't even give me the decency of looking into my eyes. "You can't tell her, Evie. It'll kill her. I know she's your sister, but you can't ever tell her."

Then choose me, I want to scream at him, but I know it's fruitless. He's already standing up; he's already walking away from me.

CHAPTER SIXTEEN

"Evie. There you are."

I curse inwardly and make to leave the room.

"Hey, no, stop, don't leave."

It's been three days since Austin and I fell apart. I've been avoiding everyone. I go to class; I avoid looking at Austin when he walks into Art History and takes a seat in the front row instead of his usual seat behind me. We've already turned in our term paper so there's no excuse for me to speak to him. I go to work and run through the line-ups and clean the locker room. I am on autopilot and I'm fine with that.

I've never felt like this before. When Jesse and I broke up all those years ago, it felt like my world had completely ended. It felt like the worst thing that could ever happen and I had to keep it all to myself. I cried alone at night, in the bathroom, when Lucy was asleep. I spent way too much time away from my home, staying with Drew and Sydney as much as possible. I didn't think I could ever feel worse than the way I felt at the end of that summer.

I was so completely wrong. I miss Austin. I miss him

more than I ever thought I could miss a person, and it's made worse by the fact that I see him almost every day. He's not talking to me. He won't even look at me, and he might as well be a thousand miles away.

I feel too much. It's overwhelming and it's so much that I just push it down and I've become a numb shell of who I was. Everyone keeps trying to get me to talk, to do something but I don't want to do anything except to go to class, and do my job, and go back to the dorm. This is the life I had planned on having when I came to this stupid college and I just wanted to go back to that. When I decided to go to this college—though, really, I didn't have much of a choice—I'd resolved to get through the four years with nothing but classes and work. I wanted to go in and out as easily and quickly as possible. No making new friends. No dating. No baseball. It's all I wanted and I broke those rules over and over again by working with the team and falling in love with Austin. It was just easier to go back to that original goal. It was the easiest way to escape all this hurt.

Sydney and Drew were working hard to bring me out of that.

I force a smile at Sydney. "Sorry, I didn't know you were in here. I'll go study in the library."

"Go study in the library? Who are you?" she says, sounding irritated. "When have you ever not been okay studying in this room?"

"I just didn't want to bother you," I say after a moment.

"Cut the bullshit, Evie, I know you better than pretty much anyone," Sydney spits out. She pushes past me and slams the door to our dorm closed. I wince at the loud noise it makes and look up at her. "You've been avoiding me for the past three days. All I want to do is find out what happened, but you won't even talk to me."

I step around her and resign myself to studying in our

room. At this point, I wouldn't put it past her to follow me all the way to the library. "There is absolutely nothing to talk about," I respond, setting my textbooks down on my desk. I turn to face her. She's watching me, waiting. "What?"

"Talk to me," she pleads. "You come home looking worse than I've ever seen you. All you tell me is that Austin knows everything and that you two are over." She takes a deep breath and tucks a loose strand of hair behind her ear. "What I don't understand is how you could possibly be over if you told him the truth."

My teeth bite into the soft skin of my bottom lip and I can taste the blood in my mouth. "I didn't. I didn't tell him the truth. He just…sort of assumed."

She crawls onto my bed, crossing her legs, and leans toward me. I collapse into my desk chair. "What do you mean?"

I take a deep breath. Sydney has known so much about Austin and I, but she doesn't know everything. Sure, I've told her the good things, but I've been keeping everything hidden, again. When will I ever learn? Keeping secrets hasn't done me any good the past three years and I just keep digging the hole until I can't climb out anymore.

"He thinks that Jesse and I have been sneaking behind Lucy's back this entire time. He overheard a conversation between the two of us. Jesse was being…Jesse and he said things. He talked a lot about feelings and…" I trail off, squirming uncomfortably.

Sydney sighs. "Well, I could see why Austin would be upset about overhearing something like that. I can see why he might get the wrong idea." She sighs again, brushing her long hair out of her face. She chews her bottom lip, thinking. "Why was that conversation even happening, Evie?

You've been doing so well! You *love* Austin, not Jesse. What happened?"

I swallow hard, but it does me little good. The tears are already forming, and I can't stop them. I've been holding them in this entire time, afraid that if I started, I wouldn't stop. I kept pushing the pain and the hurt down, hoping that I could just handle it. "Because he has a video, Sydney. He has a video of Austin and I…" The words get caught in my throat. "He has a video of Austin and I having sex."

"*Excuse me*?" Sydney's voice is low but dangerous. Her green eyes flash. "How the fuck did he even get that?" It dawns on her before I can answer. "The dugout. There's cameras in the dugout."

I nod, reaching for a dirty t-shirt out of my laundry bag at the end of the bed, and use it to wipe the tears and snot now smeared all over my face. "He said he would show it to my dad and…he would ruin Austin's career if I didn't break up with him. Austin didn't overhear that part, of course. I *had* to do it, Syd. I had to. Austin's career is so important to him. I wasn't going to ruin it for him."

A fresh bout of tears spills over my cheeks. "It doesn't even matter though. Because he wants nothing to do with me. He thinks I'm this…this person that would do something like that to my sister, to him. That's who he thinks I am. And I can't change that because, one, he won't give me the chance and two, even if I do, Jesse is just going to ruin his life anyway." I raise the shirt to my face but it's so wet with tears at this point, that its completely useless.

Sydney looks around for tissues but, of course, this is a dorm room and there are none in sight. She grabs my bath towel, hanging at the end of my bed and hands it to me. I take it gratefully, wiping away the black circles left underneath my eyes from my mascara.

Sydney stays quiet for a long time, tracing circles on her

sweatpants with her fingertip. She's lost in thought, processing everything.

"Okay, well first off, Jesse is an asshole, which we already knew but we're going to do something about that video because that scumbag is not going to use it to hurt you or Austin or I swear to god, I will murder him. I don't care how important he is to the team. I'll murder him."

I blink a couple times. "Wow, Sydney…"

She rolls her eyes, but her expression immediately turns hesitant. "Evie, I think…"

"You think what?" I ask her. I'm nervous to hear what she has to say. If there's one thing that Sydney always is, without fail, it's blunt. She may not always tell you what you want to hear but she always tells you what you need to hear.

"You need to talk to Austin," she says, firmly. "He has only bits and pieces of the story. He thinks you're still in love with Jesse and that's not even true. He thinks that you're…you're this horrible person and you're not. You were naïve and misled. You had your heart broken. He needs that story. He definitely needs to know about the video and Jesse's ridiculous blackmail."

I turn away from her, facing my laptop. The screen is black, and I don't even have the energy to slide my hand across the mousepad to turn the screen on. "He won't even talk to me."

"He doesn't have to talk. He needs to listen. And you go over there, and you make him listen." Her voice is loud and fierce and it's a shock after keeping to myself for a few days. "You need to show him that he's the one you want."

I don't answer and she reaches forward, grabbing my chin in her hand and yanking my face around to look at her.

"Ow," I say, glaring at her, as her nails bite into my cheeks.

She ignores me. "He *is* the one you want, right?"

My brow furrows. "Yes. Of course. Of course, he's the one I want," I admit. Her fingers clench around my face and I resist the urge to push her off me. "I want Austin. That's not a question. But Jesse…"

"Seriously? *Seriously*?" she practically screams at me. "God, what is wrong with you…"

I yank my face away from her grip and get scratched across the cheek in the process. "Jesus, Sydney. Give me a break. I'm trying to figure things out. He has a video of the two of us having sex and he wants to use it to ruin Austin's career!"

"Figure things out? Are you insane?" She's hitting all the high octaves today, and I flinch at the sound. "You're more important to Austin than some stupid blackmail by your shitty ex-boyfriend. God, Evie, you're more important to him than his career, don't you know that by now?"

"Do you have to yell at me?" I say, clapping my hands over my ears, like a child.

"I can't do this." She shakes her head and pulls her phone out of her back pocket. She types furiously into it, before setting it in her lap. "This is way beyond me. You need your other best friend too."

Drew knocks on our door less than ten minutes later and he's so fast that I wonder if he was hanging around campus, just waiting for that text message from Sydney. He's wearing jeans and a black Quakes shirt, and a ball cap on his messy blonde hair.

Sydney practically attacks him as soon as he walks into the door and he looks taken aback. She grabs his arm and drags him over to me. "Please. Talk some sense into her. She's acting like a nutcase."

"You know, Syd, maybe calling Evie a nutcase isn't the

right way to get her to listen to you," Drew mutters under his breath.

"She's being crazy! Acting like there's an actual choice to make between Austin and Jesse." Sydney collapses on her bed and waves her hand in my direction. "I can't handle this. It's your turn."

Drew's hands are shoved deep in his pockets and he stares at me for a long moment. Sydney knows me well, but no one, not even Lucy, knows me nearly as well as Drew. Drew listens and watches when I think no one else is listening or watching and I can't lie to him. I squirm under his scrutiny. This is exactly why I've been avoiding them for days.

"Come on, let's go," he finally says, backing up toward the door.

Both Sydney and I stare at him in confusion.

"Wait, what?" Sydney asks, disbelieving.

"Go where?" I ask warily.

Drew tears his gaze away from me and looks at Sydney. I can't handle how she can't see the infatuation that is so obvious in his gaze. I've never seen anyone look at Sydney that way before and it was only getting worse. In high school, it was clear to me that he had a puppy dog crush on Sydney but that wasn't true anymore. He loves her; he really and truly loves her. I recognize the way that he looks at her because I've seen it and Sydney is completely oblivious. I'm scared for him. I'm scared that he'll someday feel exactly the way I feel right now.

I wouldn't wish this heartbreak on anyone.

"You asked me to come here to help, Syd. Now let me help." He turns back to me. "Just come on, okay? Trust me."

He's one of the very few people I fully trust so I reluctantly stand up and grab my bag, slinging it across my shoulder. I chance a glance at Sydney, who is glaring at me. "I guess I'll be back."

Her frown deepens. "I don't know where he is taking you, but hopefully it's a Jesse detox center."

"Sydney," Drew warns but she's already turned away from us, absorbed with something on her phone.

When we pull up to our destination, I feel disappointed. I feel probably exactly the way Austin felt when I brought him here just a couple months ago. "Why are we here?"

Drew opens his door and starts to get out of the car. "Because, when life is shitty, it's good to hit a few balls."

I sigh, angrily, and get out of the car, and follow him into the batting cages. "Does that mean I can hit you in your balls?"

He shakes his head. "Not today. Maybe tomorrow. I might need them today," he says, seriously, and I resist the urge to laugh. He says some of the stupidest, goofiest things but he never fails to make me laugh.

He quickly sets us up in a lane and hands the bat and helmet over to me. "Go for it."

I take them, unsure. "You don't want to talk to me? Tell me I'm crazy, or that I'm being stupid, and that I need to talk to Austin or any of that."

Drew leans forward, opening the cage door and practically shoving me inside. He sighs, as he takes a seat. "Sure. I'd like to, but I know talking to you right now is just pointless. You've been avoiding me, and Sydney, and pretty much everyone all week. The last thing you want is to listen to us." He points at the machine. "Just hit some baseballs, okay?"

I think about it for a few seconds and then pull the helmet snug over my head. I feed money into the machine, and get into stance, ready and waiting.

I lose track of time. I know I go through more than a

few rotations, but I don't care. My muscles ache and I'm sweaty but it feels amazing to be in that batting cage. It felt good coming here with Austin but now? Now I remember how much I genuinely love doing this and how good I am. My connections with the ball aren't beautiful, but each satisfying crack is a small accomplishment. I'm not thinking about anything, except hitting the ball each time it comes flying at me.

With my muscles now aching and a new bead of sweat dripping down my temple, I stop and lean against the fence. I'm exhausted and disgusting but I feel much better. I look over at Drew, who hasn't moved from his seat. His arms are crossed over his chest and he's looking at me, a small smile on his face. I return it.

"You're still so damn good at that," he says.

"I know," I answer, and he laughs. "I want to play, Drew. I miss playing."

"You should play," he replies, simply, and I take a moment to let that sink in. It should just be that simple. I want to play. I should play.

"Thanks," I eventually say.

He nods. "Feel better?"

I still feel like someone reached into my chest and yanked my heart out and stomped all over it. The ache of missing Austin is still there. Everything feels so much clearer though. Spending time in that batting cage has taken all the scrambled thoughts of Austin and Jesse and made them feel more manageable. I need to speak to Austin and explain. I need to talk to Jesse and tell him that he can't keep doing this to me, to Lucy. I do feel better. I have a plan and I know what I need to do. Swinging a bat and hitting some balls has helped relieved a lot of the stress and anger and the feeling of just not knowing what the right thing to do is. I can take a breath and face it head on. It doesn't feel like chaos in my head anymore. "I think so."

"Good, then are you ready to listen?" he asks, standing up and taking the bat and helmet from me. I nod. "You need to talk to Austin."

I open my mouth to protest and he immediately interrupts me.

"You know I'm right, Evie. You knew that Sydney was right too. You have to talk to Austin and set the record straight. You need to tell him about Jesse and Lucy and the video, and you need to tell him how you feel about him—how you *really* feel," Drew points out. He hands the equipment back and we head outside. He bypasses the door and walks to the back, hopping onto the trunk. I follow him and lift myself up. Our hips are pressed together, and his arm comes around me, holding me tight against him.

"I don't know if he's going to believe me," I whisper, pressing my forehead against Drew's arm, and he squeezes me tighter.

"He might not," Drew admits, "but he loves you, Evie. Any idiot with a pair of eyes can see that. I'm willing to bet that he'll believe you." He lets silence fall between us before continuing. "Secrets are what caused all of your problems and trouble three years ago. You know that. So much could have been prevented if there had been a lot more honesty going around back then."

He was so definitely not wrong about that and I nearly laughed at the thought.

"The last thing you want now is all these secrets that you have to keep from everyone." Drew's eyes meet mine. "You're crazy about him, Evie. How much worse can it get if you tell him the truth? You have to take risks when you love someone."

I feel much better, like a weight has been lifted off my

shoulders but I still feel like I'm being knocked in the chest with a baseball bat repeatedly. "What about you and Sydney?"

Drew growls, frustrated, and his fingers tighten their grip on his knees. "I can't make Sydney do anything she doesn't want to do."

I raise my head from where it's resting on his shoulder and look at him in shock. Ever since Sydney moved to Santa Isabella, he's been denying it up and down that he has feelings for her and now...

"Drew?" I ask, hesitantly.

He smiles wryly down at me. "Come on, it's not like it was a secret."

I purse my lips together to keep from smiling but I can't help it and it bursts through. "It was obvious. I *am* your best friend, you know. So, where's all your talk about risks and love when it comes to her?"

His jaw tightens. "I told you. I can't make Sydney do anything." I wait for him to continue but he doesn't. He just stares out across the parking lot. You can see part of the boardwalk from this parking lot and a tiny sliver of the ocean, shining in the midday sun.

I think of the way Sydney has been acting like lately and pieces are starting to fall together. "Did something happen between you two?"

Drew laughs, but there isn't a whole ton of humor in it. "You'll have to ask Sydney about that." I open my mouth to ask another question, but he cuts me off. "It's fine. Stop worrying about Sydney and me. Just worry about you and Austin, okay?"

I sigh, leaning my head against his shoulder again. "Okay, Drew. If you say so."

"I do say so," he says, looking grateful that I'm dropping the subject. He pats my thigh a couple times before hopping off the trunk. He holds his hand out to me. "Jump down. I have something for you in the trunk."

I raise an eyebrow at him, taking his hand, and letting him help me off the trunk. He pulls his keys out of his pocket and presses the trunk release. He rummages around for a while—my god, his car is always an absolute mess—before finally letting out a triumphant cry and backing up out of the trunk. I see what he's holding, and I can't help it. Tears spring up in the corners of my eyes.

"Take it," Drew says, holding it out to me. "It's yours, it's been waiting for you."

I reach for it and clutch it tightly to my chest. It smells the same as I remember, like old leather. I haven't laid eyes on my old mitt in three years. I thought it was gone forever. "Where did you…I threw this away!"

Drew shrugs. "I dug it out of the trash. You threw it away when you were upset. You were so upset, and you tore down your posters and threw away your pennants and so many things and I knew one day you'd regret it." He shrugs again. "You love baseball too much. I knew you'd be back one day."

Tears are streaming down my cheeks and I've never been more grateful in my life to have Drew in my life, to have him as my best friend. He truly does know me better than anyone to have gone digging in the trash to save the one possession that means the world to me. I haven't thought of my baseball glove in so long but holding it here in my hands brings instant regret at throwing it away. "Drew, I can't—thank you."

He smiles, sheepishly. "There's no reason to thank me. Though you could come back and play. I'd call it even then."

I consider this. "I just might be able to make that happen."

CHAPTER SEVENTEEN

"Blue or red?" Sydney asks, holding up two dresses in front of her. I can't see much difference between them other than the actual color and I shrug. "Seriously, Evie? Just choose one, please."

"The blue one then," I say, pointing at it from my perch on her bed.

"Perfect," she trills, tossing the red one on the bed next to me and pulling the chosen dress over her head. She pulls her long hair from the collar and it goes flying everywhere. She's the only girl I know that can pull off wild red hair like that, but she works it.

"Where are you going?" I ask her, leaning back on her pillows.

"On a date." She smiles mischievously at me before grabbing her perfume off the top of her dresser and spritzes it on her wrists.

I raise my eyebrow. "With Drew?"

She whirls around to look at me, and there's no mistaking the look on her face. She's pissed. "Why on earth would you think it was with Drew? What did Drew tell you?"

I fight hard to keep a smile off my face. I shouldn't find this so amusing, but something has obviously happened between the two of them and I'm dying to find out what. "Should he have told me something?"

Her face flushes a bright red but her firm expression remains in place. "No. Of course not."

I remind myself, not for the first time and certainly not the last time, that she'll come and talk to me when she's good and ready. She's avoiding something right now and I have one very good guess that it's Drew. I let it go for now. "Who are you going out with then?"

She waves her hand dismissively, her anger disappearing as fast as it appeared. "I don't know. Some guy from my biology class."

I roll my eyes, but I don't say anything other than "be safe". She laughs, kissing me on top of the head before heading out the door.

The room is always much quieter without Sydney's presence, and I reach for my laptop. There's probably something on Netflix that I can watch and if not, I haven't killed a couple of hours on Pinterest in a while so that might be a nice way to shut out the deafening silence in the room.

I've barely typed "*Netflix*" into the address bar when there's a loud knock at the door. I frown, setting my laptop aside. I wasn't expecting anyone, and I wonder if Sydney has left behind her keys again. I cross our small dorm room and open the door, peering outside. My eyes widen and I take a step back.

"Can I come in?" Jesse asks.

I nod wordlessly and step backward towards the bed as he makes his way inside. "No, leave it open," I say quickly, as he starts to close my door. He studies my face, as if he were getting ready to argue with me about it before just shrugging and leaving the door propped open.

"What are you doing here, Jesse?" I ask him, folding my arms across my chest. There isn't much space to move in here and I can feel the heat of his body so close to mine in this small area. "Did you come here to blackmail me some more?"

He shoves his hands in his pockets and looks around nervously. He's never been in here before and he looks incredibly out of place. "I heard about you and Austin. I am glad to hear it, but I still wanted to see if you were okay."

I snort and it's loud and unattractive. "Did you come here to gloat?"

"Of course not, Evie," he says, softly, taking a seat on the edge of my bed. "I just wanted to talk to you." I don't say anything, and he continues. "Come sit next to me."

I hesitate. "I don't think that's a good idea."

Jesse looks hurt. "Come on, Evie. I'm not going to hurt you."

Not intentionally, I think to myself, but I take a few steps and sit next to him. My palms are pressed together, held tightly together in my lap. "What do you want to talk about?"

"I see things so clearly now. Things are falling into place. There have been scouts coming to the games; ones from Houston and San Francisco, and all kinds of teams. It's finally coming together, you know?" He looks up at me as if expecting me to agree. He continues, hastily. "Now that baseball is finally where it needs to be…I realize more and more what I want."

There is a lump in my throat, and it feels like my heart has dislodged itself from its normal spot in my chest and settled in a new home in my stomach. "What is that?" I whisper.

"It's you, Evie." His voice is soft and fierce. "I love you. I've always loved you. You have always deserved the very best, much better than a guy like Austin, who, let's face it, isn't going anywhere."

I pull back. The comment about Austin not going anywhere pisses me off but I'm confused. This isn't how this should be going. "Wait. Is that what this is about? Do you actually love me or are you just jealous of Austin?"

Jesse stares at me, confused. "What? No. No way. I know how I feel about you, Evie." His gaze drops down to his lap and back up to mine. "I messed up, but I'm here now."

"Jesse, I don't know…" I start to say but he's leaning across the space dividing us. His hand wraps tightly around the back of my neck and he pulls me into him. My lips connect with his for the first time in years. His lips are still so warm, soft, and full and they part for me, our tongues meeting. There is a low groan in the back of his throat. "Evie…" His tongue swipes against my lower lip and he pulls me tighter against him, greedy.

"Wait, *wait*…" I say, pulling away from him. "This is too…this is too fast for me."

He raises an eyebrow at me, but he's breathing too heavily to properly speak. "I don't want to wait for you anymore." He's back on top of me, and I fall back, sinking into my soft comforter. His kisses are fast and rushed and I'm finding it hard to breathe and not in a good way. Fingers are tugging at the low collar of my shirt, already dipping into my lacy bra. Nothing about this feels sexy. It feels possessive and rushed and completely wrong.

"No," I say, firmly, yanking my face away from his. "Stop."

He raises his head and looks down at me, perplexed.

"Come on, Evie, what's wrong? It's you and me, again. We're meant to be."

I shove an elbow into the empty space between us and manage to squeeze myself out from underneath him. I stand up, running a hand through my messy hair. I feel slightly out of control from the brief encounter and there is a sick feeling in my stomach. "We are *not* meant to be, Jesse. You're with Lucy. You've been with Lucy. This is wrong."

Jesse shakes his head. "It's always been you. Always, and I know I messed up but I'm here now." He sits up and reaches for me.

I step back again, right out of his grasp. I'm suddenly angry. Everything that I've been feeling the past few years comes rushing at me and it's overwhelming, but I know exactly what is going on.

I don't love Jesse Valdez anymore. I haven't for a very long time. Part of me wonders if I ever did or if I'd had my head up in the clouds, thinking that the giddiness I felt when I was around him was love. I don't know anymore.

"No," I say firmly. "That means nothing to me, Jesse. That means *nothing*. You broke my heart three years ago, and I kept thinking over and over again for years: What if there wasn't a baby?

What if, what if, what if.

I never stopped to think about was that things would have been so different if you just would have been honest to begin with."

He stares at me, his arms hanging uselessly on his sides. His hair is messy from our brief tussle and his shirt is rumpled and he looks nothing like the boy I was convinced I was so massively in love with when I was sixteen years old. "What?"

"From day one, Jesse, it was all about *you*. You were the baseball star and that's all that mattered to you. God, that's all that mattered to me! You wanted to keep me a secret and I went along with it because I was young and naïve, and I loved you. I loved you so much. You also never believed in me. The only thing I wanted, the only thing I *ever* wanted, was to play baseball and I was good. You know that I was good, but you made me feel silly and stupid and I thought you loved me, so I started to think it was silly and stupid. I quit the one thing that has always made me so happy."

I take a deep breath and continue. "Don't you understand? Keeping me a secret? It ruined *everything*. You kept me a secret and you just did what you always do. You just take whatever you want. You wanted both Cordova twins. Well they both had to keep it a secret—keep *you* a secret, so no one would never know."

A sob escapes my throat and I swallow hard. I will not cry in front of him. Not anymore. He has seen way too many of my tears. "I kept thinking Lucy getting pregnant was this tragedy that got in the way of our epic love, but I was so wrong." The revelation hits me as I speak. "I was so wrong! You were selfish, and you wanted both of us and you kept us both a secret. You broke my heart and you broke Lucy's. You knew you could never leave her after the baby, but you kept me hoping for years."

"Evie, I didn't..." Jesse starts to say.

"You did," I interrupted him. "What is wrong with you, Jesse? How could you do that? How could you sit there and tell me you loved me and promise me the world and then turn around and say the same things to my own twin sister? My best friend?"

"I was young. I was stupid," he says.

I face him. He looks defeated but his gaze doesn't waver. He never looks away from me. "I'm the same age as you were back then. Yeah, I'll agree with you. I'm young and

I'm stupid and I've made a lot of stupid mistakes. But I would *never*, ever do that to someone I supposedly loved."

"I did love you!" he says loudly. He stands up and walks toward me, but I hold my hands out to him. "Evie, of course I loved you."

I shake my head. "Not enough—never enough. You made all the wrong choices and forced me to give you up because you knew I love Lucy more than I could ever love you. You *ruined* my friendship with her. You ruined baseball for me. The last three years of my life have been *hell* because of what *you* did."

Jesse is quiet. I've never spoken like this to him, ever. The short amount of time that we spent together was all under his control. I was meek and shy in his presence, agreeing to whatever he said, to whatever he wanted, because he was older, and I thought he knew better. I had tricked myself into believing that he had wanted what was best for me. "You're the one I've always wanted."

I choke out a laugh. "Well, you certainly had a funny way of showing it, Jesse. You chose her, and you got her pregnant. When she gave up that baby, her heart was broken, and you made me promise never to tell her what a total scumbag you are—and I made that promise because I knew it would kill her."

Jesse opens his mouth to speak but another voice, a voice that I know as well as my own, that rings out in the silence between us.

"What the fuck is going on in here?"

Lucy and Austin are standing in the doorway of my dorm room. Both are staring at us, in shock.

"What are you doing here?" I ask them.

It takes a moment before either of them answers. Lucy's eyes are on Jesse and it's like Austin and I aren't even in the room. They stare at each other for a long time before Lucy finally speaks up. "Jesse said he was going out with some guys on the team tonight and I figured I'd come and keep you and Sydney company." Her voice is flat, like she's not even aware of what she's saying.

Austin seems to wake out of his stupor, and he lunges for Jesse. Jesse stumbles back, and nearly falls on the bed.

"Austin, what are you doing?" I shriek, jumping out of the way.

He's not listening to me. His face is red and he's staring at Jesse like he's a completely new person. On the field, when they're together, they work as a team. They work off each other and make each other better. They're two of the older members of the Quakes and there's a mutual respect between them.

I can't see any of that respect right now. Austin is the one in charge and he's staring down at Jesse with a murderous expression on his face.

"Is it true?" Austin is yelling in his face. "Valdez, *is it true*?"

Jesse's collar is held tight between Austin's fingers, but he isn't even looking at Austin. His eyes are still on Lucy, who looks like she's about to fall apart at any second. I don't know who to go to. I don't know what to say.

"Lucy…" Jesse starts to say, his voice strangled.

"Answer the question," Lucy says. There are tears in the corners of her eyes and her voice wavers a little, but she remains firm. Her eyes are defiant.

I want to sink into the floor and disappear. She shouldn't have found out, not like this. My heart breaks for my sister all over again.

"Answer the question, Valdez." Austin's teeth are practically grinding as he spits out the words. "Goddammit, Jesse. If you can't tell me, at least tell *her*."

"It's true," Jesse whispers, and it's so soft that I almost miss it.

All the color drains out of Lucy's face and she looks like she's about to fall over. She reaches for the bed and lowers herself. Her breathing picks up and her hand is pressed tight against her stomach.

"Lucy. Lucy, I'm so sorry," Jesse says, trying to pull himself away from Austin.

Austin's not letting go though. "What is wrong with you?" he asks, darkly. "Why would you do that? You think it's fun to take advantage of two teenage girls?"

It's impressive how well Jesse is managing to ignore Austin, who is inches away from his face, and has a firm grip of Jesse's shirt in his fingers. "Please, look at me," Jesse begs.

"I think…" Lucy says, sounding surprisingly calm. "I think you should leave, *now*."

Austin finally looks away from Jesse and throws an incredulous look at my twin. "Lucy…"

Lucy's eyes meet his and I see a degree of affection in her eyes. There's something about this that makes me happy, like an unspoken approval from my twin sister. She nods. "It's okay, Austin." Her tone is hard when she speaks to Jesse. "You really need to go, Jesse."

Austin lets go of Jesse, and Jesse straightens out his rumpled shirt. He heads for Lucy, who looks panicked, but Austin grabs his arm before he can reach her. "*Get. Out.*"

Jesse's eyes meet mine just once before he leaves, and I know then that there is absolutely nothing between us anymore except a shared past. I don't love him anymore. I don't. And the way he looks at Lucy, and the way he looks at me tells me exactly which Cordova girl he is in love with.

"Please. Just—just leave," Lucy pleads, the words thick with tears.

He hesitates for a moment but between Austin's death glare and Lucy's tears, he knows he's lost. He yanks out of himself out of Austin's grip, and walks out of my dorm room, leaving only silence behind him.

A few minutes pass before both Austin and Lucy both turn to me. They had forgotten about me while focusing on Jesse but now they're both looking at me and even I can't read the expression on their faces. The two people I love most in the whole world and I can't figure out what they think of me at this moment.

Austin said he wanted to know all my secrets. Now that they are all here in front of him, I'm not sure that he wanted to know anymore.

"Austin," Lucy says, putting her hand on his arm. He jumps, startled, and looks down at her. "I need to speak with Evie. Alone."

My stomach dips at the words. I wish Austin could stay in here and save me from this. I don't know what he thinks but I can lose Austin. I don't want to, it would hurt a thousand times worse than losing Jesse, but I can. I can be okay.

I can't lose Lucy. Not my sister — my twin. *My other half.* Not when I've spent the last three and a half years protecting her from this exact heartbreak.

Austin nods in agreement and moves to leave. He still looks angry and his hands and folded into tight fists. I can see the vein twitching just above his eyebrow, and I'm worried what he's going to do when he leaves the room.

"Wait, Austin," I say, quickly, before I can stop myself.

He pauses in the doorway and turns back to look at me.

"Just…don't go after Jesse, okay? Call me later?"

He thinks about it and nods, before knocking his fist once on the door and leaving.

The boys are both gone. It's just me and Lucy now.

CHAPTER EIGHTEEN

L ucy stays quiet for a long time. I climb up on my bed, bringing my knees to my chest, wrapping my arms tightly around them. I'm afraid to be the one that says anything first. I'm afraid to disturb the silence that is between us.

She cries for a while, though she's trying hard to hide it. Her hand is pressed tightly against her mouth as her body shakes. I lean my head against the wall, closing my eyes briefly. It hurts to hear her cry like this. This is exactly what I didn't want. I've been keeping so many secrets for three years. I've been holding in my own hurt and my own heart-break for one reason one reason only, and that was to keep Lucy from having her heart broken too. Listening to her sob, it feels like it was all for nothing.

When she finally speaks, it startles me, and my eyes fly open. "What?" I ask.

"Why didn't you tell me?" she whispers, wiping her tears on the back of her hand. She looks over her shoulder at me. "Why didn't you ever tell me?"

I take my time before I answer. "I never wanted you to feel like this, to feel the way I did when Jesse walked into that room and chose you over me."

"I didn't know," Lucy says. She shifts her position and turns to face me. "Evie, I had no idea."

I nod, pressing my lips tightly together. "I know you didn't. I didn't either."

She nods. Her hair swishes around when she moves, and she tucks it behind her ears. She looks defeated and I haven't seen her look like this since the baby. "Tell me. Tell me what happened."

"Oh, Lucy, I don't know if that's such a good idea," I admit.

"I need to know, Evie. I *need* to," she says, and her voice is pleading.

I take a deep breath. "What do you want to know?"

"*Everything*," Lucy replies firmly. "I want to know absolutely everything."

I fidget a bit in place before I sigh and launch into the story. This is a story that I've never told before, so I take my time, making sure I say everything. This is what I should have told her years ago. This is what I should have told Lucy from the beginning.

I tell her how Jesse and I talked for hours that night at the bonfire at the beach. I tell her about our first date and how he made me a picnic and kissed me like no one had ever kissed me before. I told her about keeping it a secret from everyone and how I thought nothing of it because it felt forbidden and romantic. I told her about the nights in his room and how we fell in love. I told her about losing my virginity to him and about how he made me feel. I told her about the promise he made me but how I couldn't keep that promise with him.

"I couldn't do it, Lucy. He was my entire world back then but…you were having his baby." I shiver. "I knew that everything was messed up but there was one thing I could do, and that was give you Jesse. I could try and let him go."

"He's an asshole," Lucy growls out angrily.

I laugh a little. "Yeah, he's an asshole. It just took us a long time to figure it out. He got in our heads, made us feel special and basically pitted us against each other." I thought about telling her about the video and the blackmail, but she was already hurting enough. She didn't need to know anything about that.

"Why couldn't you just tell me what a terrible person he was?" Lucy asks, her brow furrowed. "Why did you let me stay with him after all this time?"

"Because…" I pause. "I didn't realize how bad the situation really was back then, you know? I was so lost in the clouds with him that all I could think of was that I was losing him. And that you needed him more than I did."

"Maybe I would have just been better off without him to begin with," she mutters to herself.

"We probably would have both been better off without Jesse Valdez in our life from the very beginning," I admit. I scoot closer to her on the bed and wrap an arm around her waist. She sags against me, her head resting on my shoulder. "But Lucy, then you wouldn't have had Molly. I know you've never regretted Molly."

Lucy stiffens slightly at the mention of her daughter. "No. I don't regret her." She doesn't elaborate on that, but I can tell there is way more on her mind. "All these years of being so madly in love with this boy, and he only stayed with me because I gave up our baby."

I shake my head. "I don't think that's true. In his own weird, completely fucked up way… I think he really loved you, Lucy. I think he still does."

Lucy laughs a little. "Then why was he here, in your room, Evie? Why was he here?"

I knew exactly why he was in my room and it had nothing to do with loving me. "If there's one thing I know about Jesse is that he hates to lose. On the stupid field, and in life, you know that, Lucy. I think there was a part of him that just expected me to wait around for him forever. And I didn't. I found Austin, and he was jealous, and he didn't like that I am in love with someone that wasn't him. That's all it was."

"I can't believe how much you've been hurting the past few years, Evie. I can't believe that I was the cause of so much of it."

"No!" I interrupt her, fiercely. "You didn't cause any of this. This was on me—me and Jesse."

"God, but I should have known. As much as it would have hurt like hell to lose Jesse right after losing Molly, it would have meant nothing to having lost you the way I did the past three years. It would have meant nothing if you had to suffer this whole time."

I shrug my shoulders. My eyes are wet, but I don't think there's anything left in me. I don't think I can cry anymore.

I'm done crying over Jesse Valdez.

"You are more important to me than any boy could ever be, Evie. *Ever*. You are my *sister*, my twin, and my best friend. You are my other half."

My other arm comes up to wrap her completely in my arms.

"I just wanted you to be happy," I tell her. "You were a mess and I couldn't fix it. And I certainly didn't want to make it worse."

We stay like that, in each other's arms, for a while before she speaks again. "I have no idea what to do. I live with him. I had my whole life built around him."

"You'll figure it out. I know you will. We'll do it together."

She stays for the rest of the night. We talk a little more and eventually I pull up a movie on my laptop and we curl up in bed, watching it. Sydney comes home late, buzzed, and I'm surprised to see her. She looks at the two of us, confused, and I give her the quick overview of what happened that night. She quickly changes out of her dress and into pajamas and joins us in bed.

"Hey guys?" Sydney whispers after the third movie finishes.

"Yeah?" I ask, yawning.

"Boys are awful." She stretches her arms above her head and crawls out of my bed to crawl into hers. Lucy has curled up on my pillow and passed out. "Well, maybe not all of them." She gives me a pointed look.

"What is that look for?" I ask her, yanking a blanket off the end of my bed, and getting ready to sleep on the floor.

"You know what it's for," Sydney says. "Did Lucy say why Austin was with her?"

I shake my head.

Sydney shrugs, before reaching to turn off the light. "Interesting…" She turns on her side and she's asleep before I know it.

It takes me a while to fall asleep. Today has been one of the craziest days I've had. I woke up, went to class, went to practice, and came home to study. I didn't expect this, and now all the secrets and lies that have piled up over the years are now all up in the open.

Why on earth was Austin even there? Why did he walk in with Lucy? I wanted to ask him, but the moment wasn't about him. He just happened to be there. It was about Jesse and Lucy and me and now that I've calmed down and now that Lucy is asleep, I finally have time to think of other things. The only thing on my mind is Austin.

I really hope that he didn't go after Jesse.

I really wish he could have stayed.

I fall asleep and I dream of Austin all night.

CHAPTER NINETEEN

The next morning, the only thing I can think of is Austin.

He is all that matters.

Yesterday was not a good day for Lucy, and I know that I'm going to need to be there for her more than I ever had before. Her entire life has been completely flipped on its head. The person she's loved since she was sixteen is not the person she thought he was. I know that it's going to take her time to process this. She stayed the night but left early this morning. She wanted to get her things out of their apartment so she could go stay in our old room at home.

That's going to be an interesting conversation with our mother, I'm sure.

I asked her if she wanted me to go with her, but she said no, insisting that she needed to handle it on her own. Both Sydney and I stressed to her that we could be there in a flash if she changed her mind and needed us.

Overall though yesterday was very eye opening for me. Everything that has been jumbled up and messy in my head doesn't feel jumbled or messy anymore. It feels clear, like I finally know what to do. I'm not overwhelmed anymore.

I know exactly who I am and what I want. It feels liberating and the only thing I want to do is go and get it.

I'm not going to see Austin until game time later and getting through the day is incredibly difficult. I can't pay attention to any of my classes. I can't concentrate on anything. I need to talk to Austin. I need to talk to my dad. There are things that need to be said.

"Stop fidgeting," Sydney says, lazily. She's laying on her stomach in bed, a highlighter in her hand as she sifts through her book.

"I'm not fidgeting," I deny. I look down at my knees, which are bouncing uncontrollably and sigh. "Sorry."

"You're going to see him in an hour. You'll be fine." She looks over at me. "Everything is going to work out."

I toss my textbook to the side. Studying right now is pointless; I'm not getting anything done. I can't focus on the words in front of me. "I hope so."

The locker room is crowded when I enter, and I know this is not the time or place to have this conversation, but my eyes can't help but search out Austin. I don't see him, and I sigh, heading toward Dad's office.

He's on the phone with someone when I walk in. He waves at me, distracted, and hands me my trusty clipboard. I glance through it and then stop and look down at it again. Austin's name is not on the list, at all. He isn't starting and he's not even a backup. I look back up at Dad, waiting for him to finish his conversation. He sounds happy and ends the conversation with a laugh.

"Who was that?" I ask, curiously.

"That was the scout from San Francisco. He's here to watch the game tonight, since Jesse is pitching," Dad explained. He studies me for a moment. "Is something wrong?"

I look back down at the roster and then back up at him. "No." He nods and turns back to his computer. "Wait, why is Austin not on the roster?"

He raises his eyebrow at me, knowingly, but thankfully doesn't say anything. "He isn't playing tonight. Can you make sure they're ready to play out there?"

A rush of disappointment goes curling through my body and my shoulders fall. "Right. Yeah, sure." I clutch the clipboard tight to my chest and exit the office, back in the locker room once more.

Most of the guys are ready but some of them are still fooling around, tossing their socks at each other and other stupid boy things like that. I roll my eyes and climb onto the seat of one of the chairs so they can hear me.

"Everyone listen up!" I call out. Most of their heads turn in my direction and my eyes scan the locker room to make sure they're all here. I nearly fall off the chair when my eyes meet Jesse's.

He looks like a wreck, like he's been crying, which is something that I've never seen him do. Normally before a game that he's pitching, he has his earbuds in, and he's serious and focused. Not now. He looks tired and dazed. That is not what has caused me to stumble though. Jesse is rocking a massive black eye and I could count on one little finger the person that did it.

I clear my throat, tearing my eyes away from him, and call out the starting lineup. The guys finish getting ready and head out to the dugout. Jesse is one of the last to leave and I'm startled again at how intense the black eye looks on his face.

I hover in the locker room for a moment, sinking into a chair. I waited all day for this moment, to finally talk to him and he's not even here. I know he's not going anywhere, and I know that I can talk to him later or the next day or something. I feel let down. I'm standing up to head up to the dugout when the door of the locker room swings open and Austin walks in.

My heart slams in my chest at the sight of him. He's in a simple black shirt and jeans, and his hair is messy, like he's run his fingers through it several times. His dark eyes are focused on me and I drink in his gaze. This is the way he's supposed to look at me. This is what I've been missing all week. I see a flash of white and I look down, surprised to see a thick white bandage wrapped around his forearm.

I finally break the silence. "You punched Jesse, didn't you? Even though I told you not to."

"I wasn't going to." He sighs. "I really wasn't. You told me not to and I knew that it wasn't going to settle anything." He shoves his hands in his pockets and his arms flex with the movement. I hold in the urge to run to him, "but I went on a run this morning. I needed to get my mind straight, and I ran into him. I just lost it, Evie. He tried to talk to me, to apologize and I just lost it."

"You shouldn't have done that," I sigh, but secretly I'm pleased. As much as I know the saying '*violence isn't the answer*,' Jesse really could have used a good punch to the face. "That's why you're not playing tonight."

"That's why I'm not playing tonight," he repeats, shrugging his shoulders. "It's worth it." He pauses. "You don't have to worry about the video anymore."

I don't ask how he knows. Sydney, Drew, maybe even Jackass Jesse himself. It doesn't matter. I'm relieved, for the both of us. "Thank you."

His face softens. "Evie. Of course."

"There's a scout from the Giants here tonight," I point out.

He shrugs again. "There will be other games, and other scouts." He takes a step forward. "Besides, the more I think about it, the more that I realize…baseball isn't everything." I raise my eyebrow at him, and he laughs. "It's pretty close to everything but there's so much more in the world. Friends. Family. *You*." I suck in a breath, "and I want to finish school."

I let that settle around me. There is something incredibly, ridiculously appealing about Austin staying in Santa Isabella for one more year. "So…you're going to stick around for senior year?" I ask him, hopefully. He nods and there's a small smile on his face. "What about my dad? I'm sure he wasn't pleased about you punching his star pitcher."

Austin takes out a deep breath and lets it out quickly. "No, he definitely wasn't," he says, scratching the back of his neck. "I'm sure once he finds out what happened and why I punched him…well, I won't be surprised if he doesn't mind too much."

Yeah, he's not wrong about that.

"Besides," he says, "there are always the playoffs. And I'll need my good luck charm there. Though I hope next year, my good luck charm is sitting on the bench, in uniform with me."

I can't help it. A smile forms across my face. It feels good to know that I'm still his good luck charm. I'm cheesy enough to admit that. And I like his vision for next year. It's my hope too.

Austin fidgets in place for a couple seconds before meeting my eyes again. "Evie, I'm so sorry."

I put a hand up to stop him. "No, Austin…"

He quickly interrupts me. "No, let me talk for a second. I should have listened to you. I know you, princess. I knew there was so much more going on. I got too far ahead of myself and I didn't let you explain. And I should have."

"It's okay," I reply softly.

"It's really not. Is *this* why you don't play baseball anymore?"

I nod. "I wasn't lying about my dad; I may have made that more of the reason to people who asked. But…after realizing that my dad didn't really want me to play and then having Jesse treat me being a ball player like a joke…it just felt like too much."

I sigh and continue. "It was always more than that. He broke my heart. He took everything I loved and turned it into a painful reminder of that heartbreak. We were a secret, and he took advantage of that and had another secret relationship with my own sister. But he couldn't weasel his way out of that one once Lucy got pregnant. I thought it ruined me."

"God, Evie, I'm so sorry." His face looks so incredibly apologetic.

"Don't be." I stand up and walk closer to him. "It's not your fault. Maybe I once thought everything that happened ruined me, but it didn't." I take a step forward and there's only a foot or two of space between us. "I didn't realize that I just needed to breathe again. I just needed to remember how many other amazing people there are. People like *you*, Austin."

I take a deep breath. "It may have taken me awhile but you coming into my life brought me back to the right plan. I feel happier, lighter, and liberated. I have baseball in my life again. I want to play again. I want that." I look up at him and reach for his hand. "I've never loved anything or anyone like I love baseball. Until I met you."

"Say it. Please." Austin's voice is low and pleading.

For a split second, I'm panicked. I'm scared. I'm unsure. But the feelings I have for him are so undeniable and I know I'm ready to finally say the words. "I love you."

His free hand reaches out to my chin and tilts it up. My eyes meet his and it feels like hitting a home run for the first time to see him looking at me this way. "Evie. I love you so much."

His lips come crashing down on me and I'm reaching for him, pressing myself into his body. I never thought that I would get to do this again and I'm savoring every second of it, every single taste. I don't know how I ever thought someone else could make me feel this way—completely *head-over-heels* in love. Austin and I fit perfectly together. My arm brushes against the rough bandage on his forearm and I pull away.

"I thought you *punched* Jesse," I say, my forehead pressed against his. My fingertips drag gently across the bandage. "What's this all about?"

Austin hesitates before stepping backward. "I was afraid…I was afraid that I had ruined it. That I would walk in and see you and that you wouldn't be happy to see me. I didn't believe in you. I fucked up the best thing that's ever happened to me and I had to do something to show you that I do believe in you. I always will."

He starts unwrapping the bandage and I look up at him curiously. "It was probably the most extreme measure that I could take but I wanted to prove to you, Evie, that I'm not going anywhere. No matter what happens, no matter how easy or hard this is, I'm in for the long run."

He's almost got the bandage off and I can see a small splash of color underneath it. He tosses the bandage aside and holds out his forearm for me to see. I gasp, tears springing to my eyes, and I take a step backward.

"Austin, you didn't…" I manage to choke out. "That's *permanent.*"

"So are you," he says simply.

Right there, on his forearm, is a large tattoo of a baseball. It looks like a simple baseball, white with red stitching, until you look closer. One of the lines of stitching is actual letters, red, cursive, and small but they're there. They spell out one thing.

Evangeline.

"You're insane," I tell him, reaching for his wrist and looking at the tattoo closely.

"I was feeling pretty insane last night," he admits. He closes his eyes as I brush my thumb across the raised skin. "Do you like it?"

My thumb pauses over my name, and it's like it sends a shock through my fingers, up my arm, all the way to my heart. "I love it. I love *you.*"

Austin smiles, and pulls me hard, so I go crashing into him. Before I can scold him for manhandling me, his lips are back on mine and we're drinking each other up. I sigh happily, as his tongue plays at my lips, opening me up to deepen the kiss.

"Excuse me…"

We jump apart, and I laugh when I see Dad standing just outside his office, his hands planted firmly on his waist. He has a stern look on his face, but I can see the amusement in his eyes.

"Sorry, Coach," Austin says, sheepishly, taking another step away from me. My hand comes up to cover a giggle that escapes me.

"Yeah," Dad answers. "Right. Both of you need to get out to the dugout so maybe you guys can wrap this up."

"Both…of…us?" Austin repeats slowly.

Dad nods. "Yeah. You can't play, Young. You hit a teammate and whatever the reason was," he glances at me before continuing, "it's still unacceptable. But I want you in uniform and in that dugout. You're still a member of this team."

Austin's face lights up and he looks like a little kid on Christmas. He places a firm kiss on the top of my head and speeds off to get ready. He stops just before he turns around the corner. "Thanks, Coach." Dad nods again and Austin disappears.

Dad looks at me. "Do I even want to ask what this is all about?"

I laugh, loudly. "You know, Dad, it's just baseball." He turns to walk away from me. I hesitate but it's way past due to say this. I have to do it. "Dad?"

He looks back at me, a curious look on his face. "Yeah?"

"I don't want to be a sports reporter. I've never wanted to be one. I just latched onto that because I felt like you thought it was the only respectable career for your daughter that was still baseball and I thought, well, at least it'll keep me close to the one that I love more than anything, the one that I actually want to do."

He looks speechless but I can tell that he wants me to continue.

I take a deep breath. *It's now or never, Evie*, I tell myself. "Dad, I want to play baseball. I want to try out for the Quakes."

EPILOGUE

The boys come sprinting off the field, cheering and yelling. I've never seen them look this happy before but I'm not really looking at them. I'm looking at one boy and he comes straight for me, lifting me up in the air and placing a firm kiss on my lips.

I pull away, laughing. "Congratulations."

Austin's smile widens. "Thanks."

"College World series winner, Austin Young," I say, trying the words out. "How does it feel?"

Austin looks around him. The team is celebrating, and the friends and family and fans that have traveled to Nebraska, where the College World series is held each year, from Izzy are running on the field like a bunch of little kids. It is beautiful and it's the perfect moment. I'm proud of this team, I'm proud of my dad for achieving another winning season and I'm proud of Austin and Drew for being champions for the first time. There were plenty of moments during the season where we—myself, my dad, the team, the entire town—wasn't sure if we'd make it here.

We are here though, and it might be the best feeling in the entire world.

It feels much better than it did three years ago.

Austin is on the same page as me. "It feels pretty damn good." His lips are back on mine and a shiver goes running through me. I push his hat off his head and run my fingers through his sweaty hair. It's been a couple months that we've been together and while every moment hasn't been perfect, it's everything that I've ever needed. "It'll feel better when you're with us next year, princess."

I grin at the thought of that. My dad had been nothing but shocked when I told him that I wanted to play baseball again. We couldn't have a full conversation because a game was about to start but we sat down later and talked.

And talked and talked and *talked*.

It was not an easy conversation, but, it was a necessary conversation to have. My dad *had* thought that playing baseball was a hobby for me and had wanted to encourage me in what he thought was my real dream, sports journalism. He was surprised to hear that I wanted to play but he was enthusiastic to hear that I still did. He thought that I always had the talent to do it.

He told me it was going to be hard, that people were going to give me a hard time because I'm a girl and that if I thought it was hard for a man to be successful, it was going to be even harder as a female. I have to earn my way onto the team, just like any other player, but he's going to give me a chance.

A chance is all I can ask for.

I'm feeling less than confident about my ability to even make the team, let alone prove myself enough to get playing, but I'm surrounded by a team of people who do believe in me. Austin has already started to whip me back into shape, since it's been three years, and Drew has been right behind him.

Who knows? Maybe I'll be in a Quakes uniform next year.

Austin's hand is snaking up my leg, sliding underneath my dress.

"Hey now," I warn, grabbing his hand and pulling it away from its intended destination. "We're in public."

"Dammit, we are," he groans, winking at me. "But you know what?"

"What?" I smirk.

"I'm loving the boots you're wearing."

A flush runs through me and I look up at him, biting my lip. I'm wearing the same cowboy boots I wore months ago at Sydney's birthday party. I know how much he loves them.

"Oh yeah?" I ask, mischievously.

"Later," he whispers in my ear, his tongue at my earlobe, "when we're alone," his lips travel down my neck to my collarbone. I can hear everyone around us but it's so hard to concentrate when he does this, "I'm going to take you in every way possible."

"Oh yeah?" My voice is faint when I ask again.

"Oh yeah," he agrees, his hand just above my ass, pulling me in tighter to him. "And you're going to wear nothing but these boots." His lips latch back on to mine as he lays another knee weakening kiss on me. "Do you like the sound of that?

A shiver runs through me. "I *love* the sound of that," I say.

"Good." The corner of his mouth tilts up, and he sets me back down on the ground. "Love you, princess."

I pick up his discard hat on the ground and hand it back to him. "Love you, cowboy."

"Evie! Austin! Come on!" Drew calls to us, jumping up and down like a little kid before sprinting out to the party that is now taking place in the middle of center field.

"You ready?" Austin asks, holding out his hand to me.

I smile widely at him and take his hand. "I'm ready for anything."

SNEAK PEEK

Turn the Page for a Sneak Peek of Book Two in the
Benched Trilogy:

STRUCK OUT

Featuring Sydney and Drew!

PROLOGUE

There are only two things that I'm absolutely sure of right now.

One, I'm drunk as hell.

Two, I can't find my shoes.

It's my nineteenth birthday, but according to the pretty little fake ID sitting snugly in my bra, I just turned twenty-three years old. My friends have all turned up to celebrate and I grab the arm of the person closest to me, positive that it's my best friend, Evie. It turns out to be one of the boys from the baseball team and I frown in confusion. The music continues to bump loudly around me, but I pause, looking around for her. She was just dancing with our other best friend, Drew, just a few minutes ago.

At least it felt like a few minutes ago. I can't really remember.

"She went home!"

The voice is loud and comes from my other side. I turn around and see Drew standing there. There's a glass clutched tightly in his hands and I know that the dark liquid in the glass is probably a Dr. Pepper. Drew never drinks during the season, and he usually stays sober around me.

"What are you talking about?" I ask him, yelling to be heard over the music.

"Evie. She went home. She wasn't feeling well so Austin took her home," he explains.

My heart sinks a little. I like Austin. I do, a lot. He's the first boy that Evie has even looked at in the past three years. He's good looking, and he's obviously crazy about her. Even so…she hasn't been around much since meeting him and I miss her.

Then again, it was my fault Austin was even here tonight anyway. *You invited him, remember, Sydney?*

I shrug my shoulders and the movement proves to be too much. I start to tip to the side. Drew's hand reaches out to grab me before I can completely lose control of myself and end up sprawled out on the sticky floor of the bar.

"I think it's time you get home too," he says, helping me to get back upright.

"But it's my *birthday*!" I protest, even though I know he's probably right. The world is spinning around me, and I don't exactly remember what I had to eat before we came here, but I have a feeling I'm about to find out. Without realizing it, I had slumped against him.

"It's one fifteen in the morning, Syd, so technically, it's not your birthday anymore."

I pout at him, but it has no effect and I let him pull me through the crowd. Somehow Drew manages to locate my shoes and helps me put them back on. A rush of friendly affection runs through me. Drew isn't as close to me as he is to Evie, but he's always there to take care of me. Especially when I get myself into situations like this.

I don't remember the drive home much. Drew deposits me into the passenger seat of his car and makes sure I'm buckled in safely before climbing into the driver's seat and driving us back to campus.

Drew lives closer to the baseball field, a good distance away from my own dorm hall, where I live with Evie and a few hundred other students. I dimly register that he's not taking me there, and that we are heading toward his own dorm.

"Where are you taking me?" I ask, my voice slurring. I narrow my eyes as my vision blurs.

"I don't trust you by yourself in your dorm. Not when you're this drunk." Drew's voice stays even as we drive, and I am grateful for it. He never judges even though I know he doesn't like that I get drunk this often.

"Evie is there. I'll be fine," I assure him.

He shakes his head, turning into a parking lot and swinging into a parking spot. It's a fair distance away from the dorms but I suppose that's what we get for being out this late while most people are sticking close to campus. I remember its midterms and inwardly grown. I haven't studied for my biology exam at all.

"Austin took Evie home because she was drunk off her ass too. She can't even take care of herself right now, let alone you."

Damn.

"What about your roommate?"

"He went home tonight. He's spending time with his mom before we hit the road soon." Drew plays for the Quakes, our college baseball team. That team is literally the most important thing in this town. "You can sleep in his bed tonight."

I want to argue more but opening my mouth seems like an awful idea at that moment. I'm hit with a sudden bout of nausea and I don't care anymore where I sleep as long as it's a bed. It'll probably smell like stinky jock straps, but I spend most of my time around baseball players, so I'm used to it.

"You always take care of me, Drew," I say, sleepily.

There's a long pause before he responds. "Yeah, I know," he replies, softly. His hands tighten on the steering wheel, but he merely gets out of the car and helps me out. I'm pretty sure my dress rides up my thighs enough so that he sees my panties. He looks away but I'm hardly bothered. It's *Drew.*

Drew scans us into his dorm hall. His hand is wrapped tightly around my arm, and he guides me through the front lobby and to the elevator. Just like the one in my own dorm hall, it takes forever to make its way down to the ground floor.

When it finally arrives, we shuffle into and I practically collapse against the wall. Drew leans casually against the wall opposite from me and tucks his hands into his jean pockets. He looks uncharacteristically serious and I take a moment to look at him.

Drew is beautiful, but he's beautiful in that way where you have to look more than once. I've known him since we were sixteen years old, when I moved next door to Evie and wiggled my way into their twosome. Damn, those kids were in desperate need of some fun. Drew was a gangly kid but talented on the baseball field and in Santa Isabella, that might as well have been a million dollars.

He's still thin but he'd grown into over the years. Instead of being gangly, he was just tall, lean, and muscled. He had to be, to be a Quake, and you could see the muscles in his arms from all the work he put in pitching. His blonde hair was styled, like usual, but it didn't make him look like he put too much effort into it, just that he cared enough for it to not be a mess. He had the greenest eyes I had ever seen. It had always baffled me how he managed to stay so single. He hadn't so much as looked at another girl since he and Evie had dated in high school…

"You're staring," Drew interrupts my thoughts.

"You know, you're kind of beautiful," I blurt out. I immediately feel myself blush, which I know can't be attractive. Red cheeks just clash *horribly* with my red hair.

Drew doesn't say anything for a moment, and I hope to god that he didn't hear me. Why do I always have to say the stupidest things when I'm drunk?

Finally, after a long awkward moment that feels like years but was probably only about five seconds, Drew raises his eyes and his green eyes meet my own. He studies me curiously and I suddenly am very aware of how little dressed I am. Drew has this way of looking at you, looking right through you, as if he knows you better than anyone.

"Thank you," he finally whispers. We reach the seventh floor and the doors slide open. Neither of us make a move to exit the elevator and soon, the doors close again, and we stay suspended.

My body seems to move on its own, like I've completely disconnected from myself. I've never really felt the need to move myself closer to Drew but he's too good looking for his own good. He always makes me laugh and he takes care of me and he's one of my best friends and right now, I want him.

It's probably because I'm drunk. Evie doesn't always approve of my ways, but she's only been with one guy, *ever*, and he cheated on her with her own twin sister, so I try to ignore her disapproving comments. I'm looking for love, isn't everyone? But in the meantime, I like to have a good time, and I have a lot of good times. It's not often that I make my way back into my own bed at the end of the night.

"What are you doing, Sydney?" Drew sounds tired but he doesn't move as I make my way across the small space of the elevator. I'm right in front of him. I'm tall myself but Drew towers over me, makes me feel small. His eyes don't look away, though they do a fair appraisal of my body. It sends a tingle up my spine and I'm happy he does it.

My hand reaches out for him, my palm pressed against his chest. I can feel his heart beating in my palm and I know that despite his calm face, he likes having me close to him. I step closer and am grateful for the heat that is rippling off his body.

"Sydney…" His voice is strangled. "Seriously? What are you doing?"

"I want to kiss you," I tell him. His eyes widened but he shouldn't be surprised. I'm bold. I don't hold back. I don't play games. If I want something, I go for it.

"I don't think that's a good idea," Drew finally manages to say. His eyes dart to the doors of the elevator but they aren't opening anytime soon.

My fingers trace a line down his jaw, and he swallows hard. My thumb grazes his full bottom lip and I pull at it for a moment, wanting it pressed against mine. And now. "I know you want to, Drew. I know you watch me."

His eyes narrow and his skin flushes red but he doesn't say anything. He just watches me warily. His hands are out of his pocket and on my waist and I love the way they feel. The fabric of my dress is thin, and I can feel how rough his hands are. I want them on my bare skin.

I'm tired of waiting. My hands reach up for him and I pull him down to me, pressing my lips firmly against his. Drew is still for a split second, barely a breath, before his fingers dig into my skin and he pulls me hard against him. Our mouths slide easily against each other and my hands are lost in the wispy blonde hairs at the back of his neck.

He spins us around so fast, I nearly lose my balance, before my back is pressed tightly against the cold wall. He's firm and warm in all the right places. This kiss is good, hard, and bruising and I can feel it all the way down to my sore toes.

Drew pulls away and I reach for him. "Sydney, no, you're drunk."

"No, I'm not," I say. My lips feel full and tingly and I want to pull him back into me. I want more.

His hands are lost in his hair and he sends me a knowing look. "Yes, you are. I don't want to do this when you're drunk, Syd." His voice is soft, and his chest moves quickly. His eyes cut back to me and he curses under his breath. "I want it to be real."

I laugh, and the sound is loud and echoing in the elevator. "That's not going to happen, Drew."

His anger is quick, and I know I've said the wrong thing. My brain is fuzzy and I'm not even sure I remember what I just said but it was wrong. It was the wrong thing to say. "Great. Just great, Sydney." His hand punches the open button of the elevator, hard, and the door slides open almost instantly. He practically sprints out and I stay there, my back pressed against the wall, my heart pounding in my chest.

A shaky hand is reaching for the Floor One button when he suddenly reappears. His hair is disheveled, and he looks upset, but his eyes just meet mine evenly. "Come on. Let's go to bed."

ACKNOWLEDGMENTS

Writing acknowledgements is always one of the hardest parts of writing a novel. This novel took about a decade of my life to write and, because of that, there are so many people to thank. I will do my best to remember everyone.

Thank you to my dad for his never-ending support, even when I write smutty novels, and for giving me my never-ending love of baseball. To my mom, for always having romance novels around for me to devour. My siblings – Robby, Jessica, Dink, Joey and Stevey – for being my best friends and for providing inspiration for all my characters. Scout, the best dog on the planet – you were the best writing partner ever and I miss you so much. To my kitty babies, Kaz and Kai, for stepping up as writing partners – yes, lying on the keyboard *totally* helps.

Thank you to my boyfriend, Daniel, for his support and for making sure that I don't forget to eat when I'm writing or editing and being *mostly* understanding when I glare it at him for interrupting me while I'm reading. You're the best! I couldn't have done this without your support and patience.

To my best friend, Meghan, for always believing in this book when I didn't. Thank you for being my biggest fan, for being an amazing friend, for always being there for me and for loving my book boys. I try to make them the best, just for you!

A huge, gigantic, ginormous, everlasting thank you to my dear friend/editor, Alyssa Barber. She has been such an amazing friend and support in the past handful of years, and she's been a champion for this book. I am not exaggerating when I say that this book would not be as great as it is without her tireless work and her dedication to making this book the best that I can possibly be. *Benched* is so much of me but its so much of Alyssa as well.

Thank you to Ryder Lyne , of Ryder Lyne Books, for doing an epic job on the interior of the book and for helping me to navigate the sometimes-bumpy road to self-publishing. To Kelley York of Sleepy Fox Studios, thank you for taking a cover I loved (but didn't realize was exactly like someone else's book…whoops!) and making it even better – the cover is gorgeous!

Thank you to the sports romance and college romance novelists that inspired *Benched* and helped me to finally figure out how to write this book after years of trying – Cora Carmack, Sarina Bowen, Elle Kennedy, Ginger Scott, Jennifer L Armentrout, J Sterling, Jay Crownover, Alexa Martin and more.

To the people in the book community – bloggers, authors, librarians – that I have met over the years who have supported me and been my inspiration, my motivation and my friends – Courtney Saldana, Allison Tran, Nicole Maggi, Jessica Brody, Gretchen McNeil, Leigh Bardugo, Alethea Allarey, Morgan Matson, Cora Carmack, Jeff Garvin, Sara from Sara's Reading Adventure, Mina from My Fangirl Chronicles, Mary Weber, Nicole Mainardi,

Stacee from Eleven Thirteen PM, Elana K Arnold, Christy and Kelly from BookCrushin', Vivi Barnes, Kasie West, Robin Reul, Demetra Brodsky, Brad Gottfred, Emily Griffin, Julie Buxbaum, Romina Garber, Cindy Pon, Megan Beatie, Joel Lawrence, Laura Fox and so many others that I know I am forgetting.

A huge shout out to my two best and favorite teams – the Los Angeles Angels and the Cal State University, Fullerton Titans. The Angels are forever my favorite team and the Titans inspired so much about the Quakes. Thank you to movies like *Bull Durham, A League of Their Own, Field of Dreams, Everybody Wants Some, Summer Catch,* and more for giving me inspiration.

I know I've forgotten someone so if I haven't mentioned you, please know that I love you and that you're amazing and I'm so grateful for you!

Lastly, a huge thank you to YOU, holding this book in your hands. Thank you for giving Evie and Austin a chance and thank you for your support. I hope you enjoyed the book and that you'll be back for more in the future!

BONUS! BENCHED PLAYLIST

Time-Bomb - All Time Low
  Without You - Issues
  Trust - Jonas Brothers
  Get It Right - Issues
  No Problem (Keep it Alive) - Issues
  COMA - Issues
  Fourth of July - Fall Out Boy
  Backseat Serenade - All Time Low
  Every Single Time - Jonas Brothers
  Dial Tones - As It Is
  Around the Clock - The Rocket Summer
  Remembering Sunday - All Time Low
  Shot Out of a Cannon - Andrew McMahon in the Wilderness
  Fall - Something Corporate
  If I Ever See You Again - Grayscale
  Let Me Go - Sleep On It
  Get it Right - Issues

ABOUT THE AUTHOR

Sara is a young adult and new adult fiction writer. She has worked as smoothie artist, Disneyland cast member, restaurant supervisor, photographer, nanny, pizza delivery driver, and barista but writing is what she loves most. She is obsessed with reading, baseball, cupcakes, tattoos, running and peach green iced teas. She runs her own nerd girl/book review blog, What A Nerd Girl Says. She lives in Southern California with her boyfriend and her two cats, Kaz and Kai. *Benched* is her third novel.

MORE TITLES FROM SARA ELIZABETH SANTANA

The Awakened Duology

Young Adult Science Fiction

The Awakened: Book 1

The Sanctuary: Book 2

Available in Paperback and eBook